*A Small Sacrifice for an
Enormous Happiness*

# A Small Sacrifice for an
# Enormous Happiness

⊣⁛ STORIES ⁛⊢

## Jai Chakrabarti

ALFRED A. KNOPF · NEW YORK · 2023

THIS IS A BORZOI BOOK PUBLISHED BY ALFRED A. KNOPF

www.aaknopf.com

Knopf, Borzoi Books, and the colophon are registered trademarks of Penguin Random House LLC.

Several pieces first appeared in the following publications: "A Small Sacrifice for an Enormous Happiness" in *A Public Space*; "Daisy Lane" in *Slice*; "Searching for Elijah" in *Michigan Quarterly Review*; "Mendel's Wall" in *Coffin Factory*; "Lost Things" in *The Collagist*; "A Mother's Work" in *One Story*; "Prodigal Son" in *Electric Literature*; "Lilavati's Fire" in *Conjunctions*. "Lessons with Father" was commissioned by Symphony Space's *Selected Shorts,* and was published in *Small Odysseys* by Algonquin Books.

LIBRARY OF CONGRESS CATALOGING-IN-PUBLICATION DATA
Names: Chakrabarti, Jai, author.
Title: A small sacrifice for an enormous happiness : stories / Jai
    Chakrabarti.
Description: First edition. | New York : Alfred A. Knopf, 2023. | "This is
    a Borzoi book"—Title page verso. |
Identifiers: LCCN 2022012709 (print) | LCCN 2022012710 (ebook) |
    ISBN 9780525658948 (hardcover) | ISBN 9780525658955 (ebook)
Subjects: LCGFT: Short stories.
Classification: LCC PS3603.H33548 S63 2023 (print) |
    LCC PS3603.H33548 (ebook) | DDC 813/.6—dc23/eng/20220317
LC record available at https://lccn.loc.gov/2022012709
LC ebook record available at https://lccn.loc.gov/2022012710

Jacket photograph by Alex Plechko
Jacket design by Janet Hansen

Manufactured in the United States of America
First Edition

*For Surya*

# Contents

⚟ ⚟ ⚟

*A Small Sacrifice for an*

*Enormous Happiness*

## A Small Sacrifice for an Enormous Happiness

From his balcony, Nikhil waited and watched the street as hyacinth braiders tied floral knots, rum sellers hauled bags of ice, and the row of elderly typists, who had seemed elderly to him since he'd been a boy, struck the last notes of their daily work. Beside him on the balcony, his servant, Kanu, plucked at the hair that grew from his ears.

"Keep a lookout for babu," Nikhil shouted to Kanu. "I'll check on the tea."

Kanu was so old he could neither see nor hear well, but he still accepted each responsibility with enthusiasm.

The tea was ready, as were the sweets, the whole conical pile of them—the base layer of pistachio mounds, the center almond bars that Nikhil had rolled by hand himself, and on the top three lychees from the garden, so precariously balanced, a single misstep would have upset their delectable geometry.

When he returned to the balcony he saw Sharma walking up the cobbled lane, his oiled hair shining in the late-afternoon light. The typists greeted him with a verse from a Bollywood number—Sharma's boxer's jaw and darling eyes reminded the typists of an emerging movie star—and Sharma shook his head and laughed.

Kanu limped downstairs to let Sharma in, and Nikhil waited in the living room while the two of them made their way up.

"And what is the special occasion?" Sharma asked, eyeing the pile of confections with a boyish grin.

Nikhil refused to say. He allowed Sharma to have his fill, watching with satisfaction as his fingers became honey-glazed from the offering.

Afterward, when they lay on the great divan—hand-carved and older than his mother's ghost—Nikhil breathed deeply to calm his heart. He feared the words would be eaten in his chest, but he'd been planning to tell Sharma for days, and there was no going back now. As evening settled, the air between them became heavy with the sweetness of secrecy, but secrecy had a short wick.

"My dearest, fairest boy," he said. "I want our love to increase."

Sharma raised his eyebrows, those lines thickly drawn, nearly fused. Who better than Sharma to know Nikhil's heart?

"I desire to have a child with you," Nikhil said.

Nikhil had trouble reading Sharma's expression in the waning light, so he repeated himself. His fingers were shaking, but he took Sharma's hand anyway, gave it a squeeze.

"I heard you the first time," Sharma said.

A rare cool wind had prompted Nikhil to turn off the ceiling fan, and now he could hear the rum sellers on the street enunciating prices in singsong Urdu.

He touched Sharma's face, traced the line of his jaw, unsure still of how his lover had received his news. Likely, Sharma was still mulling—he formed his opinions, Nikhil believed, at the pace the street cows strolled.

Nikhil waited out the silence as long as he could. "Listen," he finally said. "The country is changing."

"A child diapered by two men," said Sharma. "Your country is changing faster than my country is changing. What about the boys from Kerala?"

They had learned about a schoolteacher and a postal clerk who had secretly made a life together. Unfashionably attired and chubby cheeked, they seemed too dull for the news. A few months ago, locals threw acid in their faces. Even in the black and white of the photographs, their scars, along the jaw, the nose, the better half of a cheek. Ten years since man had landed on the moon, and still.

"We are not boys from Kerala. We are protected."

No ruse better than a woman in the home, Nikhil had argued over a year ago, and eventually Sharma had agreed to a marriage of convenience. Kanu, who had loved Nikhil through his childhood and even through his years of chasing prostitutes, had arranged for a village woman who knew about the two men's relationship but would never tell.

Nikhil rummaged through his almirah and returned with a gift in his hands. "You close your eyes now."

"Oh, Nikhil." But Sharma did as he was told, accustomed now perhaps to receiving precious things.

Around Sharma's neck, Nikhil tied his dead mother's necklace. It had been dipped in twenty-four carats of gold by master artisans of Agra. Miniature busts of Queen Victoria decorated its circumference. A piece for the museums, a jeweler had once explained, but Nikhil wanted Sharma to have it. That morning, when he'd visited the family vault to retrieve it, he'd startled himself with the enormity of what he was giving away, but what better time than now, as they were about to begin a family?

"Promise you'll dream about a child with me."

"It is beautiful, and I will wear it every day, even though people will wonder what is that under my shirt."

"Let them wonder."

"You are entirely mad. Mad is what you are."

Nikhil was pulled back to the divan. Sharma, lifting Nikhil's shirt, placed a molasses square on his belly, teasing a trail of sweetness with his tongue. Nikhil closed his eyes and allowed himself to be enjoyed. Down below, the rum sellers negotiated, the prices of bottles fluctuating wildly.

Afterward, they retired to the roof. Their chadors cut off the cold, but Nikhil still shivered. When Sharma asked what the matter was, Nikhil kissed the spot where his eyebrows met. There was another old roof across the street, where grandmothers were known to gossip and eavesdrop, but he did not care. *Let them see*, he thought, *let them feel this wind of enormous change.*

The next morning, while Sharma washed, Nikhil said, "I want you to toss the idea to your wife. Get Tripti used to the matter."

Sharma dried himself so quickly he left behind footprints on the bathroom's marble floor. "Toss the idea to my wife. Get her used to the matter," Sharma repeated, before he changed into his working clothes, leaving Nikhil to brood alone.

Tripti would have few issues with the arrangement of a child, Nikhil believed. After all, at the time of her marriage to Sharma, her family was mired in bankruptcy, her father had left them nothing but a reputation for drink and dishonesty, and she herself—insofar as he recalled from his sole meeting with her, at the wedding—was a dour, spiritless creature who deserved little of the bounty that Nikhil had provided her. What little else he knew was from Kanu's reports. Extremely pliable, Kanu had first said. Then, closer to the wedding: little stubborn about the choice of sweets. She wants village kind. On that note, Nikhil had wilted—let her have her desserts, he'd said, the wedding paid for, and the matter removed from mind.

The next few days, when Sharma was away at the village and at the foundry, Nikhil paced around the house, overcome by the idea of a child. He'd always dreamed of becoming a father but had never believed it would be possible until this year's monsoon, when, in the middle of a deluge, his forty-two-year-old sister had given birth to a girl. The rain had been so fierce no ambulance could ferry them to the hospital, so the elderly women of the family assumed the duties of midwifery and delivered the child themselves. The first moment he saw his niece he nearly believed in God and, strangely, in his own ability—his *right*—to produce so perfect a thing.

He couldn't bring Sharma to his sister's house to meet his new niece, so the next week he'd spent their Thursday together sharing photos; if Sharma experienced the same lightness of being, he didn't let it show. All he said was, "Quite a healthy baby she is."

It was true. She'd been born nine pounds two ounces. The family had purchased a cow so that fresh milk would always be available.

. . .

Nikhil convinced himself that he had opened Sharma's heart to the idea of becoming a father, but the exuberance of this conclusion led to certain practical questions. Sharma's wife would carry the child, but where would the child live? In Sharma's house in the village, or in Nikhil's house here in the city? If she lived in the village, which Nikhil admitted was the safer option, how would Nikhil father her, how would she receive a proper education?

These questions consumed the hours. When he went to check on his tenants, he was distracted and unable to focus on their concerns. A leaky toilet, a broken window, the group of vagrants who'd squatted outside one of his properties—all these matters seemed trivial compared to his imagined child's needs.

The next week, the afternoon before he would see Sharma again, he stepped into a clothing store on Rashbehari Avenue to calm his mind. It was a shop he'd frequented to purchase silk kurtas for Sharma or paisley shirts for himself. He told the attendants he needed an exceptional outfit for his niece. They combed the shelves and found a white dress with a lacy pink bow. He imagined his own daughter wearing it. From his dreaming he was certain a girl would come out of their love— Shristi was what he'd named her—Shristi enunciating like a princess, Shristi riding her bicycle up and down Kakulia Lane.

Early on, they'd agreed that Nikhil would avoid the foundry, but he was feeling so full of promise for Shristi that he did not deter himself from continuing down Rashbehari Avenue toward Tollygunge Phari, nor did he prevent himself from walking to the entrance of Mahesh Steel and asking for his *friend*.

Sharma emerged from the uneven music of metalworking with a cigarette between his lips. His Apollonian features were smeared with grease. His hands were constricted by thick welding gloves, which excluded the possibility of even an accidental touch. When he saw Nikhil, Sharma scowled. "Sir," he said, "you'll have the parts tomorrow."

Though he knew Sharma was treating him as a customer for good reason, the tone still stung. Nikhil whispered, "See what I have brought." He produced the perfect baby girl dress.

"You have lost your soup," Sharma whispered back. Then, so everyone could hear, "Babu, you'll have the parts tomorrow. Latest, tomorrow."

Nikhil tried again: "Do you see the collar, the sweet lace?"

"You should go to your home now," Sharma said. "Tomorrow, I'll see you."

But that Thursday Sharma failed to visit. Nikhil and Kanu waited until half past nine and then ate their meal together by lamplight.

. . .

They met on Thursdays because it was on a Thursday that they had first met three years ago, at that time of year when the city is at its most bearable. When the smell of wild hyacinth cannot be outdone by the stench of the gutters, because it is after the city's short winter, which manages, despite its brevity, to birth more funerals than any other time of year. In the city's spring, two men walking the long road from Santiniketan back to Kolkata—because the bus has broken and no one is interested in its repair—are not entirely oblivious to the smells abounding in the wildflower fields, not oblivious at all to their own smells.

He supposed he had fetishized Sharma's smell from the beginning, that scent of a day's honest work. The smell of steel, of the cheapest soap. The smell of a shirt that had been laundered beyond its time. The smell of his night-bound stubble. He allowed his hand to linger on Sharma's wrist, pretending he was trying to see the hour. An hour before sunset. An hour after. He did not remember exactly when they parted. What did it matter.

What mattered were the coincidences of love. The day he saw Sharma for the second time he counted among the small miracles of his life.

Sharma was drinking tea at the tea stall on Kakulia Lane. He was leaning the weight of his body on the rotting wood of the counter, listening to the chai wallah recount stories. Later, he would learn that Sharma had landed a job at a nearby foundry and that this tea stall was simply the closest one, but in that moment he did not think of foundries or work or any other encumbrance, he thought instead of the way Sharma cradled his earthen teacup, as if it were the Koh-i-noor.

Oh, he had said, did you and I . . . that broken bus . . . What an evening, yes?

A question that led to Thursdays. Two years of Thursdays haunted by fear of discovery, which led to a wedding, because a married man who arrived regularly at Kakulia Lane could not be doing anything but playing backgammon with his happenstance friend. What followed was a year of bliss. He considered this time their honeymoon. They were as seriously committed as any partners who'd ever shared a covenant, and shouldn't that show?

.  .  .

Sharma did visit the following Thursday, though the matter of his absence the week before was not raised. Instead of their usual feast at home, they ate chili noodles doused with sugary tomato sauce at Jimmy's Chinese Kitchen, along with stale pastries for dessert. Sharma was wearing Nikhil's family necklace under his shirt, with just an edge of the queen's image peeking out from the collar. Seeing his gift on his lover's body released Nikhil from his brood, and for the first time that night, he met Sharma's gaze.

"You're cross with me," Sharma offered.

It wasn't an apology, but Nikhil was warming to the idea of a reconciliation.

"Anyway, Tripti and I have been discussing the issue of the baby."

*Tripti and I.* He so rarely heard the name Tripti from Sharma's lips, but that she could be in league with him, discussing an *issue*? Unjust was what it was.

"It's in part the physical act. We eat our meals together. We take walks to the bazaar or to the pond. But that, no, we do not do that."

"Don't worry," Nikhil said. "I shall do the deed. I shall be the child's father." While it was unpleasant to imagine the act of copulation itself, he'd studied the intricacies of the reproductive process and believed his chances were excellent for a single, well-timed session to yield its fruit.

"But you can barely stand the smell of a woman."

What passed over Sharma's face could best be described as amusement, but Nikhil refused to believe that his lover wasn't taking him seriously—not now that he'd opened his heart like a salvaged piano. "Sharma," Nikhil said. "It shall be a small sacrifice for an enormous happiness."

"Oh, Nikhil, do you not see that we are already happy? Anything more might upset what we have. We should not tempt the gods."

Nikhil ground away at the pastry in his mouth until the memory of sweetness dispersed. The things Sharma said. As if there were a cap on happiness in this world. It was Sharma's village religion talking again, but there was something more. He sensed in the way Sharma held his hands in his lap, the way he kept to the far side of the bed when they retired for the night, that Tripti had wormed something rotten into him. He was vulnerable that way, Sharma was.

When Nikhil awoke the next morning, Sharma had already departed, but in the bathroom, which he'd lovingly reconstructed from Parisian prints, with a claw-foot tub and a nearly functioning bidet, he found Sharma's stubble littering the marble sink. Sharma had always been fastidious in the house, taking care to wipe away evidence of his coming and going, and the patches of facial hair offended Nikhil. He studied their formations, searching for patterns. When nothing could be discerned, he called for Kanu to clean the mess.

. . .

Only one train went to Bilaspur, a commuter local. For two hours, Nikhil was stuck next to the village yeoman, who'd gone to the city to peddle his chickens and was clutching the feet of the aging pair he'd been unable to sell, and the bleary-eyed dairyman, who smelled of curd and urine. The only distraction was the girl with the henna-tinged hair who'd boarded between stops to plead for money, whose face looked entirely too much like the child he envisioned fathering.

When he reached the Bilaspur terminus, he was relieved to see the rows of wildflowers on either side of the tracks, to smell the bloom of begonias planted by the stationmaster's post.

It wasn't difficult finding Sharma's home. With money from the foundry and regular gifts of cash from Nikhil, Sharma had purchased several hectares of hilltop land and built a concrete slab of a house, garrisoned with a garden of squash, cucumber, and eggplant, and with large windows marking the combined living and dining area. Nikhil found the structure too modern, but that was Sharma's way—he had never swooned over the old colonials of Kakulia Lane.

From inside the house, Nikhil could hear the BBC broadcast, which was strange given that Tripti didn't understand English. Nikhil tiptoed toward the open living room window, and from there he spied. Sharma's wife was holding a book on her lap, mouthing back the words of the BBC announcer.

"BER-LIN WALL," she said. "DOWN-ING STREET."

She had a proud bookish nose—adequately sized for the resting of eyeglasses—a forehead that jutted too far forward, reminding Nikhil of a depiction of Neanderthal gatherers, and the slightest of chins, which gave to her appearance a quality of perpetual meekness. Her sari was stained with years of cooking. Her only adornments were the bright red bindi on her forehead and the brass bangles that made music whenever she turned a page.

There were certain topics Nikhil and Sharma had left to the wind, foremost the matter of Sharma's marriage. In the beginning, Nikhil experienced a shooting pain in his abdomen whenever he thought about Sharma and Tripti coexisting in domestic harmony, though over the past few months that pain had numbed; the less he'd thought of Tripti, the less she existed, but here she was now—the would-be mother of his child. He rapped on the grill of her window.

"Just leave it there," Tripti said without looking up from her book.

It was the first time she'd ever spoken to him. Her voice, which was composed of rich baritones, seemed rather forceful, and her demeanor, that of the lady of a proper house, left him feeling uncertain about his next move. At last, he said in a Bengali so refined it could have passed for the old tongue of Sanskrit, "Perhaps you've mistaken me for the bringer of milk. I am not he. Madam, you know me but you do not know me."

The words had sounded elegant in his head, but when spoken aloud he flushed at their foolishness.

She looked up to study his face, then his outfit, even his leather sandals now rimmed with the village's mud. "I know who you are," she finally said. "Why don't you come inside?"

He had not planned beyond this moment. He had allowed his feet to step onto the train at Howrah, imagined a brief meeting, a quick exchange at the doorstep, ending with a mutually desirable pact.

"I can't stay long," he said. Sharma would be home in another hour, and Nikhil had no wish to see him in the same vicinity as his wife.

While he settled into the living room, Tripti puttered around the kitchen. The house was decorated with wood carvings and paintings of gods and goddesses. Parvati, the wife of Shiva, smiled beatifically from a gilded frame, and her son the remover of obstacles was frozen inside a copper statuette. From the plans Sharma had shared with pride, Nikhil knew that a hallway connected the three bedrooms of the house— one for Tripti, one for Sharma, and the last a prayer room— and he wondered now how their mornings were arranged, what politics were discussed, what arguments were had, where the laundry was piled.

Tripti brought two cups of tea and a plate of sweets. "Homemade," she said. He'd been raised to fear milk sweets from unfamiliar places, but out of politeness he took the first bite—a little lumpy, only mildly flavorful.

"Sharma is always praising your cooking," he said, but it was a lie. They never bothered to discuss Tripti's cooking; in fact, Nikhil had teased that they were lovers because of his own talents in the kitchen. Still, it felt appropriate to compliment this woman, and he continued in this fashion, standing to admire the Parvati painting, which he described as "terribly and modernly artful."

"Nikhil-babu," she interrupted. "Are you here to discuss the matter of the child?"

He sighed with relief. Until that moment, he'd been unsure about how to broach the subject.

·

"You know," she said. "We discuss our days. We may not be lovers, but we are fair friends."

He experienced what felt like an arthritic pain in his shoulder, but it was only the collar of his jealousy. At least they were not *best* friends.

She pointed to the book on her coffee table, an English-language primer. "Unfortunately, it's just not on our horizon. You see, I'm going to university. I shall be a teacher."

"University," he said. "But you did not even finish eighth grade."

"That is true, but at Bilaspur College, the principal is willing to accept students who display enormous curiosities."

He found it improbable that she would be able to absorb the principles of higher learning, but he had no particular wish to impede her efforts. Education was a challenge he understood. "You want to improve yourself? Wonderful. If you are with child, I will have tutors come to you. Not professors from Bilaspur College. Real academics from the city."

But it was as if she had not heard him at all. She submerged a biscuit in her tea and stared out into the garden.

"Whose happiness are you after, Nikhil-babu?" she said. "Yours and yours only?"

He found himself grinding his teeth. The great bane of modernity. Though the country had opened itself to the pleasures of the other world—cream-filled pastries, the films of Godard, a penchant for pristine white-sand beaches—he did not care for the consequences, the dissolution of ordering traditions, with whose loss came poor speech, thoughtless conduct. A village woman addressing him without the slightest deference.

"Perhaps you should enroll in a school for proper manners," he said.

Tripti eased her teacup down. He followed the geometry of her sloping wrist, but there was no break of anger in her face.

"Listen," he said. But how could he explain that his want for a child had become rooted in his body, in the bones of his hands and the ridges of his knees, where just that afternoon the girl on the train who'd emerged from the rice fields to beg in the vestibules, whose outstretched palm he would normally loathe—there was no way to lift the country by satisfying beggars—had touched him. Had he not smiled back and touched her hair?

"If you're planning to catch the last train back," she said, "it's best you go now."

He chewed another of Tripti's lumpy sweets. When properly masticated, it would have the consistency to be spat and to land right between Tripti's eyes. But Tripti had turned away from him and resumed her studies. Soon he was all chewed out; he had to show himself out of the house.

. . .

By the time he reached the train station, the six o'clock was arriving at the platform. He squatted behind the begonias by the stationmaster's post and waited to see if Sharma was aboard. With the afternoon's disappointment, he felt he deserved to see Sharma's face, even if only covertly. See but remain unseen. In that moment, he could not have explained why he did not peek his head out of the tangle of flowers, though a glimmer of an idea came, something to do with the freedom of others—how, in this village of Sharma's birth, unknown and burdened, Nikhil could never be himself. Sweat pooled where his hairline had receded. How old the skin of his forehead felt to the touch.

As passengers began to disembark, those who were headed for the city clambered aboard. He looked at the faces passing by but did not see Sharma. The first warning bell sounded, then the second, and the stationmaster announced that the train was nearly city bound.

He saw Sharma as the crowd was thinning out. He was walking with someone dressed in the atrocious nylon pants that were the fashion, and perhaps they were telling jokes, because Sharma was doubled over laughing. In all their evenings together, he couldn't recall seeing Sharma laugh with so little inhibition as he now did, so little concern about who would hear that joyous voice—who would think, *What are those two doing?* He watched Sharma walk along the dirt road toward his house, but it was an entirely different progress; he was stopping to inspect the rows of wildflowers on the path, to chat up the farmer who'd bellowed his name.

He kept watching Sharma's retreating form until he could see nothing but the faint shape of a man crossing the road. It was then he realized that the city-bound train, the last of the day, had left without him; he sprinted into the stationmaster's booth and phoned his house. It took several rings for Kanu to answer. "Yello?"

"Oh, Kanu," he said. "You must send a car. You must get me. I am at Bilaspur."

The connection was poor, but he could hear Kanu saying, "Babu? What is happening? What is wrong?"

There was no way to express how wounded the afternoon had left him, and he knew the odds of securing a car at this hour, so he yelled back into the phone, "Don't wait for me, Kanu. Make dinner, go to bed!"

He asked the stationmaster if there were any hotels in the village. A room just till the morning, he said. The stationmaster shrugged and pointed vaguely in the direction of the dirt road.

. . .

There were no hotels, he soon discovered. Either he would sleep underneath the stars or he would announce himself at Sharma's house to spend the night. He was certain he couldn't do the latter—what a loss of face that would be—but the former, with its cold and its unknown night animals, seemed nearly as terrifying.

He paced the town's only road until he grew hungry. Then he headed in the direction of Sharma's house, following a field where fireflies alighted on piles of ash. He had no wish to be discovered, but in the waning daylight that would soon turn into uninterrupted darkness, he felt as anonymous as any of the mosquitoes making dinner of his feet.

When he reached the entrance to Sharma's house, he could smell the evening's meal: lentil soup, rice softened with clarified butter. He could see the two of them together in the kitchen. Sharma was slicing cucumbers and Tripti was stirring a pot. The way Sharma's knife passed over the counter seemed like an act of magic. Such grace and precision. Soon, he knew the lentils and rice would be combined, a pair of onions diced, ginger infused into the stew, the table set, the meal consumed. He watched, waiting for the first word to be spoken, but they were silent partners, unified by the rhythm of their hands.

They moved into the dining room with their meal, and he crawled to the open kitchen window. Sharma had left his mother's necklace on the kitchen counter, next to the cheap china atop the stains of all meals past. What he was seeing couldn't be dismissed: Sharma had treated his greatest gift as if it were nothing more than a kitchen ornament. Nikhil's hand snaked through the window to recover the heirloom, and he knocked over a steel pan in the process.

Sharma rushed to the kitchen and began to yell, "Thief, stop," as if it were a mantra. Nikhil scurried down the hill, the necklace secure in his grip, and when he paused at the mouth of the town's only road and turned back, he thought he saw Sharma's hands in the window, making signs that reminded him of their first meeting, when in the darkness those dark fingers had beckoned. Nikhil almost called back, but too much distance lay between them. Whatever he said now wouldn't be heard.

## Lilavati's Fire

Aparna unlocked and opened the garage door, pushed the crates inside with her son Sanjay's help, then shooed him away. Out of breath, she flicked on the light. The pieces of her airplane winked back under the fluorescent overheads: a Lorenza twin-speed engine, a vintage wood propeller, an aluminum frame, the sheer tarpaulin that stretched into four-foot wings. She'd bought the parts one by one and rigged a pulley system to lift and place the heavier pieces. Now, here they lay, well-arragned. Settled on the floor, they reminded her of the musterings of storks that would gather in her father's garden in Kolkata.

When Sanjay had moved out—in those first days when it seemed impossible to fill the hours—she had rediscovered two books from her childhood. The first one was by Bhaskara, the twelfth-century mathematician. Bhaskara had written a text in honor of his daughter, Lilavati. *On an expedition to seize his enemy's elephants*, Bhaskara wrote, *a king marched two leagues the first day. With what increasing rate of daily march did he proceed if he reached his foe's city, a distance of eighty leagues, in a week?*

The second book she'd found was by Lilavati herself. It was no more than thirty pages and fraying at the covers, but in the middle section, there was a diagram of a flying machine. Aparna's father had once claimed that Lilavati was the pioneer of flight, and with Sanjay gone, Aparna had vowed to test the theory herself. Harish, her husband, would be home soon, so she picked up her wrench and went to work, fixing an axle onto the plane's rear wheel.

Before the first shipment had arrived, she'd made a show of dragging an easel and paintbrushes into the garage. "It will be my private studio," she told Harish, who was eating a single piece of roti before the evening news, a ritual he'd performed without fail every day of their twenty-year marriage. "Painting is a fine pastime," he said, though he knew nothing about the subject. His expertise was his job: fuels for military aircraft. Harish turned up the TV one notch to suggest that the conversation was over.

Aparna continued anyway. "What if you don't like what I paint?" she said. "What if I paint odd things?"

"Odd things," he said, tilting his head sideways as he did when pondering a challenging engineering problem. "What do you mean?"

"For example," she said. "What if I paint nudes?"

"As you like, Mrs. Dutta. You'll find no quarrel from me."

She went into the kitchen and clanged two of her pans together, but when she came back into the living room, Harish was sitting just as he'd been, a piece of buttered roti stuck to the side of his lip.

. . .

Next evening, when Harish came home for dinner, she could tell he was in a dark mood. If his mood were lighter, he would've walked into the kitchen with his bare feet. That was his way: he had grown up with the muddy ground underneath his toes, passing a football between his ankles. Instead, as she reheated some curried potatoes, he stormed about the living room in his office shoes. "So, Mr. Dutta," she called. "Did they strike or did they not?"

He threw his tie on the floor and peeked into the kitchen; the cumin smell nearly brought a smile to his lips. He explained how the union was still giving them hell and the negotiations were on the wrong track. She murmured in sympathy.

"So, did you see Sanjay today?" he asked.

"I did. He is quite well, Mr. Dutta."

Since the night of their wedding, they had called each other Mr. and Mrs. Standing on the wedding altar, she'd been terrified of him, despite his boyish smile. His smile that revealed to her that he knew nothing about women, confirmed he was committed to worshipping her, expressed to her just how beautiful she was, how beyond his reach she should've been. Their first night, she thought he seemed like an ogre with those outsized hands, that sweet pepper breath. Seated on the wedding bed, he saw her confusion and granted her a reprieve: *We don't have to bed each other yet*, he said. *You can call me Mr. Dutta. I will wait until you wish to.*

That she had not wished to the first week hadn't elicited a single objection from him. They were headed to America, which was already a kind of cleaving. That she hadn't wished to the first month was attributed to the stresses of the new country, though when she was still Mrs. Dutta after six months of marriage, when her husband still forbade using the familiar form because they weren't to each other man and woman, the questions his family raised couldn't be ignored.

. . .

*While making love, a necklace broke. A row of pearls was mislaid. One-sixth of the pearls fell to the floor, one-fifth on the bed. The lady saved one-third of them. One-tenth were caught by her lover. If six pearls remained on the string, how many were there altogether?* She had memorized all of the problems in *Lilavati*, but this was the one she whispered to herself the first time they tried to conceive Sanjay.

It happened on the first Sunday of the seventh month, when Harish no longer seemed like a stranger. She came into the bedroom and started learning what was needed of her. For this task, she used Bhaskara's *Kuttaka*—the method of dividing a complex problem into parts—and she did as Lilavati would have done: she erased the answer from her brain and set about solving the formula afresh, each time Harish set his hands on her body, with that touch that both tickled and bruised—she was sure he did not mean to wound, but of course he did, in his curious and ungainly way, grateful for whatever she would give him, which in the autumn of year three, when they had been trying for a year and five months, was everything and nothing at all.

By winter she brimmed with a new life; when she saw the beautiful webbed feet in the ultrasound, she cried. Here was her life's work, composed in a single piece. It squirmed toward the light of the camera, as if searching for warmth. All of the pain she'd endured had transformed into a thing without eyes.

Later, when Sanjay was old enough to leave trails of cigarette ash in their backyard, she would remember this singularity, a moment not unlike happiness.

. . .

In her drawings, Lilavati had called it an *air chariot*: an open carriage with side struts that extended four feet from the body. At first, Aparna was distressed that the drawings looked nothing like the Wright brothers' first model, but she countered her doubts by doing the thrust-to-lift calculations so many times her fingers became stained with the numbers. On a good day, she was sure that Lilavati's airplane would soar through the air.

After she glued and wired on the tailpiece, which in Lilavati's model had functioned as a rudder, she spied on Harish from the safety of the garage. The man had decomposed himself into his Sunday clothes, Bermuda shorts and a size-small tank top, to mow the lawn. As he turned to avoid the hedges, his shirt caught in a branch and revealed his paunch. It was a consequence of middle age from which even she hadn't been spared. No, she had not grown heavy like her sisters, but her skin had still given way.

Perhaps that was why Harish had stopped. Maybe she was simply too old to be desirable. After the birth of Sanjay, they had tried for a second child, but it came to nothing more than two miscarriages. When Sanjay was making words like *Abracadabra* with his delicate, impish mouth, it was Harish who suggested the possibility of two separate beds.

"Will it not be better for us?" he'd said.

Her sisters had been blessed with a pair of children—a boy and a girl each—but she and Harish wouldn't now. From now on it would be Sanjay and the two of them: Mr. and Mrs. Dutta. She swallowed the shame and agreed it would be better to sleep apart. They traded their teak frame queen for a Spartan pair of twin beds, and she bought floral-print sheets to brighten up the new room.

. . .

As June wore into July, Aparna struggled to find private time. The engineers had gone on strike at Harish's plant, so he was frequently home. Because he was prone to loneliness, he asked her to sit on the couch with him; she did as he wished, but they did not talk. Instead, he went through his papers and silently studied his upcoming work.

Years ago, before Sanjay had been born, there had been another strike, but that month it had been different. With a mug of lemonade in her hand, she'd spent the afternoons listening to her husband reminisce. She loved the way he talked about his childhood in Maniktala, the exploits at the public pool at Haldiya, where he told raucous jokes and dove from makeshift springboards into the shady green water. In his time, Harish had been a social force, a teller of ribald stories, even a singer of Tagore's sentimental songs.

She hadn't noticed until Sanjay had moved out, but these days he was quieter, less prone to either stories or songs; the office work seemed to have pacified, or else muted, his soul. She wished he would discuss things, even if it was regarding the aerospace fuel. At dinner, after a few days of his being home and her being on the couch with him, inhaling his mint aftershave, which he still bought from the local Indian grocery, she spoke up. "Well, Mr. Dutta," she said. "I happened to read some papers you left in the office."

"Oh?" he said.

"Yes, I found the notes regarding the Fischer-Troph fuels project and—"

"Oh, that boring business," Harish said. "Don't worry your head about it."

"But I have an idea."

"Mrs. Dutta, please. I don't want to talk work with you."

Before he interrupted, she was going to add, *I have an idea, regarding how to achieve the highest fuel efficiency, not by changing the fuel, but simply by changing the placement of the engine relative to the fuselage.* Instead, she kept her mouth shut; she chewed her food.

"By the way," Harish said, between bites of a fluffy samosa. "How is your painting coming?"

"Fine," she said. "Terribly fine."

. . .

That Friday, when Harish went to play golf with his bosses, Aparna called her son. "Beta, there is a big problem. Can you come quickly?"

He arrived fifteen minutes later in his delivery truck. From inside the garage, she watched him smooth his rumpled trousers before slouching toward the house. She unlocked the garage door and led him inside. They stood in the darkness, for a moment in the smell of paint and freshly shaven wood.

"Ma, did you seriously bring me here to show me paintings? You realize I have a delivery schedule, right? If I don't keep to it they might—"

She turned on the light and watched him study her creation: he sucked in air as his eyes darted from the moped wheels to the frame she'd painted with the sign *Lilavati's Fire* to the nose propeller to the side flaps, which would bear the ratio of lift to resistance.

"Remember I read you Bhaskara's book when you were a boy? This is my creation. Made with Lilavati's drawings." Long ago, when he could fit on her lap, she had sung him Lilavati's puzzles as if they were lullabies.

"Ma, you can't be serious," he said. "You put this together?"

"Beta, I have not been painting this and that. What I have been doing is what you see."

He stepped toward the airplane and poked at the frame with the edge of his shoe. "It's something," he said. "And what do you intend to do with it? Put it on eBay? Sell it for a few bucks? I could help with the online stuff."

"Why would I want to sell? What I want is to fly it. *Lilavati's Fire* will take to the air. I have done the researching—pilot's license not required for tiny aircraft."

He looked at her as if she were a stranger. "Ma, are you okay?"

She could not bear to see him looking betrayed, so she tugged on his nose as she'd done all the years of his childhood. It always got a smile out of him. "Beta, don't look so bruised. I am quite fine. Your mother is simply bettering herself."

"I don't get it. Last summer, you didn't know what the internet was. I had to explain the difference between 'single click' and 'double click.'" He brushed the hair off his forehead. He'd developed an unsightly patch of dandruff; she would need to advise him on the Ayurvedic remedy for healthful hair.

"This is not the internet, Sanjay. This is Lilavati's master creation."

"It's Sammy, Mom. Sammy."

Sammy, her careless failure. Sanjay, her extraordinary blessing. She knew both better than anyone. Sanjay got a little blue in the winter, and sometimes walked into bars and wasted himself. At twenty-three, her boy had turned into a man. The slender neck, the fine, long fingers, the need for loneliness. Those he'd inherited from her.

"Sammy," she said. "Your mother needs help to put the engine. She needs a hand."

The engine lay on the floor. It would take the whole of their effort to hoist it underneath the pilot's seat.

"What does Baba think about this? Does he know?"

"What do you think, beta? Could I have shared such a thing with your father?"

"I didn't think Indian women went through midlife crises." Sanjay circled around the engine slowly as if it were the body of a dead relative. "I know I shouldn't, but I'll help you."

When he turned to leave, she offered him the leftovers she kept in the garage fridge. "It's not just lunch, this is to show my love," she said, and this time, he accepted.

. . .

That night Aparna prepared Harish's favorite meal. Since the discovery of his high blood pressure, she'd put him on a special regimen involving lots of steamed creations—leafy, American recipes that avoided oil—but tonight she scooped several dollops of ghee into the pan and allowed the onions to find their footing with the garlic. She crisped a bit of hilsa fish, then dressed the pulao with raisins and cashews imported from home. At first, she'd known none of the ways to please a man by the culinary arts, but now she knew enough to write a history of how her spices could shift Harish's moods. It still gave her pleasure, once in a while, to see him dig in with his hands. They barely spoke at the table, but she could feel the weariness of his work, where the strike had just ended, lift as he chewed. When he was finished, he burped in appreciation and reached to hold her hand. She did not refuse him, though his palm was greased with turmeric and sesame oil.

The night of her first miscarriage, after Harish had driven her home from the hospital, he set two bowls on the table and boiled chicken in a pot. He fed her the broth spoon by spoon. Then he helped her to the den and sang a Tagore melody they both knew, which sounded like "Auld Lang Syne." He sang it over and over, each time more earnestly, as if it were the mantra that would keep them whole. It was his own version of homesickness; somewhere in the middle of the night, she relaxed in his arms.

She could not remember when the feeling of that night left them, but it did, not long after. Then he was the old Harish again, and she was doing for him what she'd always done. She kept little Sanjay from taking too much of his time, and, in return, Mr. Dutta continued his streak of promotions. She wrote letters to aunts and added their recipes to hers. She cleaned the house with dedication. It had been good enough to go on like that, for quite a while.

. . .

In the field behind the town pond, Sanjay helped her unload the airplane. They used a rope to slide it from the bed of Sanjay's delivery truck into the damp grass, where the impact scattered a group of frogs into the thicket. The field was all hers, an awesome stretch of three hundred feet that ended in a line of maple trees. She would need to rise after the halfway mark. The plan was to circle around the town twice, thrice if the air wasn't too rough, and then return to this very spot. She told Sanjay to angle the nose of the machine eastward.

"Ma," he said. "What are you trying to do here?"

"Isn't it clear, beta? I am trying to fly this plane."

"No, I mean, is this some way to get back at Dad?"

"Beta, be careful when speaking about your parents. Your Ma and Baba are the sturdiest couple on the block." She tied the end of her sari to her hip, fixed the helmet on her head, and adjusted herself into the seat of the plane.

Sanjay puttered around the wing, tapping here and there with his fingers. "This is crazy," he said. "You could really hurt yourself. Ma, please."

Aparna looked at her son. When he got serious, his lips puckered too thoughtfully, as if he were giving a speech he didn't believe in. From whom had he inherited this expression? There had been an Uncle Puntu who had started with drink and ended with God, but her son would not follow that path, if she had anything to say about it.

Sanjay took hold of her hands. "You and Dad should go to couples counseling," he said. "You can work stuff out. You don't need to fly a plane to prove a point."

"You know, beta, I don't often regret having raised you in this country, but when you begin to use such words as *couples counseling*, then I think perhaps you missed something." She took her hands from his and knocked on the side of Sanjay's skull the way her family had done with Uncle Puntu. "Wake up, beta. This is not our way. Now, please, stand aside."

All this talk of Harish had soiled what should have been a day of considerable joy, but in the air, she believed she would feel a sense of perfection. She turned the ignition key and was met by the pristine sound of the engine, its sweet, lulling hum. Overhead: a troop of well-behaved geese. Her fingers, she found, were shaking a bit and there was a lump of worry at the back of her throat. She turned from Sanjay and mouthed one of Lilavati's truths: *Objects fall due to the great force of attraction. Therefore, the earth, planets, constellations, moon, and sun are held. To break this force—*

Aparna pressed on the throttle. *Lilavati's Fire* waddled forward. As the machine picked up speed, she saw the scurrying of frogs; soon the plane was carving the grass too fast for her to see anything. A little shiver. Hair streaked into her eyes. The hem of her sari caught on her heels. She bent, untangled her feet. Then she opened the side flaps to catch the air, hoping for lift—for momentum to exceed resistance—but the plane sped forward without release. When she looked up again, the geese were leagues above where they'd been, and she was still on the ground. Yards from the maple grove, she tapped the brakes and let the wheels wade through the damp grass. At this distance, she could see what the termites had done to the maple bark: the puckered skin, the telltale grooves of rot. She cut the ignition; the machine exhaled a single plume of smoke before coming to a dead stop.

. . .

When she asked Sanjay if he would take her home, he didn't say a word, though he had every right, she supposed, to call her a real *pagal*, to laugh at her airplane, which hadn't managed a moment in the air. Instead, he pulled the machine into the back of the truck and drove slower than usual. She sensed his sympathy, and was buoyed by this pouring of his love, though as they drove on, she felt bruised and incompetent. That she had not experienced flight was difficult; worse was the feeling that her calculations were wrong—Aparna Dutta was a competent housewife, and not much more.

Sanjay pulled up to their house as the sunset was coming down from the sky and the cicadas were waking, channeling their calls from body to body—this mass of life from under the earth—many of whom would soon be eaten by squirrels or frogs. She was enjoying the sound the cicadas made when her son stopped the truck a few feet behind Harish's sedan.

"Should I come inside, say hi to Dad?"

"No, beta, you don't have to. You are a young man. Do something good tonight. Be with others your own age. Don't worry about your old parents."

"Ma, don't be this way. Just because it didn't work the first time, doesn't mean you can't fix it. Seriously, look around. How many moms on this block would put together an airplane from scratch?"

She surveyed the street. A few neighbors were walking. The older and the younger, some holding hands, one stopping to pick up trash. She looked at all the lit windows and imagined inside them colonies of moths, setting their wings against the linoleum floors, the soft, velvet drapes of bedrooms. She imagined their long hours of pacing, the waiting, the ways in which the American women would speak to her. But they would not—they did not—make time for Aparna Dutta. Long ago, she had built herself a fortress on this block. She was grateful for it now, that sublime feeling of one's own silence.

Carefully, they unloaded the airplane. Harish's car was blocking the garage, so they left it on their driveway. They had made a great deal of noise and Aparna thought she saw flashes of her husband through the window, but she was too exhausted to care whether Harish noticed or didn't.

"Beta," she said, as her son turned to go.

"Yes, Ma."

She wanted to ask him so many things, but mostly she wanted to know if he believed in her abilities, if he saw her as anything more than a caregiver. There was something between them, though, which later she would describe to herself as the rift between mothers and sons, so she only put a hand on his forehead to bless him. "You will overcome, beta," she said. "Don't worry. You will do good things, great things, in this world."

"See you guys for breakfast on Sunday," he said. Then he was gone.

. . .

When she opened the door to the house, she found Harish waiting on the couch. Before she could say a word, he spread his arms out and said, "Surprise," then led her into the kitchen, where several plates of food were arrayed on the table. There was a reddish pasta dish, a bowl of scalloped potatoes, and the grilled body of a carp.

"My goodness, Mr. Dutta. What is all of this?"

"Well, Mrs. Dutta, your husband has been learning of American cooking. He has been taking online classes."

"Classes?" she said.

"Since you were learning painting," he said. "I thought I also should better myself. This is my first proper attempt."

She imagined him scouring the internet in search of the perfect class. Oh, Harish. His pasta had a sour aftertaste and the potatoes were clumped in cream, but then she'd never had the right tongue for American food. It could have been extraordinary, this gelatinous creation that was swimming around in her throat, making its way to her belly, and in fact, there was a sweetness to every part of the meal.

"It is truly good, Mr. Dutta," she said. She pursed her lips in the approximation of a smile.

They continued with knife and fork. Then he brought out a bottle of wine. "1997 Merlot—absolute best taste. Flavor of the woods," he said.

They did not have alcohol in the house unless they were entertaining Harish's boss, but Aparna went along with it. She drank a few sips as she picked at the overdone carp.

He drained his first glass and said, "Why aren't you eating more? You do not like the food?"

"It is tasteful," she said. After a pause she said his name out loud. "Harish." She'd imagined speaking his name over the years but hadn't since they'd stopped sharing a bed, when she'd learned that marriage was about keeping your honesty at a distance. It was not lying, exactly. With a love as old as theirs, the truth simply counted less and less—it began to meld into another world, and what was left was the history of the unsaid.

"There is something I would like to show you."

For some time, he did not look up from his food, which had mixed on his plate into a sort of casserole, but when he finally met her eyes, she could tell he was afraid and was trying not to let it show. It was probably the sound of her voice: she had spoken too firmly, too directly, used the familiar form without shared consent. "Husband," she said, rising from the table. "Please come with me."

He loped behind her. They stood together on the driveway before *Lilavati's Fire*. A car alarm sounded in the distance; a few dogs howled their own chorus. She looked at her husband's face and tried to discern what he saw in that streetlamp light, but it was difficult to say: even after so many years, he was unknowable in moments—a man of some unsolvable inner mystery. "Well," she said. "What do you think?"

"Oh, I don't know," he said. "These last few weeks you were acting so strange. You were going into your garage and every day painting so much, I thought—" He stopped, cleared his throat. She reached to hold his hand, but he refused. "I thought you were going to leave me," he said. "I thought you had tired of me, but now I see, you've been assembling some kind of vehicle. I suppose I am relieved."

He didn't look relieved. Instead, in that moment, he looked old, all the lines of his face converging into a surface of worry. She imagined him beyond his middle age: his hands tremulous, his mind a little loose. No, he had never meant to harm her; he had never meant to wound.

"Is it for Sanjay's birthday?" he said.

They would walk in the morning sun. He would lean on her. For steadiness.

"Aparna?"

"Yes, Harish," she said. "That's all it is."

Later that night, when she had retired to her bed and Harish had retired to his on the other side of the nightstand, she stayed awake for a while to hear the music of the cicadas, but Harish's snoring was supreme. So she went outside in her nightdress and heard them on the lawn. She sat on the grass and smelled the honeysuckle planted next door. As a girl in Kolkata, she had sucked the honey from the beaks of these flowers, living inside their smell, drunk with life.

She stared at her air chariot on the concrete; it seemed to stare back with derision. She had used the drawings of an ancient mathematician, who had never known of Newton—of his third law of action, equal reaction—and when the miracle of flight had not come and she was still on the ground, she did not think of Newton or Bernoulli's principle, of how curves under pressure create the most important form—*lift*—she thought instead of that first moment, when Sanjay had come out from her body and the nurse had passed him into her

arms, as if he were the most precious gift; and all she had
thought then, as Harish looked on weak-kneed and teary-eyed,
was how ugly her little boy seemed, how covered with blood
on his sagging skin, but she held him anyway, with his cave of a
mouth, with his arms outstretched like a fledgling bird.

## Lost Things

One afternoon as the boys were crossing from the football field to the cricket green, Mrs. Gupta emerged onto her balcony to scream. I am certain that this was the first time I had heard a grown person scream, at least in the way of impolite grief, in that prehensile way I mean, though we had known her earlier, a perfectly respectable woman. But during that year (how long did it last?—a monsoon, or into winter, when we would have played in collared sweaters) we understood, or rather I understood, that I did not know her at all.

First, I would hear the sound of her third-story door being flung open, as if hurried by a fierce wind, then she would appear in her widow's white sari (though she was not a widow) and she would run from the lip of the balcony to the railing that overlooked the aging mango tree, return inside, then sprint back again, six or seven times, it seems now, was the right number.

I cannot tell you why I remembered Mrs. Gupta's ritual while comforting my wife in a clinic that promised wanting couples a child. Except that we had just lost, yet again, the possibility of a child (an amorphous shape when it stopped being of this world) ourselves, while Mrs. Gupta had lost more—her three-year-old son, to be precise. But grief, it seems to me, brings with it imprecise analogies.

I won't (or rather I can't) tell you why the past rose up in me like the debris of a long-forgotten war, except that this is the way in which we become more circular to ourselves, in which we diminish our perceptions as narrow, purposeful things, composed of destinies, and return to the simple ways of remembering.

For the sake of our child, my father walked ten miles up a mountain so close to the Himalayas that when he recounted this story to strangers, he said he climbed the Himalayas proper, but no matter, he is nearly seventy, and ten miles for a seventy-year-old man is no small distance. Certainly not for a man who has hardly performed a ritual in his life, who has made a living of classical and nonclassical logic, studying and teaching around the globe. For such a man to climb a mountain and to leave an offering for a goddess (or rather an amorphous rock near the mouth of a cave) was a divine stroke, or so I thought.

I believe that Mrs. Gupta searched for her son with every facility available. We know that he was lost in the circus. We know the circus came to town once every year, for two weeks, and that the final day brought the most people, perhaps a quarter of the southern city. I had been there myself—I had seen, at the least, the garish elephants and the wearied lion tamers—all amuck in the noise and flight of the obscene grandeur of the living world, the two-headed boy, the girl with a tongue so long she could curl it around a glass of beet juice.

I don't know exactly where Mrs. Gupta's son disappeared,

though I believe it must have been in the great tent, where the quarter of the city adjourned, and there I believe he fell away, or perhaps he was coerced by someone, or something, and followed that inclination toward its own story.

During the nine weeks our to-be child was known as an embryo, we referred to it (here, finding a pronoun is challenging) as "the bright spot."

Those afternoons when Mrs. Gupta emerged onto her balcony, we viewed her ritual in part with the same fascination we viewed the girl with the enormous tongue. Though, there was something else, which even then with the simplicity of childhood, I understood in my belly as a kind of churning up—a warning sent by my own future self.

Plants have not fared well in our house. Even the desert plant that requires nothing more than mist was doomed. One day it was knocked over and crushed by a neighbor's dog, who came alongside the neighbor, when we held a party for our birthdays, which are, as it turns out, only two days apart. It seemed fitting to bury the bright spot in one of these plants that did not fare well, whose survival was like the arc of life itself, at first full of eagerness and bloom, then a slow, leveling off, a browning at the edges. Sometimes, an unexpected return to form.

My father, the Hindu, who climbed that mountain, would tell you that we may be reborn as plants, as elephants, anything composed of soul. We buried our bright spot in the garden by our house. It was fall. I remember the sun was not unkind, showering us with its warmth. My wife dug the dirt out with her hands and put the bright spot in. I kept my eyes shut. I remembered Mrs. Gupta's voice, the way it would echo from building to building, those days we lived so close together like ants. I remembered the terrible pitch and thunder of the aging mango tree, as it leaned in the monsoon. I lay my hand on my wife's on that tissue of unborn thing, unprepared for prayer.

## The Import

Right away Raj could tell Rupa apart from the other passengers. Even though he'd encouraged his mother to send her in American travel gear, she'd arrived in a homespun sari that looked like a hand-me-down, beleaguered and wrinkled as it was from the long journey. She clasped her hands together in greeting and tried to touch his feet, which alarmed Bethany.

"Oh, no, that's all right," said his wife. Like Rupa, she wore a nose ring, a little gem that once upon a time had set her apart.

Rupa blinked in response. The question of how well she understood English was a hotly debated topic. Raj's mother had claimed that she had enough education to be a barista, though any claim made by Raj's mother was inevitably questioned by Bethany, who still believed that Rupa knew little English and even less the ways of the world. He had tried his best to stay out of the fray. They'd made a decision, and for the next six months they'd have to abide.

Raj located Rupa's luggage; when Bethany was out of earshot, he spoke to her in Bengali. "It's all right," he said. "Don't mind Bethany-didi."

When she smiled at him he could see a winsome gap

between her two front teeth, slight enough to at once be memorable and charming.

They'd left Shay at home with his temporary babysitter, also a college-age girl but one who spent more time on her phone than watching Shay's antics, which as he'd turned three had grown increasingly more complicated, the turns of his imagination both rousing and enervating. Shay ran to the door as soon as he saw them, though when Rupa entered, dragging her one large duffel bag, he retreated behind the cover of Raj's legs.

"Who's that one?" shrieked Shay.

"This is your new babysitter," Bethany said. "Her name is Rupa, and Rupa is going to be staying with us."

"Oh, why is she wearing that?" asked Shay.

"Ask her yourself," Raj said.

"No, I won't," said Shay, but he came out from Raj's legs and tugged at Rupa's sari.

She held the fabric tight against her body. "Hello, friend," she said in staccato English.

"You're not my friend," Shay said.

"That's not how we treat our guests," Bethany said.

Raj thought he heard a pleased note in her voice. When he'd first revealed the plan, she'd laughed, thinking it a joke, then, on realizing how committed he was to the notion, had argued at every turn. One of her fears, he believed, though she'd never said it outright, was that of being usurped, but here was their little boy showing his loyalties.

That night he put Shay down as Rupa looked on. He demonstrated how much milk to pour, which books to read for bedtime, what songs to sing. At Bethany's insistence they'd installed a nanny cam in Shay's room, so they watched from their bedroom as Rupa lay next to his crib, stroked his forehead. Once or twice Shay called for his parents, but the day had been long and he had little fight left. Rupa sang her own song when Shay cried. Raj recognized the tune, thinking at first that it was one of those film numbers, until he heard the song for what it was—a harbinger of rain, of harvest.

"Let's go on a date," he said.

"You're crazy," Bethany whispered, though Rupa was out of earshot. "We barely know her."

"We've got the baby monitor," he said. "Don't worry so much." He was forever lampooning her child-rearing anxieties, though truth be told Bethany had loosened up. Anyway, it made sense, given all the trips to the fertility clinic, resulting in a quick succession of two miscarriages. When Shay finally came, those early months, each crawl, step, and then dash had felt like a disaster in waiting. There was only so much baby proofing one could do. Shay had survived, seemingly no worse for a few falls.

"Okay, but I'm keeping the monitor open the whole time," Bethany said.

They ended up having two cocktails apiece at their favorite local bar, which was just two doors down and close enough perhaps to even hear Shay crying if it came to that.

"He asked me where the moon comes from," Raj told Bethany. He knew dates were meant to exclude talk of Shay, but he couldn't help but reminisce about all that his son was saying.

She smiled as if confronted with a fading beauty, which meant that she wasn't listening to him. Maybe she was thinking about work or the roses he'd once ordered her from Kyoto. Time was passing her by. She was on business trips a quarter of the year, which meant she missed Shay more than he did. Time was passing him by, though he couldn't account for the reason. He chugged his cocktail and asked, "Now do you think it's a good plan?"

"Darling," she said, coming back to him, "your mother is always right."

It was, in fact, his mother's plan. Rupa was part of an entourage of servants that hung around their old colonial home in Kolkata. He didn't know her from Adam but trusted his mother's judgment. She'd suggested that live-in help would restore domestic bliss and offered up Rupa, for whom the six-month salary was equal to several years' wages. Not only that, but she'd offered to arrange for Rupa's visa, her flight costs, and even her salary. Inch by inch Bethany had caved in.

"We can actually go out again. We can go out on the town and be who we were," he said.

"Trust me. We can't be who we were, this village girl or no."

"Just you wait," he said. "Just you wait and see."

He had visions of reliving his early New York life, only this time with Bethany in tow. They'd met eleven years ago speed dating at a speakeasy. He won her favor by holding her gaze. Now they were parents, living through the weather. Ever since Shay had been born, they'd tried to leave the city, but something held them there. Some vital force prevented egress, and even though they'd had their fill of dazzle and moonshot, even though their bank accounts said nothing for their time toiling away, they remained as they were.

"What does *The Import* eat?" Bethany asked. Two cocktails in, she'd found a nickname for Rupa that tickled them both.

"Mac and cheese?" he asked. "Cocoa Puffs with chocolate milk?"

. . .

That first week he stayed home to help Rupa acclimate. Their house in India knew little of modernity's offerings, so Rupa marveled at the many settings of the dishwasher and the washing machine. Mostly she admired the wide variety of snacks that were available to Shay at any time. Looking through her eyes, he could see how it might feel overwhelming for his little boy, as he was posed with choices at every hour—organic strawberries or cheese sticks or veggie straws or Goldfish. Perhaps it was like that for Rupa now.

"Goldfish is not really fish. It's more like a cracker," he explained.

"GOLDFISH IS NOT FISH," said Shay, who was already lording over his new babysitter. He was off preschool for the summer, which had expedited the need for childcare.

That first morning they went to Prospect Park. Rupa bonded with Shay as he ran around a playground with a statue of a dragon, whose mouth spewed water instead of fire. Up the stairs she walked, and down the slide she came. He could tell that Shay loved the singularity of the attention. She was speaking Bengali to him, which had always struck Raj as a child's language, full of soft, cooing sounds, and Shay seemed to be following along fine enough. That was the other reason for Rupa. Raj's mother had wanted her grandson to learn her language. Raj hardly spoke to Shay in Bengali, so it was Rupa's task to bring the language to his son.

After the park and lunch, he put Shay down for his nap.

"There's some business I have to attend to," he told Rupa when Shay was asleep.

"Of course," she said. "I'm here now."

It was a thrill to leave his boy with Rupa. He wasn't sure if he could, but now he had. That she wouldn't tell Bethany was the sweetest part.

He walked to the other side of the park, where rents were a little more affordable and the greenery less plentiful. It had been here that during one of his early-morning runs as a new father he'd met Molly Choi. She was running as he was, and they matched each other's pace on the straightaway and struck up a conversation. Even though they were measuring a good clip, he could smell a cloud of lavender every time he leaned close to hear something she'd said. She was neither as pretty nor as worldly as Bethany, he came to discover, but she was better in bed. Though he wore a wedding ring, she never asked about his story. Back when he was enjoying press junkets and finding himself in the occasional one-night stand, there was no expectation of further intimacy, and the same was true of his encounters with Molly. Their get-togethers confirmed his feeling that he was simply acting out his nature. He had only recently begun to think this way, believing that there was little choice for him to do anything else but to respond to Molly's text that read *U Free?*—for it was in his constitution.

This afternoon, even though he'd explained to Molly in advance that he'd be free all week during the day hours, even though he knew that she herself had arranged to "work from home," he desisted. Ten feet from the musty hallway of her prewar building, he texted her back, *Kid won't go dwn. Sorry!* The kid he'd told her about, just not the wife. He jogged back across the length of Prospect Park, nearly trampled at one point by a spandex-clad cyclist. He realized he'd left his child—his most precious, voluble creature—in the hands of a person he barely knew. His jog turned into a sprint.

When he got home, Shay was up from his nap and roaming in the kitchen. He was trying to explain that he only wanted to eat animal crackers. Rupa was cutting the fig-sized grapes Bethany had bought into little pieces.

"He just got up," she said, continuing to slice even as she held his gaze, a display of culinary competence he found endearing. "He only wants to eat sweet things."

"We have to be careful about that," he said breathlessly. There was no fire to put out. He was relieved, though no fire to put out was also a little disappointing.

"Once he finishes his snack, would it be possible for me to make a call?" she asked.

"To India?"

"What's India?" Shay interrupted. He seemed to enjoy the challenge of having to learn their new language.

"It's the far, far-away place where Rupa and I came from," he said in English.

"Where did Mommy come from?"

"The far, far-away place called Missouri. They speak strangely there and barely know how to spell."

"It's just that it's getting late," Rupa said. "Over there, I mean. You could just call your mother on video. She'll have everyone come over."

"Hold on, skipper," he told his little boy. "We're establishing cross-Atlantic communications."

His mother answered the video chat, her face so overly close to the camera that he was level with the blackheads on her nose. "Beta, it's almost midnight. What is the matter?"

"I didn't realize it was so late," he said. Most of the times they connected it was she who called at times that suited her.

"Ma," Rupa said, squeezing beside him so he could feel the press of her hip on his. "Can I speak with her?"

"Who?" Raj asked.

"Hold on," his mother said, grumbling as she pointed the camera away and began to dress.

"Is that Grandma?" Shay asked, trying to burrow between their bodies.

"Oh," Raj's mother said, returning moments later. "It seems they've been waiting by my door."

"Who?" Raj asked again.

His mother panned the camera to show all the faces that had entered her room. He hadn't been home in over a decade and didn't recognize a soul. There was a gang of them, squinting into the screen.

"I don't see Lakshmi," Rupa said.

A little girl's face emerged into the camera. She was wearing a lacy dress that could've been used for a christening, entirely too hot for the weather. "Hi, Ma," she said.

"Who's that?" Shay and Raj said almost as one.

"That's my daughter," Rupa said. "She's turning five next week. Can I have a minute to talk with her? I want to introduce her to little Shay."

"Your what?"

"My child. Did Ma not explain?"

"Of course! Ma, I'm going to call you on your cell." He locked himself in his bedroom and considered what he'd say to his mother. This was her idea, though he'd been the one to sell it to Bethany. Apparently, she'd left out a little detail. He had assumed that Rupa was unattached, not a mother herself. They'd contracted someone to watch their child while her own remained a world away.

"Completely unacceptable," he said, when he'd gotten hold of his mother on his cell phone. "Why didn't you tell me she had a little girl? I thought she was like twenty-two or something."

"She is twenty-two," his mother said. "It just so happens that she started early. Pretty common for village people, actually."

"But you didn't tell me!" he said.

"You didn't ask," his mother replied. "Anyway, what does it matter? She has a history. All people do. That is why she is doing the job. With the money she gets she'll start sending Lakshmi to private school. Six months is not a long time, you know. There's hardly a change in that time."

Perhaps that was true of him. Once he'd landed his job at the *Times* he'd steadily put in enough hours to be neither fired nor promoted. *Do enough* was his mantra. It had been like that for most of his life, until Shay was born, and he'd decided to go part-time to become the primary caregiver, a duty he'd come to regret. In his life, little seemed to change in six months, but for Shay the same period of time had meant the difference between incoherent babbling and semi-coherent speech. Lakshmi was a little older, but still. "There's something not right about it. I'm dreading telling Bethany," Raj said.

"Why would you tell Bethany?" his mother asked, as if he were the dunce in the room.

"We don't keep things from each other," he said, thinking of Molly Choi's violet bedsheets.

"Then you are stupider than you look," his mother said. "Anyway, what will you do? Send her back? If you want, I can arrange her ticket to return home next week."

"Oh," he said, feeling a shiver run through his heart. Besides Molly Choi he'd planned a host of activities that were to be timed with Rupa's visit. The potential loss of those afternoons at the bar, or at the beach, or winding his way through the couples intimacy workshops he'd signed himself and Bethany up for, was too much to bear. "It's just that I need to wrap my head around this. Anyway, it's late over there. Goodbye, Ma."

When Bethany came home that night, she flashed a smile that signaled just how bone-tired she was. They'd entered the news world at the same time, but she'd desperately wanted to climb the ranks. So she had. From running features to becoming managing editor of a travel journal and then editor-at-large of a magazine that did travel entrepreneurship, a term he still barely understood. Whatever it meant she still paid the bulk of the rent.

They'd prepared dinner in her honor. When motivated, Raj knew how to make a meal delight all the senses, and tonight he was. Motivated, that is. They'd all three made a trip to the market, where Rupa had marveled at the ubiquity of every fruit and vegetable, wrapped her sari around her shoulders as they passed through the frozen aisle. She made a few suggestions along the way, picking up bitter gourd, which he'd tempura-battered as an appetizer.

"What's that saying? The fastest way to a girl's heart is through her stomach?" Bethany said, relishing the gazpacho he'd made with heirloom tomatoes and fresh lavender.

"We had such a nice day," he said. "Didn't we, little man?"

Shay vehemently shook his head, *no*.

"We went to the park, we got groceries, we acquainted Rupa with the neighborhood."

"Yes," Rupa added. "Yes, very good."

"Oh, I'm so glad things are working out!" Bethany said.

That night Rupa again put Shay to bed, and this time his boy put up less of a fight. Raj thought of telling his wife that he'd learned something of Rupa's history, but the dinner had gone so well that he let the moment pass.

He lay with Bethany in the dark of their bedroom, cluttered from the detritus of their travels, the trinkets all around him— the stars from Mexico with little inner lights, which they'd hung in the ceiling. Occasionally they lit those lights and had sex, though this had been abated by Shay's coming, or simply by the exhaustion of their bodies, the familiar smells and snores. This night he tried again by stroking Bethany's thigh. She murmured something.

"What is it, darling?" he asked. But it passed like a signal from a faraway planet.

. . .

The summer burned on. Bethany took a trip to Iceland, where her ancestors came from, for the sake of covering a music festival, and reported that even the far north was suffering from a heat wave. When she returned she seemed more relaxed, rejuvenated even. In her absence, Rupa had continued to learn the neighborhood. A month into her tenure, she'd even improved her English. She'd made friends with the bodega owner down the block, who regally opened the door just for her and Shay.

Raj and Bethany had reached the age where most of their friends had either tied the knot or committed to the single life the city offered. There were, however, still a few in-betweens, divorced men and women who threw potlucks to celebrate the second coming, or partnerships that were made for the sake of the children promised. It was to one of these that they'd been invited in Maine.

When he suggested that they try to leave Rupa alone with Shay for the weekend, Bethany threw her shoe at him.

"She hardly speaks English!" Bethany yelled. "What if something happens? How will she communicate?"

"She'll call me on the cell, and I'll translate," he said. "Besides, she's been picking up a few words." *Give me two mangoes for price one*, he'd heard her say to the bodega owner, who mysteriously had complied. He'd enjoyed the role of translator, his language the primary link to the person who was safekeeping their child. This frustrated Bethany, he knew that. She spoke three languages but not the one she'd need to understand what her son was now beginning to learn.

So Rupa came along, as did Shay. Raj's mood soured from the moment he picked up the minivan, which was the only rental left that could fit all of them. Driving it through the Palisades and onto I-95 he felt ancient. He'd turned forty the year before, but the gray had started to accumulate in his beard seasons earlier. Every time Shay cried or had a tantrum in the car, he felt another little strand of himself wither into old age.

Helen, the bride-to-be, had attended Bethany's alma mater, and in bygone summers Bethany had spent weeks at their house on the lake. Now they'd rented a cabin next to the wedding plot. It was also on the lake but allowed for more privacy. There'd been an option for them to stay with other families at the wedding, but Bethany had declined. He suspected it was because she was embarrassed about Rupa, who still rotated through the same three saris she'd brought from India, fastidiously washing each day's garments in the bathtub.

They'd arrived on a Friday afternoon. With the wedding not until Sunday, they had a whole day to laze around the lake. The water felt too cold to him and to Rupa also, who for once declined to follow Shay as he ran from the beach into the clear water, instead letting Bethany run alongside her son. His wife was at home here. Even in Iceland, she said, she'd bathed in the fjords, and their son had inherited his mother's gift for cold waters.

"Have you ever been to the sea in India?" he asked Rupa.

"I was in North Calcutta. I was in my village, and now I'm here. Nowhere in between."

"Oh," he said. He was going to tell her a story about the time his parents took him to a seaside resort as a child, which no longer felt apropos. "Well, do you like it here?"

"The lake is beautiful, yes."

"No, I mean America," he said. "Do you like being with our family?"

She looked at him for a long moment. Even in the hour they'd been outside, her skin had bronzed in the sun. "Your little boy has a good heart," she said. "But I miss my Lakshmi."

Since that first call with his mother, he'd almost forgotten about the existence of her own child. She hadn't asked to see her daughter again, and he hadn't offered. It had seemed for the best. Once the time to tell Bethany the truth had passed, a gentle forgetting was all anyone could hope for. Even when his mother had called to check up on Shay and Rupa, they'd never again discussed Lakshmi. He wondered now who was taking care of her—a grandmother, an aunt, the uncle who chauffeured his mother around?

"We can call her again when we get back to Brooklyn," he said. He would have offered they try this weekend in Maine, but his cell phone didn't work and neither did the Wi-Fi, Helen's family having chosen to forego installing a satellite dish or doing anything that would interrupt their connection to the bucolic setting.

When Shay took his nap, Raj and Bethany visited Helen and Rob, her husband-to-be, in their house. Rob fixed margaritas for everyone, and Helen shared their honeymoon plans for Tahiti.

"A bungalow on the beach is exactly what I need after all this. It's on stilts, so it sways whenever there's a wave, which means you sleep more deeply."

Rob licked the salt off his margarita glass. He was into watches that told him things about his body. At the moment he was testing and wearing three separate ones, one of which caught the light from the lake and glowed like an orb. "So who's the refugee?" he asked.

"Hey, that's not nice," said Helen. "Unless, of course, she is a refugee, which is perfectly fine, of course. There are countries where horrible things happen, and we shouldn't close our doors to everyone."

"She's not a refugee. She's here on a legal visa," Raj said.

"More to the point," Bethany said. "She's here to take care of Shay. Plus, she's being paid for by Raj's mother, so cheers to that."

They all clinked glasses, including Raj, who pretended he was enjoying the joke as much as anyone. Slowly he zoned himself out of the conversation, smiling at the right times so no one would notice. There was an extraordinary amount of pink Himalayan salt on the lip of his glass, and he took his time to surreptitiously lick it off.

It was nearly evening when they thought to return to their cabin. Bethany was the one who'd realized, even though she'd had one margarita more than he, that the afternoon had flown by. "He's up from his nap, I'm sure, our little man," Bethany said. The tequila failed to mask the anxiety in her voice.

"Don't worry. The Import's there, and she's more responsible than both you and me," he said, which he'd meant to elicit a chuckle, but no one joined in.

They walked back to their cabin as the sun began to set on the lake. Even the old house next to theirs where no one lived, which was being subsumed by the land, seemed as if it were made of impressions and follies, the nails on the clawed wood of the docks shining like white teeth.

The door to their cabin was open—no one bothered to lock doors here—but the house was quiet.

"Shay, baby?" Bethany called. She couldn't help but sound chirpy whenever she was worried, but Raj knew the difference.

"Maybe they're playing hide-and-seek?" he offered.

They searched through all the rooms. Shay's stuffed octopus was in his crib. His diaper bag with its travel toys was missing, as was Rupa's pea coat, which was too warm for the weather but which she'd brought anyway.

"Obviously they went for a walk," Raj said. Even he had begun to feel it in his belly, the beginning of trouble. He'd always had a knack, as a reporter on the beat, for knowing, for instance, when to leave a protest before it became unruly. He thought of himself as a survivor, someone who made it through life's turbulences through the grace of this sixth sense.

Once again Bethany restarted her cell phone, but there was still no service. "One of these houses must have a land line. We could call the police, get them to help us," she said.

"That's a little premature, isn't it?" Raj said. He led them into the twilight, unsure of how to begin their search.

"We'll split up," Bethany said, taking charge. "I'll go get Helen. You look in the other direction."

The other direction meant the road that led off the island. "Road" was an exaggeration, though. It was a graveled stretch of land; there weren't even barriers to keep cars from falling into the water. As it darkened, he used his cell phone as a flashlight. The lock screen photo was one of Shay at seven months, an epoch before, when they'd barely been sleeping through the night and when he'd questioned his life choices, as he was doing now, walking alone on that path where few of the cabins were lit.

He kept telling himself that Rupa was a village girl, which meant she knew something more about the darkness than he did. Probably she was not even afraid, wherever she was.

Nearing the end of the island, he saw a canoe in the middle of the lake. He couldn't tell if it was Rupa and his little boy until he shined his light toward them and heard a response.

*Oar in the water*, Rupa called.

"Okay, you stay where you are!" he yelled back, as if they had a choice.

He ran back toward the cabin and found Helen, Bethany, and Rob carrying life vests and a giant flashlight.

"I found them," he said triumphantly. "They went out on a boat and lost their oars, so they're just floating there. They're perfectly safe."

"You saw Shay? He's all right?"

"I heard Rupa. She said everything was fine," he said. In fact, he hadn't seen his boy or heard from him, the boat too far in the water to make out faces. Years later, sitting with his therapist, he would also begin to question whether in fact he'd heard Rupa. *Oar in the water.* He couldn't think of the Bengali phrase for that, and Rupa wouldn't have said it in English.

"I'll get our boat," Rob said.

They all squeezed into a motorized dinghy that had been beached on Helen's dock. The oar-less canoe was still there, floating perhaps a little farther away from the island.

"I've got some rope, so we can just tie them to us," Helen said.

They seemed so capable in a crisis, these two. He hoped it

would make for a memorable nuptial story they'd embellish with humor and retell for years to come.

For what seemed like minutes, Bethany hadn't said a word. He held her hand, felt her quickened pulse. She would as rather choke him now as give him the time of day. A reckoning was what she was planning, though he didn't know the details. He wanted to calm her and seem strong. She flexed her wrist and took his hand away as if it were a soiled napkin.

Nearing the boat, Rob dimmed the lights. It was still hard to see, but there was Rupa waving at them.

"You will go into that boat," Bethany said quietly. "You will bring my boy back. I don't care if you leave her there."

Rob steered the boats close together. When he lurched into the canoe, Raj saw Shay asleep in cat pose. Rupa had a hand on his forehead. She didn't seem at all surprised to see him. That's when he noticed the oar lying in the middle of the canoe. He kneeled to examine it for any defects, but it seemed right as mud.

"What are you doing out here?" he asked.

"I didn't want to remain inside," she said. "He was having a fit. We needed air."

"But it's dark, and I called you from the shore. Didn't you hear me?"

She gazed into the dark water. The slant of her face reminded him of a hunting knife held in shadows, a thin, sharp instrument. His knees began to shake. The stars edged closer to the lake, or so it felt, as if on this night the cosmos was aiming to suffocate him.

Finally she returned to him and spoke in a voice so low that only he could hear, "You worry at the wrong times and about the wrong things."

"What is she saying?" Bethany shouted. "What did she do to my son?"

"What you should worry about is a woman who fails to love you," said Rupa. She put the hood of her sari over her head, rocked in her seat as if muttering a prayer.

"Bring him here right now," Bethany called.

Rupa stood to her full height. Perhaps, there'd been a river in the village, for she balanced in the canoe like a natural. She bent to pass him Shay. For a moment her callused hands met his before he brought his boy back into the dinghy. Helen attached a rope to the canoe and they set off for the shore.

Back in his mother's arms, Shay awoke. He seemed startled by the moonlight. The night was alive with the chorus of bullfrogs and crickets and the hums of a myriad of other insects. For a long moment he remained quiet. "Why are there so many frogs?" he finally said.

The love roared out of Raj for his little boy. "There are a million frogs here," he said in his first language, which had become for them like a secret tongue, but Bethany was holding Shay to her breast, cooing into his ear, as if he were a baby newly emerged from the womb. Behind them he could see Rupa clearly: a cheap nose ring, a dark face in the pale light. They were pulling her toward the shore as if she were their prisoner, but it was not like that at all. She had come of her own intent. It was that you could know a person only so well. Then their own ideas would muddle the water. Then you'd have to return them to where they belonged.

## Prodigal Son

Fourteen hours on the plane to Kolkata gave Jonah ample time to feel superior to the other travelers, especially those parents who were bringing along their hapless toddlers. He was traveling to visit his guru in a village that no one knew of. Predictably, the cabdriver tried to cheat him, even though he'd taken this route many times over the past fifteen years. He was still disappointed by the inflated rate, his whiteness announcing itself long before he could switch to a Bengali slang, convince the driver of his adopted roots. His wasn't a perfect vernacular but should've been good enough to avoid the tourist's fare.

Guruji lived near a sweet shop in a house whose electricity Jonah paid for. With his meager earnings in America, he paid for the gardening as well—a bed of azaleas bright in the sun—and for diabetes pills for Guruji and the education of Guruji's son. It was his guru's son who came to greet him.

"Oh, Uncle," Karna said, touching Jonah's face as if he were blind. It had been two years since they'd seen each other, and now Guruji's son seemed more urbane, his face strikingly angular, a fine moustache having found its way onto his upper lip.

Suparna, Karna's mother, emerged. She was fussing about

his suitcase, though it was mostly empty, and fussing about his weight, too. Since his boy had been born, Jonah had been so busy he'd skipped meals more often than he cared to admit.

"You've come back to us a ghost," Suparna said. "But no worries, we'll fatten you up again."

Guruji came out, leaning on his cane. "What a ruckus," he said, though it was clear that he was happy to see his second son.

. . .

Jonah had found Guruji at that time in his life when nothing seemed permanent. Twenty-three years old and grasping to call something his own. He used to play folk music at the Bitter End on Bleecker, money out of a hat enough to tide him over from couch to couch, a drink and a lover to boot. He could always play the life out of his guitar, but he never had the voice to attract a label.

Guruji said as much when they first met in Kolkata, all those years ago. "Your voice has a demon in it," he'd said. "But there is still music in you."

The flute calmed him. He found he could play for an hour and escape his anxieties for the day. He became Guruji's first international student and eventually his most devoted, practicing in the mornings and late into the evenings. Year after year while he freelanced in America and pursued a degree in music theory, he'd return to Kolkata to show what he'd learned and to learn the next difficult thing, and every year Guruji would say, "Almost, beta. You are almost there."

He remembered those words as Suparna poured him tea and asked about Samuel, who'd just turned two.

"It was hard to leave the little guy," he said, though that was not entirely true. He loved his boy, but once he'd set foot on the plane, he hardly paused to think about him. What he'd thought of instead was sitting with his guru again—one last time, he'd promised his wife. To learn not only from Guruji but also from Karna. "Play something," he said, smiling at Guruji's son.

Karna's lips found their way onto a melody they'd once learned together, an afternoon raga that cut through his jet lag, his sense of city self. When Karna played it sounded like a younger version of Guruji, the plainly hopeful notes breaking through Guruji's more skeptical, sparse turns.

"Splendid," Jonah said, his eyes shut, the music leaving the taste of honey in his mouth. When they'd first learned this raga together, Karna had been a five-year-old boy. Now he was months shy of becoming an adult, though even in the early years he'd been serious enough to sit by his father's feet, for the little boy had no demon in him—he had only song.

"Too sentimental, beta," Guruji interrupted. He was always harder on his biological son, but Jonah knew what perfection sounded like—the boy wasn't far off, not at all.

"When do we record the album?" Guruji asked.

"Soon, Baba," Jonah said. He'd brought along recording equipment to produce an album of Guruji's best compositions. Though he was surely a gem of his generation, his guru had never made the headlines. He'd never toured the big cities in America or Europe. Instead, he'd worked his whole life as a tax collector, playing music on the evenings or weekends.

That hadn't mattered to Jonah when he'd first heard his guru play a concert in Kolkata. A maestro, Jonah thought, though Guruji's style, even then, was antiquated, a throwback to a time of courts and minstrels. Jonah would make the album for Guruji, but he doubted that it would bring fame. A few years into his apprenticeship he'd accepted the hard truth that Americans didn't care for flutes or ragas; the music they played required a commitment to do nothing but listen, and listening was in dying supply, even in Jonah's own house, where sometimes he'd catch his wife's eye, her love for him and her doubt of his art; oh, she'd never discouraged his flute playing, but sometimes in the early mornings when she'd mosey into the living room where he practiced, he could sense her bewilderment: *Why keep on?*

As Karna stopped playing, the weariness of Jonah's long travel returned. He was shown to the guest room, where Karna had arranged hyacinth petals on the pillow. "For beauty sleep," Karna said expectantly. From the beginning, Karna had needed acknowledgment for the smallest acts, hanging on to his father's dhoti for scraps of praise, and now Jonah obliged, stroking the fine hairs on the back of Karna's neck, before he slipped under the sheets. Karna sat by him on the floor, playing another melody, nothing serious, just whatever came to his lips. There were a few raw notes in the composition, but Jonah didn't mind. "Play until I fall asleep," he said, not intending to sound like he was giving a command.

When he awoke from his nap, night had fallen on the village. The house was quiet, and someone had slung a mosquito net over his bed, which he felt grateful for. Guruji's family might have made a stop at the village temple; they were always throwing flowers into fires, hoping for rain. He needed to call Melanie, so he headed to the phone booth in the village center, with its pay meter that clicked every few seconds.

"Hello," she said, her voice caught between layers of static.

"I made it," he said, trying to subdue the elation that he felt. She was three months pregnant with their second child and wouldn't appreciate the joy he'd felt leaving home. "How is baby?"

"Which one?" she asked.

She was not happy with him, though she'd agreed to give him this week between a toddler and a newborn for himself. *One last trip to your motherland*, she'd said. The only time she'd joined him in Kolkata she'd caught a case of dysentery so severe she'd spent two days in the hospital; ever since, India had been his motherland, not hers.

"I love you," he said, watching the pay meter jump with every word he spoke. If only there were such a meter for life itself, you would feel how little time was left in this world; you would say the things that mattered.

"Goodbye," she said. "I know it's a fortune to call."

After she hung up, he imagined her in their railroad apartment in Brooklyn, a coffee in one hand and a cloth diaper in the other. It was much too small now that they had a child and another on the way, but that was true for most anyone in New York. The day before he'd left they'd been trenched in all morning, the branches outside snapping from the wind and the weight of the falling snow. He had strapped his son to his chest to walk into the blizzard. When they returned, Melanie started a bath, and he lay in it with her and with Samuel, who curled close and sucked his thumb. There was still sweetness there, though not as often, not nearly as often as when they'd first called each other beloved.

"Two hundred forty rupees," someone called, knocking on the booth.

Heading back to Guruji's, he could see that the family had returned, and they'd put Bollywood songs on the antique turntable. Through the window, he could see Suparna dancing, which was mostly a stationary business with a coquettish flutter of the hands.

"There you are," said Guruji.

Inside the house, everyone was wearing festive clothes. Someone had put eyeliner under Karna's eyes, dressed him in a red kurta that was too big for him. It was a party in his honor, Jonah guessed, a welcoming home. Sweet that they'd taken the trouble, though he could've done without the music, the lilting high-pitched voice of the playback singer too tawdry for his taste.

"Well, tell him the good news," Suparna said.

"We were waiting till you returned to us," Guruji said. "This is engagement party. We are marrying our little boy."

The sentence confused him. He imagined Guruji marrying his own son, though that was not it, for Suparna was smiling. Now he realized why Karna was dressed for the occasion and why the sweets were finer than any he'd ever been offered.

"She's just passed her exams," Suparna said. "The family is well established, living in Howrah. They own two rickshaw repair shops and one shoe store."

"Karna's way too young," Jonah said, unable to control himself.

"Why? He is the age I was married," Guruji said, the smile on his lips beginning to waver.

"Karna should become a musician who tours the world. He has the talent, Guruji."

"He will play the music that is in his heart after he finishes his job. I will find a civil service post for him, do not worry."

"He's not even twenty-one. Don't sell him out."

Guruji lowered his voice. "You are my second son, but not even you can disrespect me in my own house."

The blood rushed to Jonah's face, then left it; he worked his jaw from side to side to bring the feeling back. This was a different rebuke than the ones he'd received trying to master the flute. This time Guruji had spoken quietly, as if no one else should hear him being shamed.

"I apologize," he forced himself to say. He couldn't make himself meet Guruji's eyes. He packed his things and left for the village hotel.

He hated the hotel, having stayed there the first few times he'd come to the village, before he and Guruji's family grew close. At night the roaches would leave their hiding places to crawl over his bedsheets, and in the early mornings the hotel staff would knock and then immediately burst through his door to deliver tea, the enthusiasm of seeing a white man enough to throw propriety out the window. He tried to fall asleep, but the clock in his body was still on the other side of the ocean. Instead, he watched old videos he had filmed of Karna. Whenever Guruji napped, he and Karna would roam the village. Sometimes, Jonah would teach him English. He'd do this by having Karna sing old folk covers.

*To everything turn, turn, turn*, Karna crooned on the video.

At least, when it came to folk songs, Jonah had the upper hand. He'd always wanted to be his guru's finest student, but from the moment that Karna played the scales, he knew he'd never measure up. There was something Karna had that ten thousand hours of practice hadn't given him. Sometimes, he blamed his whiteness. Sometimes, he blamed his city life. These days, he mostly blamed the duties of fatherhood, which he'd begrudgingly embraced with body and soul, unlike Guruji, who'd never changed a diaper. It was not in his stars to become a musician, he'd decided with Melanie, so she'd allowed him to visit India a final time. This trip was to be a goodbye to that life. But it needn't be for Karna, who, from the beginning, quickly progressed from repeating a melody to transforming it into his own language, imbuing feelings he was too young to name.

Someone knocked on his door. "Go away," he said.

"It's only me," Karna said.

It was not so late to consider a visit out of the ordinary. After all, he'd come from a whole continent away. He let Karna in.

For years afterward, he would search for the smell of Karna on the other side of the door, that sliver of life, that musk, and he would remember the aluminum taste in his mouth, his knees frozen. Now he looked for a place to sit. Only the bed was suitable. Jonah fixed the rumpled sheets, searched his bag for snacks, and offered Karna a granola bar.

"I'm totally full," Karna said. "But why did you leave so quickly?"

Now that he was out of the blankets he could feel a chill in the air, not cold, what in his world counted as the first sign of autumn, though back home he knew it was snowing; he knew Melanie had been out that morning with her shovel while Samuel watched from the window. He shivered a little, tore into the granola bar himself. The gesture felt rude, but he was already halfway through. It was chocolate peanut butter, which stuck to his teeth.

"I don't care for the idea of marriage for you," Jonah said. "You can be one of the great musicians of our, I mean *your*, generation."

"You are too kind, Uncle. The problem is that the girl's family is very rich, and dowry is very good," Karna said.

They were forever lampooning their lack of wealth. Along with perfect pitch, Guruji had passed on his miserly attitude to his son, his belief that they were to always live in lack, though over the years Jonah had done his very best to scrape away money for them, delivering a monthly check to Western Union as if it were a piece of his heart.

"I understand money is hard. I just don't want you to throw your life away." He had almost said: *I just don't want you to end up like your father.* A tax collector with few fans and a single, poor, devoted student.

"Do you remember when you played *yaman*? Like, when you really understood it? It made me remember the one time I was in Greece, swimming in the ocean at night with the fish glowing greenish blue in the water. The only person who can transport me like that is your father."

Jonah grabbed one of his flutes and tried to draw out the notes the way Karna had, and though he was capable of a technical fluency he still lacked the fortitude of Karna's turns. Within the notes were the many microtones, too many to

write down; you'd have to remember them in your body. Jonah
tried, but it came out a simulacrum.

"Yes, yes, it's like you're floating in the ocean a day before
the storm," Karna said. He took Jonah's flute to his lips
and began to play. *Yaman* was the evening song, and it was
meant to be played in the twilight, in that ambiguous hour
where dogs appeared like wolves. Karna played slow and fast,
bringing in melodies Jonah had never heard. He teased the
rhythm structure, which was in twelve beats, and it seemed
for moments that there was no ending, no beginning. When
he hit a particular low note, it felt to Jonah like the music had
changed the work of his heart so that it was beating in time
with the music.

Afterward, Jonah sat in silence while Karna cleaned the
flutes, but he still heard the music. No one had ever played
*yaman* as Karna just had, Jonah thought. And he had been the
one to witness it.

"So, what are my options, Uncle?" Karna said. "We are not
people who can change our lives so easily."

"You must come live in America with us," Jonah said. He
hadn't meant to speak these words, but as soon as they'd come
out he recoiled at how familiar they were. It was no more
than a fantasy he'd played in his mind for many years, the
prodigy coming to live in their house, Melanie accepting Karna
completely. In that moment, he didn't think of his burgeoning
family, their lack of space or funds, or even Melanie's
hardening heart, he thought only of how Karna played the
scales, how those refrains traveled up his spine.

"Oh, Uncle," Karna said. "I feel you've unburied me."
Jonah used fingers that still smelled of chocolate to wipe away

Karna's tears. As he did so, he found that Karna's eyes looked more beautiful with a smudge of black.

Someone lumbered down the hallway and entered the adjacent room. He held his breath. When he laid his hand on Karna's chest, he could hear Karna's heart as clearly as when they'd bathed in the village stream together, let the current play on their bare legs. Next door someone tuned the television to what sounded like a Bollywood movie. He breathed again, thankful for the cover, and let his mouth find the boy's.

Next door, it sounded like a car chase musical: an automatic rifle announced itself, and then a woman began to sing a throaty conniption. He kept his hand by Karna's heart until its rhythm matched his own. "Don't call me Uncle," he said, laying the boy on his bed.

. . .

The next morning, he awoke alone with a note on his pillow. *Thank you for everything, Jonah*, the note said in a fine cursive. He blamed his jet lag for his transgression. His lack of sleep from being a new parent plus the sleeplessness of the plane—he was always wearing dark circles under his eyes—which had meant that once again his lips and hands had roamed where they shouldn't. It was not only that. For a few hours they'd basked in the possibility of their America. He would take Karna to his stomping grounds, introduce him to the regulars. One of his old contacts might launch the boy on an illustrious career. He imagined Karna at Carnegie Hall as he and Melanie beamed like proud parents from the front row.

But in the morning, he saw the filth of the room, the old

stains on the sheets, the desk chip-toothed, the floors cracked. The thin walls between the rooms did little to dampen the snoring that came in stereo. A used condom lay on the floor. Now, he would have to undo that which he'd promised. In the shared hotel bathroom, he dumped a bucket of cold water on his head. A moment of passion—when he'd been with Karna, it had felt as if he were in the center of that glorious, sweet music—was all it had been.

He headed to Guruji's to triage the situation. He found Suparna in the living room, cleaning the wicker mats where he'd once sat for lessons. "Oh, beta," she said. "I am so sorry for the disturbance last night."

What did she know of their tryst? Even those afternoons in the village stream when ankle had grazed ankle, when he'd dried Karna's back with his towel, his affections hadn't been more than avuncular. What he'd known of Karna was through the family life, the evenings spent listening to classics on the turntable. But now Karna was older; his music had been like an enchantment. The dogs at dusk had turned into wolves, and the muscles of Karna's shoulders had been strong enough to sink his teeth into. They'd proceeded through the ritual slowly, for he believed in so doing he might remember the particulars years later. "I had no right to challenge what will surely be a beautiful union, Auntie," he now said. "It's not my place."

"Of course, it's your place," Suparna said, looking at him as if he were slow. "You are family to us. Do not wonder about that. Anyway, all this morning Karna has been dancing something happy. Now he's gone to tell Guruji the good news. Guruji had an errand at the post office, but Karna simply could not wait."

"The good news—you mean about the wedding?"

"Oh, no, the wedding's been canceled," Suparna said. "Who needs a little dowry when your boy's going to America?" She yelped in delight and kissed his cheeks.

"Oh, America," he said, as something vile caught in his throat. Of course, Karna would already have told his parents about Jonah's offer. Now Jonah would have to explain how America was mostly a distant possibility, not only to Karna, but also to Guruji and his wife.

"Why don't we all go celebrate?" she said.

"Celebrate?" he winced.

She took his head onto her bosom, stroked his thinning hair, and cooed into his ear: *Thank you, thank you, beta.*

. . .

The post office was the grandest of buildings. Long ago, in the lore of the village, the British had imagined that this spot of land was to become their capital in India, only to change their mind once they saw how the post office sunk a centimeter into the mossy swamp the village had always been known for. Still, it remained as the last act of gallantry—a stroke of accidental beauty, with Greek balustrades and verandas of marble, and an old mahogany door that could've protected a medieval castle.

Given that the locals didn't receive enough mail to warrant such a building, they'd turned the institution into a mall of sorts. Vendors from nearby villages set up their wares on foldout tables. One could purchase a samosa, try on a faux-silk scarf, or even arrange a marriage with the local matchmaker. They found Guruji and his son at a table that offered thermal underwear and coats.

"Oh, beta," Guruji said, giving him a great hug. "All my life I wondered why one would buy such a great big coat. Now I know the reason. It is for America." He held up an ugly green winter coat that looked to have been salvaged from consignment. "Karna will need such a thing, no?"

"It does get cold in New York," Jonah said.

That afternoon he returned to the phone booth and metered a call to Melanie. "How is everything at home?" he asked.

"Why are you calling again?" she asked. "Your son puked three times last night, and I had to clean the mess three times. Anyway, he's better now, if you're one to care."

"I am one to care. I am definitely one to care," he said. He tried to imagine how he could broach the subject of bringing someone home with him. "So, Karna's doing really well."

"Yes, and?"

"Well, I thought it would be a good time for him to launch his career in New York."

"Oh no you don't," she said. "No way am I spending another dime on that carnivorous family."

"They're all vegetarians," he said.

"Your son's smearing poop on the walls," Melanie said, hanging up the phone.

"Very expensive call. Two hundred seventy rupees," the attendant said, and Jonah fished out of his wallet the exact amount.

He could've guessed what Melanie would say. Now, when he returned to America, it would mark an end to his amphibious nature: he would be known not as *flautist*, nor even as *lover*, but merely as *dad*. He would be expected to earn a suitable income. There was a preschool back home that needed a music teacher, and he had a degree for that, if not the desire.

He walked to the river and dipped his toes into the shallows. All around him the birds that had migrated south for the winter flattered themselves and those that remained yearlong carried their own cacophony. A few feet away an old, rotten jackfruit too heavy for its host fell to the earth with a piece of branch. Here, the trees grew heavy with offspring but hardly shed their leaves, a country of perennial sun; even in the so-called winters, there was a significance of bloom.

That night, he arranged his recording equipment in Guruji's living room, and though there was no video involved, Guruji emerged in his wedding finery with his oldest instrument in hand. He played an evening raga that soon left Jonah in tears. Before Samuel and before this other baby to come, they'd had a miscarriage. He did not know why the way Guruji played, which that night was perhaps the finest he'd heard, made him think of that crawl of life in his wife's body, the work of the pregnancy he'd been jealous to inhabit, that being so easily scratched from the world. That was why they hadn't arrived at a name for Samuel till days after he was born. As Guruji caressed the low notes, Jonah longed for his child and wife and their small apartment. Somewhere in the song Karna joined in, providing harmony, though that was not their usual way. Even Suparna lent her song to the chorus.

"Do you think it will be well received in America?" Guruji asked when they were finished with the cuts.

"Very much," Jonah said.

In the early morning, he awoke to find everyone else still asleep, Karna's head on his father's lap, a trio of snores

interrupting birdsong. He felt miserable but clear in what
he needed to do: he should have known he was ruined the
moment he'd stepped on the plane to Kolkata. A quick peck
on Karna's lips before he repacked his things; Jonah left
behind his granola bars and his recording equipment, which
he imagined would sell for half the cost of a ticket to the
States. It wouldn't be enough, but perhaps it would count for
something.

. . .

Soon after he returned home, they moved upstate. It was
so much cheaper, and there would be a yard and deer to
glimpse through the trees. While Melanie worked five days a
week, Jonah cut his teaching load to take care of Samuel and
Gandharva, their second son, whose name meant "music."
When Gandharva was still small enough to be carried in a
sling, Jonah took the boys into the woods, and one day his
second son matched the call of a passing loon with his own
sweet voice, note for perfect note. Jonah thought then: *Here
is the one*, though over the years that memory faded into
confusion. Even with tutelage from two maestros, Gandharva
exhibited no further musical talent. Instead, he became known
for writing limericks that made his teachers blush and in
second grade changed his name to Gary. Jonah's boys loved
him with a fierceness he found frightening. Sometimes, he'd
pretend to be deeply asleep just to feel their anxious hands on
his face, cajoling him back to life.

Jonah never responded to Guruji's letters, or Suparna's
postcards, or even Karna's emails, which shifted over the years
from bewilderment to an imperious rage. Karna had believed

that their night together had meant something more than it had. *I put my hopes on you*, Karna wrote in his last email. *Only to find you lack a heart*. Jonah had touched his chest when he read the line to confirm the anatomical truth.

A decade later, he found their last recording in his garage, which by then was filled with strollers, bicycles, and the detritus of children growing older. It was the thick of winter, with snowmen arranged on their property like sentries. Only deer walked the woods, though he yearned to hear the forest music that meant the season was finally set to change. As sleet knocked against the garage door, he played Guruji's tracks, and his heart began to race. Oh, those old familiar notes: evening's song. For a moment he struggled to breathe as a terror coursed through his chest—what had he done?

*Lessons with Father*

I wanted to know something about my father's art, though by then he was already dying. His last days were like any of the days after my mother had passed, and I had come to his house to assume his care, which meant, as I remember it now, two things: cooking a lentil and tomato soup that would last him several meals, and replenishing his supply of comics—*Tintin* and another series that was surely inspired by Melville, because for years the same crew had been adrift at sea, searching for an island that would give them power and a reason for having devoted their lives to the search.

My father was a painter at a time when art was central to our country's fight for independence, and I supposed my own entry into music had as much to do with the communities of youths who'd barged into our flat at all hours, that sense always that my father, wild-haired and loose-tongued and smelling of his sandalwood cologne, and all the others— Satyendar Bose, Jatin Sanyal, Triveni Chatterjee—were knocking on the door and by their knocking alone would freedom be possible. I suppose I grew up with the sense that oppression was always temporary. By the time I entered school, my father's paintings had been displayed in London, New York, and Madrid. And India was a free country.

I had turned fifty when I told him I wanted to learn painting. Behind me and ahead of me I could see the great repetition of my life. But what did he know of my unhappiness? He only said that I should stick to my music, that at this age there was no reason to learn anything difficult.

. . .

It takes courage to be angry at a dying man, especially if that man is your father, but I loved him well enough to be angry with him then. For days we were cold to each other. A week passed and I did not trim his fingernails, a ritual I knew he secretly enjoyed: the taking of his hands, the studying of the tremulous life line. At his age the nails had brittled, become glass-like, but still they grew like weeds. Were it not for my ministrations, they'd turn into claws.

In response he stopped bringing me the paper, which he'd usually open to the cinema section, tolerating but never quite understanding my love of a good Bollywood number.

I explained all this to my husband. He appreciated my paintings. At least, he complimented them in as many ways as he knew how, which was not a great deal, but still, when learning something new, any encouragement will suffice. Ever since we'd given up trying to conceive, almost ten years ago, he'd encouraged me in areas great and small. Our childlessness brought out in him a desire to praise, in his way—to nurture.

The next week I told my father that if he didn't teach me

I would seek the help of his juniors (over the years, he'd apprenticed nearly a dozen painters, a couple of whom now held their own fame).

No, he finally said, let me.

. . .

I grew up in a country accustomed to death. It was no special privilege. So many of us witnessed riots, mothers dragged by their braids, skullcaps burned, so many heads lifted onto pyres and, with all the vigor of public ceremony, set to flame. Still, it is different when you see the slow unraveling. Today when I was drying him after his bath my father handed me a tooth. It had come undone in the night, but he'd plied it in place for as long as he could, until finally he surrendered it into the warmth of my palm; a bit of his gum tissue still stuck to the dulled enamel.

. . .

We began our lessons on a Thursday afternoon. I made him his milk tea. I brought out a couple of my own brushes—using his would have felt too familiar—and set the colors in a row. A few examples of my drawings, landscapes mostly, I put on display.

He reviewed my landscapes, studied them with that expression he wore when touring the National Museum, an expression that suggested indifference, amusement, and, alternately, a deep curiosity. So it was impossible to know what he thought of any piece of art, including mine.

He assembled the canvas by the window and put my

brushes in order. Then he said, Wait. I pulled my chair close
to the window, where I could see what he saw every day—the
light over the family across the lane. In this part of the city,
the streets were wide enough to allow only bicycles, no cars,
and often we could see every detail of what happened in their
house, as surely they could in ours. They were a young couple
with a daughter, the woman rather pretty, the child with
pearl drops in her ears, though she could not have been older
than six months. For hours, the mother, a housewife, would
hold the child in her arms on the old, colonial roof, which
was leaning dangerously, every few weeks another piece of
stonework gone missing.

What is the difference between this light, my father said,
and the light when we first sat? I tried to remember. There was
the wind. There were the baby's cries. At one point the mother
had brushed her own hair and it seemed like black gold. Now
close your eyes, he said, and paint the difference.

. . .

When my father passed away, there was a great deal to do.
Much of it concerned money, with which he'd never been
proficient. I handled his most pressing debts, and I left his
studio intact. For days, I returned to that window to spy on the
young mother and her child. By now, the child could balance
on the mother's thighs by the balcony's balustrade, open her
pink, impish mouth, and peek over the gulf.

Yesterday, I found the last painting my father made. It was
behind the gramophone, somewhere I wouldn't have thought
to look. Maybe he wished to keep it from me, maybe it was a

gift he never completed. It's the face of a woman, or rather, half of her face, drawn with a few brushstrokes. Was it the woman next door, who kept my father company each day, or was it me, or was it no one that I knew?

I painted where his hand had been. I made the lines whole.

## Daisy Lane

When Shira first heard about Daisy Lane, she experienced a moment of bliss before Harold argued away any notions of charitable grandeur. There would be no daisies on Daisy Lane, and the orphanage, named after the street, would repulse them. They would wish to leave as soon as they'd arrived, he'd proclaimed, but still they had come, having flown across the world, largely due to the breadth and force of her desire to bring into their life what had not come after years of trying naturally—a child of their own.

She was nervous when Ravi, the orphanage's main caretaker, answered the door, surrounded by several of his curious children, a few toddlers toddling and two teenage boys sporting pencil moustaches, and though she was disturbed by the peeling paint, the discord of broken toy parts, the sheets hanging off cribs stained an old, nebbish yellow—a scene that seemed to confirm Harold's suspicions—she did not look away.

"Your future son is sleeping," Ravi said. "May I offer you something to drink?"

"We're fine, thank you," Harold replied. He'd convinced her to avoid all food or drink that they themselves hadn't brought from America or purchased from their four-star hotel. Except tea was all right. She'd read that in the *Everything India* guidebook. She didn't say no when Ravi offered again, even though Harold gave her a look like he'd wring the clay cup from her hands. Now in the twelfth year of their marriage, they should have entered a phase of steady sweetness; instead, they'd begun to quarrel over the right sort of wine, politics, and even what to name their child. Not uncommon, but still. From a first year of ecstasy that included the muddy pits of Woodstock '69, in an age when no one compromised on love, their marriage now stood on arthritic knees. No affairs, no extraordinary fights, just a malaise developed over the years. They'd married in their early twenties, so it was hard to find anyone to blame. A child could save the bones, illumine their house and gazebo with unfettered love. But *she* would need to lead them out of the fog.

"I want to see my baby," Shira said.

"If you don't mind, madam, Boone is sleeping—shall I wake him?" Ravi asked. He had a strange way of pronouncing their chosen name, more like *Bon*.

The first time they'd met Ravi was at a farmer's market in Westchester. He had stitched together a little stall, as if adopting a child were like buying the perfect orange. Still, there was something comforting about his manner. He was from the north of India and had eyes as green as her own.

"Let him sleep," she said, trying to cull her anticipation. She'd waited four months and now could wait the length of a nap. She released herself from the company of the two men to wander the main room of the orphanage. There was a single large window that brought in the smell of the sewage that was piled above the clogged gutters, but the light through the grills of the window was beautiful. A little girl, perched on the windowsill, was drawing with colored pencils, filling in the trunk of an elephant a rich blue. When she saw Shira, she stopped.

"That's pretty," Shira said, hoping that her smile would translate the words.

The girl wore a pink frock patchworked by many odd stitches and flaps. When she shook her head, a plume of dust floated between them. "No," the girl said, returning her attention to the elephant, coloring its ears and tail with amber.

Ravi joined them and led Shira away from the window. "I knew you were the perfect parents when I first heard your voice. There is in you people something very kind, something very serious. You don't know how many families I rejected."

Every time there'd been a delay in the paperwork, Ravi reminded them that he'd just turned away another family. No one was up to snuff, or maybe, no family was willing to pay Ravi's prices. He ran a boutique orphanage. *Daily care on Daisy Lane*, his pamphlet had announced, using photographs from long ago, before the paint had faded over, the walls chipped and cracked. Like her husband, Ravi was a businessman, though his profit was made from the safe transfer of children. Still, a business could also be a calling. She watched as Ravi attended to a pimply little girl with pigtails. He took her in his arms, undid the pigtails, and combed her hair straight until she was relieved of her tantrum. Was it all for show? She couldn't tell.

Aside from the main room, which seemed to serve as a

dining, living, and play area all in one, there was a separate bedroom devoted to newborns and tots, where Ravi led her and she saw her Boone for the first time. He stirred awake and immediately fixed his gaze on her. What she noticed was the eyeliner under his eyes that made him look older than four months. He'd only just learned how to roll over, Ravi said, as he murmured something more about a diaper rash, but Shira didn't hear. She picked up her child, and he felt weightless in her arms. She'd been handed a feather, which she'd need to carry home and keep safe all her life. Boone gave a little gasp. Was he afraid or just in love, as she was? He lay the weight of his head on her shoulder. Never had she felt so ruthlessly needed.

Someone tugged on her sleeve. There again was the girl who had painted the trunk of the elephant blue. "No, no," the girl was saying over and over, each time more forcefully, stopping only when Shira had set Boone back down into his crib. Immediately Shira ached for him, a stirring in her belly, and would've taken him back into her arms were it not for the girl's long stare.

"She does not want to lose her brother," Ravi said. "But is better this way. Better the boy have a good life with you."

"She's our boy's sister?" Harold asked.

They'd signed so many papers, but nowhere had they been told that their child had a sibling.

"What does it matter?" Ravi said. "Lila is four years old. She is too old." Every child in the orphanage needed a bath and a hearty meal, but maybe none more so than this girl. It was clear she spent her days on the streets from the evidence of her hands: they were dirtied with henna and soot and ash and the skin was cracked and browned like the smokestacks the city ran through the night.

Harold gripped Shira's arm. "We've been fooled," he whispered. "This is a scam."

At first, Shira didn't know what he meant. She tickled her son's toes for comfort. "Boone," she said, the sound of his name so familiar to her now it could have substituted for any number of words that meant *jewel*. But as she processed Harold's words, she sensed that there was something between her and her precious thing. She looked hard at the girl, who refused to look away until Shira averted her own eyes. That her son and this street girl shared so much in common— unthinkable was what it was.

"Perhaps you wish for some time with him?" Ravi asked.

"Yes," Shira said. She looked over at Harold, sensing how unmoored he was here. "Do you want to hold him?"

"No," Harold snapped. Then, gazing at Boone, he softened. "I'm afraid to hold him. I'm afraid I'll break him."

"You won't," she said.

Harold sucked his belly in and rocked his boy. "Oh, my," he said.

"No, no," Lila said, pulling at the sheet that kept Boone snug, but Ravi was already shooing her away. He pushed her out the door. The girl stationed herself at the window, her face between the bars, peering in.

. . .

There was more paperwork to be handled before her son could be taken home, so they spent the night at their hotel with an undersized supply of wine.

"It's imported," the waiter announced, proudly pouring into their glasses so carefully that not a drop was wasted.

Throughout the meal that was meant to approximate American food—a slab of chicken moated by buttered corn and spinach—she thought of the feeling of Boone. Her doctor had said holding an infant elicited a serotonin response, a clinical reaction. But it felt more personal, the little bundle of him cooing for her ears alone: *I am yours to do with as you will.* The gravity that would reshape her life and Harold's.

"It's a ruse," Harold said, interrupting her reverie. "Boone doesn't have a sister. It's a hoax to make us fly another one of them home."

*Another one of them.* She was never sure how Harold felt about the enterprise of parenting, or rather, she wasn't sure how he felt about adoption, though he'd told her many times that this remained the best course. Still, there were moments when she thought she'd pushed him here, that he'd been ready to give up long ago, if not for her—if not for her happiness. Or maybe, it was not her happiness he was after. It was to preserve his idea that they should remain married. He was opposed to failure in any form, and divorce was the worst failure of all. So it began, the two-year search that led them here. They'd started with the adoption agencies that were the size of small countries and then, on a crisp fall day, found Ravi on his funded tour of New York, wrestling his brochures from the wind. She never bought her clothes from the big labels, so when it came to a child—the most important investment of all—why should she settle for what everyone already had? Ravi found children from the villages in the valley of Kashmir: babies born outside the perimeter of disease and neglect.

Here in the hotel, she asked Harold, "How do you really feel about Boone?"

"Well, he's our boy. He's what we agreed to," he replied.

She'd caught him off guard, but he'd still responded from the record. Could an agreement amount to love? For both of their sakes, she hoped so.

"But we have a bigger problem than Boone," Harold said.

"Boone is not a problem, darling. He's our baby boy, like you said."

"You're right, poor choice of words. He's not a problem, but that girl is. Lila or whatever her name is. Don't tell me you have a design on her.

"The paperwork for another child would be prohibitive," Harold continued. "Just guess how many times my secretary wrote to the government?"

"Thirty-two," she said, knowing the answer perfectly well.

"Don't worry," Shira added, mostly to console herself. What did she feel about the little girl? Ravi had told them a few details over the afternoon's paperwork. The girl had been a slow speaker, but she wasn't dumb. At times, she had tantrums. There was a scar along her right shoulder. "We don't know why it's there. A removed tumor? A cruel parent? We do not know," he'd said. She kept to herself, mostly, happy enough with her coloring book, except whenever it came time to part from her little brother. Then she'd storm. She'd let everyone hear the most powerful lungs on Daisy Lane.

Something about the girl frightened Shira, made her wish to cling to Harold, though they were both sweat-drenched in the July heat. She'd assumed that he would view the whole

business of adoption as just that, a business, but now he'd
chugged through the bottle of imported Merlot and was
searching for his next drink, as unsettled as she'd ever seen
him. He asked the waiter for ice with his gin and tonic, though
he had warned her himself that ice was a terrible choice,
formed certainly from the local tap water, filled with all
manner of malevolent bacteria. A little dirty ice in their drinks
when the sun hadn't even set. She thought of warning him,
but he'd have a hundred reasons to justify his choice. Anyway,
a little liquor would do him good. After all, they hardly drank
and almost never this early. She took a long sip of her wine
and watched a street cat tiptoe across the hotel roof.

"This is the only other place where cats roam free," Shira
said. Harold smiled and relaxed into an earlier version of
himself.

They'd met wintering in Israel with differing political views
in a neighborhood famous for its cats. Hordes of cats, all of
them dispatched a decade earlier to slay platoons of mice.
The mice were long gone, but the cats remained, wild and
predatory. On a day when she'd returned from the market,
strawberries overflowing in her basket, a striped orange tabby
had jumped through her window and into her living room. She
screamed as it rushed through her apartment, knocking over
a sculpture and a vase of lilies. Then Harold barged in. She
barely knew him then. "Do you have a broom?" he asked.

She'd nodded. With weapon in hand he chased that cat out
the door, flush afterward with the exhaustion of his heroism.
"Could I have something to drink?" He wiped his brow in a
way that reminded her of the hardworking men in her life.

She poured him a glass of white wine and told her life's story. A child of Yemenite Jews who settled in the Midwest. He was Ashkenazi: formed of Polish and Russian stock. He wiped his forehead with a handkerchief. So the climate of the Holy Land was less than suitable, he said. She still remembered how sweetly he'd enunciated *suitable*.

They drank wine on their first meeting, in the middle of the afternoon. She wasn't a drinker then either, but there was something in his face that suggested the urbanity of an afternoon cocktail, or at the least, a decent glass of wine.

"I prefer to drink what we make here," he'd said, when he'd learned the wine was imported from Italy. She still remembered how earnest he seemed saying that.

That was how he was now, sitting on the rooftop of their hotel bar in Calcutta, when the power went out. Within moments the city's electricity disappeared, but there were still the lights from all the small fires, all the kerosene tins the poor lit to cook their evening meals.

"Don't think of taking her home, sweetie," he said to that near darkness. She knew he had added the *sweetie* not as an endearment but, strangely, as a way of exerting his control. He was a man who did others favors, paid them kindnesses with the expectation that someday he would come calling.

"Don't call me that," said Shira. "If it weren't for me, we wouldn't be here."

"Well, that's true," he said.

"And our marriage went to shit," she said. "Now it has some life."

Harold raked his stubble in silence. She didn't curse often, and maybe that had tripped him up as much as the honesty of her words. Their marriage had long been unraveling. A storm that came and went, or sometimes a melancholy kept at bay, a little secret known only to them.

"Yes," Harold finally said. "Now it has some life."

Later that night, Shira awoke in the dark. She could feel the outline of their mosquito net but no Harold, though where he would have been there was a flashlight that could have doubled as a baton. She lit her way out of the room. Both the gatekeeper and the lobby boy had fallen asleep at their posts, and there was no sign of Harold anywhere on the grounds. No reason to worry, exactly, other than that he wasn't a drifter. He didn't take nighttime strolls, unless it was with his pedometer in hand to tally his daily ten thousand steps.

The orphanage—if that's where Harold had headed—wasn't far, and having grown up on two hundred acres, she had a keen eye for directions. Mostly darkness greeted her, the power still not back. Bamboo burned, an old lady brushed her teeth in an alley while holding up a lamp.

Along the walk the people in their old, crumbling houses came out to peer at her with flashlights and their oil lamps. News of a white lady walking in the power-out traveled from house to house; in that *load-shedding* night, the locals said, walking with her Bloomingdale's sandals with their gladiator straps and her straightened hair a little pasted on the side of her head from that heat. News of her spread like a film no one wanted to miss.

By the time she reached the orphanage, a small gang was following her. She had no alms, yet it seemed that whenever she smiled, another one would start to follow. They were mostly children, a few mothers with babies strapped on hip. Night crawlers. This wasn't a country for privacy, and the children following behind—as if she were leading them on a great expedition—looked as helpless as she felt.

That's when she saw Harold, squatting like a local by the orphanage's door. "Too hot to sleep?" he called out.

"You could have left a note," she said. "I almost worried."

The children behind her giggled, the sound of her English an exotic treat. Harold dispersed them with a stash of candies he'd carried in his pockets, retrieved from who knew where. Oh, but he had that light in his eye, grinning as each kid snatched a toffee from his palm and ran. Sometimes he still surprised her, the ways he could be generous.

"Let me show you something," he said.

She allowed herself to be led to the southern window, hoping for another peek at Boone. The window was open, so she lifted the curtains, and there in that space of so many cribs she strained her eyes in the dark until she thought she could see her boy. But she couldn't be sure, what with his bronze skin in that dark night, so she lit a match. In that moment of light, she saw that he was lying on his back, his mouth ajar. There were pillows in his crib, a suffocation risk, she'd heard. She wasn't sure he was breathing until the match burned down to her fingers, and she saw Lila's hand lift up to squeeze his leg—oh, she'd been lying below him all this time! Her boy gave a little cough, and the match gave way. In the darkness, she sucked the burn from her fingers. This wasn't the story she'd dreamed. A scrawny little girl who hung around her precious little boy. This wasn't the story at all.

"You see what I see?" Harold whispered, drawing the curtains back. "The girl sleeping under the boy."

"I see her," Shira said. "But what do you make of her?"

"She reminds me a little of the girl from Egypt."

Harold was talking about a street girl with a blue umbrella who, years earlier, had chased them around the corniche in Alexandria. With Harold's schedule, they hadn't traveled much together, so Alexandria had become part of their lore. She barely even remembered the girl's face now, only the blue umbrella. But there had been talk, even then, of trying to adopt her. Just talk, though, neither of them had pursued the matter seriously. Like the Egyptian girl but unlike Boone, who was too young to know the difference, Lila reminded her that there had been *another mother*, that there would always be a specter to compare against.

"I don't intend to pay for another," Harold said.

His generosity box had squeezed shut. They had the means, but with Harold there wasn't always the will. Something had ticked him off, she didn't know what, and she could feel the tension souring his breath. But she knew how to calm him. A hand slowly circling the back of his neck. Sometimes, she had to mother him, like that girl was doing for her little boy. Sometimes, Harold needed to be reminded of the late bloomer who'd trekked across the world to till a desert land. She led him away from the orphanage.

"We've seen enough," she said. "Nothing to argue about."

. . .

The next morning, she awoke before Harold and traced the graying hairs of his chest. He'd gone gray early, though so few knew, given how regularly he dyed the hair on his head. But the hair on his chest was another matter—it was a secret pleasure to see him vulnerable before her, the gray an artifact of any number of corporate tussles he'd steered in his favor through will alone, and she now the only one to behold the lasting burden. Oh, he'd confessed certain failures, kept others to himself. She'd never imagined she would become wholly reliant on his money, but a contract had sprung up between them, affording a number of conveniences.

Still, he'd courted her for the unfamiliar. Even now, he relied on her vitality, shuffling home from work numbed, hoping and thus far finding in her a lightness of being, a curiosity about his world. He didn't know that she'd had to work at it, as he had at his job. How could he? In his eyes, her world was surely simple. Breakfast together, painting afterward, tennis in the afternoons, then him again in the late evenings, if work permitted.

They didn't discuss how life would change with a child. She was happy enough to know that it would not be the same hours. In the middle of the day, she'd once called Harold's secretary with the excuse of an emergency. "I have nothing left to clean," she'd told him. "The house is perfect now." He'd tried to console her, suggesting a visit to the psychiatrist who frequented their cocktail parties. It wasn't enough, though the doctor's fees had burned, and she'd had to alter her future guest lists for fear of an awkward meeting.

"I want a day with both of them," she now told Harold, just as he was waking.

He gazed at her, terrified for a moment, then rubbed his

eyes, released his morning cough. So far, it seemed he'd
offered her everything she'd asked for, but what she'd asked
for in this epoch of their marriage—perhaps those requests
hadn't amounted to much. A stipend for tennis lessons, more
funds for a trip to a little island in Greece where she swam
each night with tribes of phosphorescent fish. Giving money
was easier than what she was asking for now: an instant family.
A baby boy. Was she asking for a little girl as well? A girl of the
gutters, a girl of the streets. No, not that, then. Permission to
take only the boy. No competition there, but what courage this
would take.

"Just one day," Harold muttered into his pillow, knowing
her well enough. "Then we're gone."

. . .

When they put Lila in the taxi she buttoned her nose to the
window for the ride, all the while keeping a hand on her
brother's swaddled legs. She was wearing her same pink
patchwork dress, though now it smelled of cheap soap, freshly
cleaned. The thing to do, they'd been told, was to go out on
the Ganges, but the Ganges had overflowed from the rain
of the past week so getting a boat was hard. Still, Harold
negotiated, drove the prices down without anyone getting
upset. This was what he'd always done. He was not all ice.
Sometimes, he could see what was obvious; he could make the
fishermen smile.

She knew Harold was willing to say no to the whole affair.
Seen from afar, they had a decent life. Better than decent.
Last summer, she and Harold had trawled the Florida coast

making dinner of clams and crawfish, astride a fifteen-foot sailboat blessed with the name *Princess Pea*. There were certain freedoms you could not put a price on.

Aboard the Ganges boat the fisherman showed them a black-and-white photo of his children. "Boy and girl," he said with a gap-toothed smile that didn't quite fit his face.

"So beautiful," she'd said, though they were not good-looking children, even in that grainy picture.

The river bifurcated the city, flowing in from a glacier the shape of a cow's mouth. One day they'd hike there, all of the family. A return of sorts. But here in the city, the river had mixed with the textile factory sluice and the refuse of the millions and the little bits of prayer offerings that bobbed innocently through the waves. It was not a picturesque river, but there was quiet and there was Boone in her arms, the condensed-milk smell of him.

Boone woke up twenty minutes in and soon began to cry. "Give me the formula," Shira commanded, and Harold took the baby formula from his cooler, watched awestruck as little Boone sucked, his sister pleased at the efficiency by which the babe was pacified. That was the first time Lila smiled back. She was a striking child, not pretty exactly, too much of a nose on her face, and with those canine teeth, that wide forehead—no, not pretty at all—but Shira could see she was full of an inner combustion that might be harnessed, if not into beauty, then, at least, into purpose.

Shira brought out watercolors and a sketch pad and offered them to Lila. Prizes in hand, the girl scampered to the bow of the boat and immersed herself in her work. It was choppy, but the girl had a sailor's feet. Had her and Boone's parents taken them out on the water? There was so little they knew, a whole history hidden by circumstances and language.

"When she speaks English, she might tell us where she came from, what her life was like," Harold said.

"When she speaks English, what do you mean?"

"Maybe, I'm softening," Harold said. "Maybe, I'm an iota more open to filling out all the paperwork. At least, if you are."

So he'd deferred to her. Unfair, but not unexpected. If she made the call, she would own the fires to come. "You can't make me decide alone," Shira said.

"You're the one who brought her. You're the one who suggested this expedition." A poor swimmer, Harold had hugged the side of the boat the whole time. He now reached a conciliatory hand toward her shoulder, which she refused.

"I wanted to see how she would react," Shira said. "I want to see who she is."

But now that she had her watercolors, Lila paid them no heed. The sweet smell of Boone mixed with the smell of the river—algae and cow dung and all the little prayer offerings everyone dumped, rotting sweetness.

"She's a child," Harold said. "Nothing more, nothing less."

As they turned back toward shore, an old barge passed by and left its wake. Even Lila had to keep a grip on the boat and little Boone gave a cry. Shira reached for the formula, but the bottle slipped out of her hand and into the water.

Lila turned toward her with accusation, and Boone began to wail. Was he hungry, or simply scared? The only feed they had for him now lay deep in the water. Boone cried so hard his face bloomed a worrying shade. She took him to her breasts, but he soon gave up, finding nothing. She'd never heard anything so fierce, so primal in need.

Harold began to yell at the fisherman, who rowed hard toward the shore, while Lila looked on, bright with anger. Already she'd failed this girl. She should've thought this through. They should've stayed at the hotel, under the air conditioner's pacific hum. Boone was crying with a volume his body seemed incapable of. Holding him close didn't soothe, nor did rocking. She'd been instructed to *shhh* but that too was ineffective. Harold came and cooed. Maybe a man's octave would do, but no, baby Boone seemed terrified, his eyes unwilling to meet his new parents'. The fisherman rowing toward shore clucked his tongue, in anger, in sympathy, it was hard to tell. Then Lila swooped in.

She took Boone in her arms, and though she was as much grizzle as the fisherman, it seemed to do. Boone stopped crying. Maybe the little girl smelled like his mother. Maybe that song she began to sing was something Boone had heard. The fisherman knew the tune. He joined her mid-chorus. The song moved like the tide of the Ganges, so many major notes, fifths and thirds. She watched Lila's open throat and tried to envision this girl turning into a woman, wondered if she would remember this moment, standing at the hull of the boat, her little brother cradled in her arms, Harold a step behind in case another wake came.

As they approached the shore, Shira watched as another mother carried a baby the size of Boone into the water. Three times the mother dipped her body halfway in and three times the baby whelped its joy and fear.

Shira gripped Harold's arm. He was watching Lila, mouth agape in awe. But she felt no victory here. Her throat parched, jaw sore, she felt too old for her body. A hag in a beautiful woman's house. But what could she do—she now loved that little boy. She kept her distance, watched as Lila held Boone in her arms well until they were off the boat. Lila's sailor's feet tiptoed up the algae-covered steps of the riverbank. Only then did she relinquish the sleeping bundle into Shira's waiting, terrified embrace.

## The Narrow Bridge

Eliza met Amit at a Brooklyn coffee shop where you could work all day and not get the boot. Her first thought was that he was too skinny for his own good, so she handed him one of the flyers she'd been carrying—*Free Bagels & Good Cheer!* He was deep into a textbook and glanced up at her with the look of someone who's been awoken from a trance. His thick eyeglasses made his lashes seem larger than life. "Best bagels in town," she said.

An hour later she saw him loitering around the entrance to the Society for Ethical Culture, looking cold on that still wintry April day, and she invited him inside. Even though the service had already begun with her partner Sarah trying to find her way on the piano, she took Amit straightaway to the bagel station, where she smeared cream cheese on pumpernickel and added several pieces of lox.

Eliza and Sarah were leaders at the Society for Ethical Culture, so named when *ethical* and *culture* could be said together without irony, and they'd helped to build a house of worship that had nothing to do with God, though they borrowed liberally from every religion, especially the Judaism of their youth. *You can worship without needing a man in the sky looking down on you*, Sarah liked to say. What she meant was that striving for peace and justice could itself be a kind of worship.

As Eliza joined in to sing *the whole entire world is a very narrow bridge*, she glanced at Sarah and believed she knew what the verse taught: especially in old age, you balanced between unbearable truths—salvation or suffering. There was hardly a moment in between.

Then she saw Amit. He looked so grateful sitting there with a bit of cream cheese on the corner of his mouth. Through the years she'd try to come back to this moment and remember him this way: a hungry boy, far from home.

. . .

At first Sarah didn't approve of Amit, or rather she didn't approve of Amit moving into their guesthouse for free, which was what Eliza suggested after he had come to services for a few weeks only to retreat, as she would later learn, to his dingy room at the Atlantic YMCA.

"This is a guesthouse, not a charity," Sarah said. After Eliza and Sarah had retired, they'd rented out bedrooms in their brownstone to long-term boarders, who shared holidays and made coffee for each other. Nowadays they had three paying guests—Herb, Zanyab, and Laura—who had also become friends. Taking in boarders had been Sarah's idea—she was the disciplined one when it came to finances, though they were both community builders—but eventually Sarah demurred, as she did whenever Eliza persisted, and so Amit moved into their basement.

"It's a cell. We can't charge him money for that anyway," Eliza said. The basement was drafty in the winter and sweltering in the summer, but it was also spacious and cozy with comfortable bedding. There was a little window from which you could spy people walking on the street, or at least you could see their legs. It had been Eliza's studio when she still painted, and there were stacks of easels against the walls.

"You can move them," Eliza had told Amit when he'd looked at the space, but he'd had no need to. All he owned in the world was a backpack full of clothes and a suitcase worth of books. He was studying applied math at CUNY, so there were lots of equations and proofs.

After Amit settled in, Eliza had the idea that she might entreat him to teach Sarah some math. She had heard that learning a new skill could help. Sarah was losing her memory, a fact that Eliza had been able to ignore until Sarah had forgotten the names of the treasurer and secretary for the Society, two people she'd met every Sunday for the past ten years. The neurologist had said the drugs were better these days, but Sarah was already moderately far along, according to the scans.

Sarah rejected the suggestion straightaway. "I would've had to have started years ago," she said. She was sixty-nine, seven years older than Eliza, and they'd been together since they'd both moved to Brooklyn two decades ago. "But I will take up Amit's help for something."

That turned out to be gardening. For years they'd let weeds take over their backyard, but now Sarah was steadfast: she planted flowers and a hardy species of kiwi that could survive the Northeast. Amit didn't know the first thing about gardening, but he was game. In a few weeks they'd set rows of beds. Not only the arctic kiwi, but they'd have a harvest with tomatoes, peppers, and kale as well.

. . .

A few weeks into their new arrangement Eliza got a call from a nurse at Brooklyn Methodist. Amit would be fine, they'd said, but he'd fallen and badly sprained his ankle. No deliveries for a while. She asked the nurse what she meant by "deliveries," and the nurse handed the phone over to Amit: "Oh, I forgot to mention, Eliza. I deliver Chinese food for a few extra bucks."

He'd taken a sharp turn on his bicycle and been swiped by a van driver who didn't pause to see if he was all right. She didn't prod further because he sounded like a kid caught in a lie. Amit liked to talk about how his family home in India had once been a cultural mecca, artists and scientists gathering in an old, crumbling parlor. That was before the money ran out, and now he was always thinking of ways to send something back. Their arrangement suited him, Eliza believed, because what would've been rent was sent straight home.

"I'm coming to get you," Eliza said, but when she hung up the phone she paused for a moment. Sarah was in the garden with a book. Eliza peered over her shoulder and found that she was still on the same page from an hour ago. Increasingly, Sarah found it difficult to concentrate on her novels. Amit had even tried to cajole her to read one of his lit texts, an endeavor that had ended as quickly as it had begun.

Eliza looked to see if any of their boarders were around. Eventually everyone who passed through their guesthouse became like extended family, but right now, no one was there.

Eliza tapped Sarah on the shoulder, who startled, losing her page.

"Anyway, it's a dull one," Sarah said, smiling.

Eliza didn't want to tell Sarah the details only to make her upset over nothing, and she didn't want to bring her along either into the chaos of a hospital. "I'll just be gone for a bit," she said. "Don't throw a big party."

It took her an hour to get Amit released from the hospital and set up with crutches, but when they got home Sarah wasn't in the garden. Eliza looked through the house, even peeking into the boarders' rooms and the basement, but there was no sign of Sarah.

"I'll help you find her," Amit said, but he was having a hard time with his crutches.

"You stay put and prop your foot up," Eliza instructed. She started to circle their block. Her neighbors waved, and she stopped to ask if they'd seen Sarah. But no one had seen her, so she kept going, all the way up to Eighth Avenue to the building that belonged to the Society for Ethical Culture.

Sarah was sitting on the steps. "Where is everyone?" she asked.

"Oh, honey, it's not Sunday," Eliza said. She walked Sarah back to their house, where Sarah made a big fuss over Amit's ankle.

. . .

As spring turned to summer, Sarah's memory continued to worsen. She walked into Herb's room while he showered and accused him of being a burglar. She took to calling Zaynab, who'd been living with them for two years, "June,"

remembering an aid worker she'd known in her time abroad.
Sarah also began to spend hours with Amit. Eliza was grateful.
All those backgammon games and glasses of ice tea kept Sarah
occupied and allowed Eliza to be out in the world.

Even so, once she'd halfheartedly nudged Amit out of the
house. "It's Summer Streets today," Eliza had said. "Your
ankle's better, so you can ride your bike again. No cars
anywhere. Get some street food."

"Not right now. We're having a good *adda*," Amit had
responded. *Adda* was one of the Bengali words they'd added
to their lexicon, which, as Eliza understood it, meant long,
meandering conversations about the state of the world.
Somehow it seemed they were both enjoying themselves, with
Sarah regaling Amit with an anecdote about a cow who'd once
blocked the tarmac in Port-au-Prince and Amit rejoining with
how familiar a story that was to him, having grown up in the
land of holy cows.

Eliza even thought of trying to set Amit up on a date, but
he'd shown no interest in that either. "Eventually, I'll be
arranged," he said with a grin. He confounded her at times
with his agreeableness—why anyway was he spending so much
time with an old lady, in this case *her* old lady—but she didn't
pursue the question further for fear of upsetting their balance.

. . .

Over the course of that summer the boarders all began to
leave. First, Herb returned to Haiti, where he'd bought a
small condo for his retirement. Then Zaynab finished medical
school and was able to afford her own apartment in the city.
Eventually, Laura from Colombia also left. When asked why,

Laura was candid. "There's so much *clutter*," she said. "I can't take it anymore."

It was true: what Eliza had once thought was a charming collection of travel memorabilia had come to dominate their space. On top of that she'd had a hard time getting rid of parting gifts from long-ago boarders: hand fans from Japan, stained-glass bowls from Italy that were too delicate to be used for anything, and a miniature gong from who knew where. None of it went together.

"I'll do a deep clean," Eliza implored.

But Laura was unmoved: the time had come, she said.

Just like that, the narrow bridge of Eliza's life disintegrated. She posted ads in the local paper and online, but she was competing with fancier, private options. She'd collected the boarders over the years, but now they were gone, and at the Society, too, numbers were dwindling. Fewer and fewer were interested in the kind of community that had you rolling up your sleeves, pausing your life for someone else's.

When Labor Day arrived, Amit started his classes again. With less of his attention, Sarah fell into lethargy. She'd wake up late in the day, sleeping fitfully at night, and spend much of the morning staring out the garden window. Where she found energy was a renewed interest in the religion of her youth, which made Eliza remember when they'd first met as teenagers at a Jewish summer camp. Sarah was a counselor and the most beautiful girl in the world despite her habit of keeping her hair in pigtails, Eliza had believed, and then they'd drifted apart, gone to separate colleges, where they'd failed to think of the Sabbath as a day of rest. When they found each other again in their middle age, Sarah sporting a gamine

cut and Eliza with her hair still long, they'd both practiced
Buddhism, weeklong meditation retreats in the Poconos,
though not the same ashram. But now Sarah was turning
back to the songs of her childhood. She reminded Eliza that
the prayer they'd sung at the Society was in fact from Rabbi
Nachman. "Kol Ha'Olam Kulo." And the main thing was not
to have any fear at all, Sarah would repeat the lyrics over and
over like a mantra.

. . .

Autumn came and Amit was around even less. Sometimes,
Eliza, who had a hard time sleeping, would hear him tiptoe
into the house at odd hours. At first, she didn't mind. Wasn't
that college—the life nocturnal? Besides, when she asked him
about his coursework, Amit seemed more confident than ever,
having upgraded his faded consignment jeans and tee shirts
for more stylish outfits. The problem was less with Amit than
with Sarah. After a few more incidents—a bath that Sarah
had started downstairs only to take a nap upstairs, the burner
she'd left on to make her eggs and never turned off—it was
clear that she needed constant attention. And without Amit
spending his days with her, it was Eliza who had to do this
work.

A few weeks into their courtship they'd discussed their
family medical histories. Back then Eliza was already
prediabetic, but aside from that they were relatively healthy. It
was one thing to know you might someday have to caretake for
your partner, another to live it. Eliza investigated the cost of
hiring someone, but without the rent from the boarders they
were digging deeply into their savings as it was. There was the

possibility of charging Amit rent, but she didn't have the heart to ask, given the situation with his family in India.

Even when they were both younger and healthier, the only time Eliza had enjoyed being at home was when their life with the boarders was in full swing, the noise and bustle of the house, the feeling that there was always someone there besides the two of them. Otherwise, she liked to be out in the world. Besides her work with the Society, she volunteered at the New American Center, helping undocumented workers learn English to find jobs and apartments. When she'd opted for early retirement from the social services administration, the expansiveness of her life had allowed her to regain a sense of youth. Now, with Sarah dependent on her, that freedom was curtailed.

One morning as he was scarfing down his cereal, she accosted Amit.

"You've hardly been around. Have you found a girlfriend?" Eliza said it teasingly but with her arms folded across her chest as if she were a disappointed professor.

"You and Sarah are still my only girlfriends," Amit rejoined with a wink, but he couldn't quite pull off the suave look. From their first meeting at the café Eliza had seen through him into what she thought of as his child self, which was always there, a layer beneath, and easily hurt. Amit headed off to school, depositing the rest of his cereal into the garbage.

That evening he returned with a box of sweets. "I went to Queens. It only took an hour and fifteen and two trains and a bus," he said, smiling, though there was a note of apology in his voice. Did he finally understand that Eliza was bearing the consequences of his newfound freedom? She hoped for as much.

Though she had to watch her sugar intake, Eliza still tried each of the little delicacies that Amit had bought. There was one that tasted like orange blossom.

"Auntie," he said, which he sometimes called her and which she still found endearing, "are you still cross with me?"

"I'm not," Eliza said quietly, though they were out of earshot of Sarah, who was watching *Jeopardy* open-mouthed. "I want you to be out in the world, doing things."

"Then what is it?" Amit asked.

"It's Sarah," Eliza blurted out. "She misses you."

Amit cocked his head toward Sarah. "I fear I've not been paying her enough attention. It's just that I've started to make friends. They invite me places. Restaurants, jazz clubs, theater productions in people's homes. I never imagined such a life."

"But you're living rent free. You're living on our good faith." As soon as Eliza spoke, she regretted the harshness of her words, but they had been welling inside her for weeks. He'd left her alone with Sarah.

She saw Amit wilt into a smaller version of himself. But the moment passed and another emerged in which it seemed like Amit had puffed air into himself, grown into the man who'd crossed oceans. "I was with Sarah for most of the summer. I thought I'd done my part."

She thought he was becoming selfish, what with his new boot-cut jeans and matching button-down, thinking less these days about the lives of others. "Well, we are just so grateful for your contribution during the summer," Eliza said stiffly.

Then she softened: who knew why, maybe out of a sense of duty, but he *had* spent so much of his summer with Sarah. "Look, if you could just spend a few hours a week with Sarah again I'd be able to go out a bit. There are cobwebs in the Society, you know."

Amit stared at her. He finally said, "Yes, of course, Auntie. It would be my pleasure."

At first when he'd arrived at their doorstep, he'd seemed so eager to please that she'd worried for him; how would he advocate for himself in this world? Now he seemed a different person, one who was growing roots outside of her home, but this premonition was quickly replaced by relief. She would be free again, at least for a few hours each day.

. . .

Eliza made a schedule for Amit. Three hours watching Sarah every weekday along with occasional time on the weekends. When she wasn't napping, Sarah liked to talk more and more about her time as a relief worker in Haiti, and Amit seemed to connect with these tales well enough, at least Eliza would see him nodding and smiling when she came home.

And how lovely it was to be out in the world. During her time away from Sarah, Eliza returned to the coffee shop to visit with old friends, and she volunteered at the New American Center, meeting people who needed her, temporarily. She still had infinite energy, she felt, and those hours outside of the house were precious.

One night after dinner when Amit had gone down to the basement and Eliza was washing dishes, Sarah said to her, "I know what you're doing."

Usually after dinner, Sarah turned soporific, but now she was sitting up straight. Eliza left the dishes in the sink and sat back at the table. "What is it, dear?"

"You're pawning me off on him, but that's not right. He's young, and really if I'm anyone's problem I'm your problem," Sarah said.

"You are not my problem; you are the love of my life." But you couldn't love someone the same way your whole life. They changed, became another person, many other persons. The woman in Haiti who lit a smoke with one hand while pulling a shawl over Eliza's shoulders with the other was not the same woman who was now sitting across from her. It would be insulting to that woman or the girl who came before to say so. Still, there was something contractual about love; whether you married or not, you agreed to see someone through their transformations. Not only to witness but also to uphold their old images of themselves.

They stared at each other a few moments before it was time for Eliza to help Sarah to bed. Eliza brought down the box of night diapers. There had been a few incidents, and it was better to be prepared.

. . .

That Friday instead of attending the dinner at the Society, Sarah wanted to go to services at the synagogue down the street. "I've introduced myself there. At least I think I have. I can't be terribly sure," Sarah said.

Reluctantly, Eliza agreed, though she hadn't been to Jewish services for many years and in her youth had resented her Orthodox upbringing. But this temple had a woman rabbi, and there was a young man with dreadlocks playing guitar. All the members of the congregation were singing. They even did a version of the Rabbi Nachman song that brought Sarah to tears.

Afterward the rabbi introduced herself and said to Sarah, "Nice to see you again. You have quite a voice. I hope you'll keep returning to us."

So Sarah *had* come here before, Eliza concluded. Perhaps Amit had brought her on one of their excursions, but Eliza had no wish to return to the Jewish life, even for Sarah's sake. This would need to be something for Amit to continue.

. . .

That night Eliza awoke with a start. There was a clamoring like her parents' radiator used to make every winter, and no Sarah in the bed. She rushed to put her clothes on and followed the sound into their garden, where under the glow of the nightlight she found Sarah clanging two pans together.

"Practicing percussion?" Eliza asked, putting a hand on her back.

"There was a deer who got into our garden," Sarah said. "I had to scare her away."

It seemed cruel to say, *There are no deer here—only rats.* Maybe Sarah was living in her memory now, from when she was a girl in Lancaster, Pennsylvania, where there were always deer about.

The commotion had made it to Amit. He came into the garden holding one of his textbooks like a shield.

"Sarah was chasing away a deer who'd jumped the fence," Eliza said plainly.

"Stranger things have happened," Amit offered.

. . .

The rhythm of their family life was interrupted by the arrival of Amit's girlfriend. She was a sweet talker and consequently also a lover of sweets, having met Amit on one of his excursions to Queens to seek out the best Indian delicatessen. Nandita worked behind the counter, wrapping everything up into little cases that could be mailed anywhere in the world.

Eliza's first thought was that Amit could do better. While she believed Amit would finish college and find himself one of those fancy tech jobs, Nandita was nearly thirty and seemed to have little ambition beyond the culinary, at least insofar as Amit's stories suggested, which tended to involve the meals she'd cooked for him, fish in the oven with a little tikka sauce, nan she'd hand-rolled herself.

But the larger problem was the pull she exerted on Amit's time. The number of hours Amit would spend with Sarah had always been an informal agreement, growing and shrinking based on Eliza's commitments that week, but there was a minimum that Eliza needed for herself.

But a month into his new relationship, Amit made a stand, out of Sarah's earshot. "Nandita wants me to spend more time with her, and there are only so many hours in the day. So . . ."

"So?" Eliza asked, forcing him out.

"Well, I think we need to revisit our arrangement. I still enjoy our Shabbat dinners and taking Sarah to services, but we might need to optimize the other parts."

That was the mathematician in him coming out, the one who'd scrimped and saved his way to a state college in this country, the one who'd *optimize* his happiness when it was under threat.

But Eliza was a fighter too. She wouldn't give up her own freedom so easily. "Nandita lives far away. What if you invited her here? We could give you Laura's old room upstairs. It's spacious enough for two."

She could see Amit recalibrate his position. "How generous," he finally replied. "But I'll need to discuss with my new boss."

. . .

Without giving her answer, the new boss invited them for a holiday dinner, an occasion that Amit explained involved a powerful demon and an even more powerful goddess. All day long Sarah had been in a mood. It was a Friday, and Sarah didn't want to take the crosstown train to Queens for an hour. Shabbat had recently become their time to reflect on the week, and anyway didn't they need to make a challah? Except, they'd never made challah before, but Sarah insisted and eventually Eliza complied. She found a recipe online and worked with Sarah to knead the dough, crack the eggs, and watched in wonder as the yeast rose.

Nandita lived in a part of Queens Eliza had never been to. As in her own neighborhood, the streets were lined with trees, but the houses were a little less grand, weathered Tudors row after row. Nandita's house seemed to have been chopped in two, a garage shared by what had once surely been a single-family home. Amit received them with open arms, enveloping Sarah in a hug. "Welcome to the palace!" he said.

It was a railroad apartment with an upstairs loft that served

as a bedroom, the kind of place where you were perennially
worried about knocking into a piece of furniture or wall art, of
which there was a great deal, mostly calendars with pictures of
gaping-mouthed Hindu goddesses.

Nandita, who'd been stirring a pot, came out to greet Eliza.
She was short and rather overweight, Eliza thought, and the
apron she was wearing, which featured various cat heads, did
little to accentuate her figure.

"We spent all day making challah. I hope it'll go with
whatever you've made," Eliza said.

Nandita stared at the misshapen bread for a moment before
she said, "It will go perfectly."

Sarah and Amit had already started chatting. Sarah was
telling Amit, for what was surely the hundredth time, about
how she'd once brought two chocolate bars to "her" kids in
Haiti and without her asking they'd split it ten different ways,
each little piece a moment of joy. "And that is what we have in
this life," Sarah said. "Remembrances of little boys smiling."

Amit nodded his head portentously, though Eliza knew he'd
received this wisdom many times before.

Nandita ushered them to the dining room table. Mutton,
peas, and potatoes in curry, a cucumber and tomato salad.
It was all too spicy for Eliza, even the salad with some
indiscernible coating, but she could see that Sarah had brought
her appetite, serving herself extra portions.

If only Sarah understood the situation as Eliza did! This
Nandita would be the end of what they had. She stewed as
Sarah continued to tell stories from her time in Haiti. She
knew Amit had heard them all before, though he seemed
happy enough to share them with Nandita, who was laughing

at all the right parts. But then, Sarah had always been a capable storyteller, born with impeccable timing.

Eliza looked at her partner of twenty years—the radiance and the forgetting—and thought: *I am no longer in love. But I am bound to you.*

Later, when Nandita carried out the dessert, a tureen of rice pudding, Eliza said suddenly, "Excuse me. I have an urgent call to make."

She stepped outside on that unseasonably warm autumn night; the leaves had fallen but still it felt like summer was trailing them. She wondered what would happen if she simply took a walk around the block, no one would notice. Then getting to the corner she saw the sunset and felt how nice it would be to keep walking. Soon enough she'd walked her way from Kew Gardens to the edge of Briarwood, where she came across an old synagogue that was being turned into a gym, a provisional poster announcing fitness under Hebrew letters.

It was only then that she realized she'd left her phone on the table, so if they looked up from their bowls of pudding, they'd see that she'd lied: not a call to make.

*I also am dying*, she wanted to tell them. *I am also deserving of your compassion.*

Nothing that she had would kill her straightaway. Rather, it was buried in the heart—an old fear that she had lived life with the wrong set of instructions (do good, do more good!) and found only in the end, impoverished in a guesthouse with only a single guest, that she'd followed the wrong blueprint.

Even though she hadn't spent much time in Queens, she still knew the outline of the city, and she knew she was walking south, back to Brooklyn. Except, it was too long a walk, and along with her cell phone she had also left behind her wallet. She couldn't go back—it had been twenty minutes, maybe more—the shame too fierce, but also she knew she wouldn't make it home on foot.

She sat on the steps of a store that sold cotton candy and Bollywood movies. No one bothered her, an old white lady far from home who began to weep, a good cry that passed quickly because she'd always been fastidious about her feelings in public. This was what it was to grieve someone still living.

A man in a turban emerged from the store carrying a stack of movies under his arm. He paused and asked, "Lady, you need a ride?"

She nodded and gave her address. "I don't have my wallet, though. I can pay you when we get there."

"Call this your lucky day."

It began to rain as they headed south toward the Brooklyn-Queens Expressway, first a light drizzle and then an unseasonal downpour, but her driver was a pro, he barely used the windshield wipers. She noticed her hands, the fine little gray hairs that had sprung up as if overnight, and there was a hint of a tremor, nothing she'd asked her doctor about, all the attention given to Sarah, but there was no denying it: she too was aging, and all the freedoms she imagined for herself would someday soon be whittled away, reshaped.

Sarah was shapeshifting as she was. It was not all darkness for her old love, not every day at least.

They turned up Garfield Street and onto Seventh Avenue and sitting under the awning of her boarders' house were the few who loomed large in her life, each of them looking damp and cold. Amit and Nandita were sharing a woolen shawl and Sarah was in her puffy winter coat. When Eliza got out of the car, they rose as one, and it was Sarah who waved shyly, like she'd done all those years ago at summer camp, who took her by the hand and led her home.

## Mendel's Wall

As soon as Shabbos ended, Mendel went for his heavy tools. He had enough sheetrock in the basement—that wouldn't be a problem—but first he made himself a coffee and added a bit of schnapps. He poured a little into his palm and rubbed it behind his ears like perfume. Sweet luck for the week ahead.

When Leah came home, she saw what he'd built and grew pale. She was holding the groceries in one hand; with the other, she took off her wig. Mendel had been imagining this moment for the past year, building and tearing the thing apart in his mind. He'd imagined it as he brushed his teeth and murmured his prayers. Now that the children were settled in their own homes, the time was right.

What had he built? Nothing more than a wall. It was made of gypsum and sheetrock and divided their apartment into unequal halves. On one side, a bathroom and the living room, with an ottoman now fitted to make a bachelor bed. On the other, the kitchen, the master bed and bath, and most of their life together: a rusty teakettle from her German mother, the candlesticks from Yerushalayim, and the raised marriage bed eased so many years ago into the sunken floor. He'd let her have the larger half.

"You schmuck. You stupid schmuck," she said.

Mendel looked at his callused hands.

"It had to happen," he said.

Later that night, he knocked on the wall. "Wife, you left some things."

Through the hole he'd built in the wall, which was almost big enough to fit his head, he shoved through her leftover possessions. A beaded necklace, the book *Honoring God and Raising Jewish Children*, the wool coat he'd bought her when they were still courting.

He couldn't tell how angry she was. The only words she said all night: "I'm going to the rebbe tomorrow and—"

Mendel latched shut the hole and heard no more. That night, he slept as well as he ever had.

. . .

On the other side of the wall, Leah read their ketubah aloud again and again.

*Be my wife according to the laws of Moses and Israel.*

*I will present you with the gift of two hundred zuzim.*

*And other necessities, for example, the dress on your back.*

*In return you agree to laugh at my anecdotes and larks.*

No matter how many times Leah read it, she failed to find the root of Mendel's betrayal. It was old; no doubt, the stubborn man had fixed his mind. How dare he, when it was she who had taken Ari and Mendel Jr. to yeshiva every morning, who'd held them when they'd cried, who'd protected them whenever he was in one of his rotten moods.

No, she would not fail. She would not let Mendel see her fail.

When Leah settled into their marriage bed, she noticed a pair of Mendel's dirty socks. They were right by the night lamp, and they produced the musty odors of Mendel himself. She picked them up with the tips of her fingers. They swayed in the air. Let him suffer a little, she thought, as she tossed them in the trash.

The next morning Leah made a chocolate babka. It came glistening out of the oven and confused the air with its warm sugary perfection. Before she left the house, she kicked the wall twice to make a dent the shape and size of her winter boot. From the other side, Mendel groaned like he was seasick.

She strode across the tundra of Sunset Park, avoiding the dogs who tended to howl viciously at this hour. They snarled at her from their turrets, but what did she care? For the first time, she felt like a free woman, free to think alone, free to read those books on the other side of midnight, free to bring home the guests she liked, free to cook the things that once made men line up around her block.

Leah decided to call on the rebbe another day.

. . .

When Mendel came home the next afternoon, he sat and admired his wall. From any angle you could see how straightly it was laid. If you were to tilt the world one hundred and eighty degrees and place a pencil on Mendel's Wall, that pencil would not roll a pinch.

He had lost the kitchen, but he'd kept the toaster. He browned a slice of rye and balanced his checkbook.

In the evening, Mendel heard the door on the other side open. Then he heard laughter rise and fall in steady waves. It offended his ears. Loudly, he cleared his throat, but it did not stop. He tapped gingerly on the wall. The noise stopped. He leaned his cheek to the wall and heard the other voice trail into hoarse whispers.

It was beyond question—there was a man on the other side.

"Rebbe, my dear rebbe, is it you?"

The wall didn't let his sound pass.

For that week's talk on the Torah, the rebbe had thrown his accusing voice around the room and then brought it back so that the families had to lean close to listen. From the back of the shul, Mendel had caught pieces. Inseparable were the two original people, he heard. They were glued together, spine to spine. And then the serpent and the apple, and the daily arguments, and the one time he hit her in the mouth, and the one time she kicked him in the knee, and the one time he scolded her over a piece of burned meat, and the one time she called his mother and smeared his good name.

. . .

The next several evenings, Mendel would roll his chair toward the center of the wall. He liked to drink next to it. A pinch of schnapps here, a shot of vodka there. This led to the counting. For each newfound day, Mendel carved a notch in the wall. There were three such notches in the corner now, and one day he hoped to fill the whole face of the sheetrock.

It wasn't all bitterness. Whenever memories of baby Ari and Mendel Jr. came into his mind, he also thought of Leah, in a way that wasn't entirely unpleasant. The two of them had lived in this apartment and they'd managed to turn two chayas into decent men. What was the straw that broke this

mensch's back? A coffee stain. A little more than a smear on
her grandmother's quilt.

In another time and place, they would have had a laugh
about it. Except this time, as she'd cleaned off the stain, she'd
brought up the way he'd smacked her cousin in Yerushalayim
years ago, and he'd started fidgeting with his tzitzit, and she'd
said, *Don't,* and he'd said, *You're not my mother,* first in Yiddish,
then in Hebrew, and she'd said, first in Hebrew, then in
Yiddish: *I just wish your mother taught you some basic things.*

All he knew was that he'd been happiest at nineteen, when
he'd crisscrossed Brooklyn on a five-speed and heaved bricks
into boarded windows. He had married at that age because he
wanted to touch a woman. That was all. Never did he bargain
that she would grow a mouth. A mouth so large it would
envelop the rooms of every house where they'd ever lived.
Husbandhood did not suit him.

"You give me zero," she'd said. "I do and do for this house,
but you, you give me back nothing."

. . .

The last few times she'd walked by Sunset Salsa, Leah had
lingered a moment to observe the men and women inside,
whose bodies moved like rain across a windshield. On this day,
she walked around the block three times, then returned to the
same spot. When she saw Chaim coming up Fourth Avenue,
she was fixing her hair, glancing through the steamed window
as if inside were nothing—a laundromat.

"Sister!" Chaim called from his bicycle. "You look terrible.
What happened?"

She shrugged and stared at her hands. Truly, they did look

old. Leah wanted to tell Chaim what her husband had done, but how could she begin to explain?

"The rebbe wants us for Shabbos," Chaim said. "And don't be late to shul this time."

It was Wednesday, which meant that she had two days before their community would learn—or wouldn't. Chaim was already halfway up the block when Leah yelled, "What if I can't come for Shabbos? What if I have plans?"

. . .

Thursday morning, Mendel was boiling with worry. It had occurred to him that he hadn't confirmed the halachic properties of the wall. In fact, it was possible that he'd committed an error by putting it up. The rebbe would know what to do, but telling the rebbe meant also telling the rebbetzin. He decided to head to Chaim's house instead, because if anyone knew halacha, it was his little brother.

When Mendel got there, Rachel was getting the place ready for Shabbos: picking up diapers, wiping away banana stains, giving a stir to the pot of cholent. He nodded to her and made his way down to the basement.

Chaim was painting again. It was one of those things he'd discovered when he was twelve and refused to give up. All around his feet lay crates of chachkis and stacks of canvases. He was mostly into painting rabbis. He'd done their rebbe in the style of Dalí and also Chuck Close. Now on a whim, he was painting the once-beautiful rebbetzin.

"Could use a little more color," Mendel said. "And in real life, her face is a bit longer. Like this." He sketched an imperfect oval in the air.

"Listen, brother, you know we are expected tomorrow."

"Shabbos?"

"Leah did not tell you?"

"You know, Chaim, we have been busy."

"Funny, I saw Leah just yesterday." Chaim sank his brush into a teacup of cerulean blue and began to work on the rebbetzin's eyes. "She said she had plans. What does that mean, *plans*?"

Mendel stared at his brother and remembered the time Chaim and he had dressed as Batman and Robin. It was to celebrate Purim. Chaim was twelve and Mendel sixteen and they'd danced together. They went along the streets of Crown Heights, floating arm in arm, until they reached the shul, where they whirled with the rebbe and drank vodka from bowls.

"Oh, that," Mendel said. "She has a kind of doctor's appointment."

"On Shabbos? Why would she have a doctor's appointment on Shabbos?"

"You know, Chaim, girls are girls and women are women."

"Don't baby me. Is something wrong with Leah?"

"It is not so serious, I think. Let us eat."

"Brother."

"Let us eat, Chaim."

Mendel left Chaim's house feeling all the more unsettled. Tomorrow at the rebbe's table, there was a chance that everyone would know what had happened between them. He hadn't planned on telling anyone, but Leah might have had other ideas. He thought they could continue to live in close but separate spaces.

On the way back home, he stopped at Lefty Pearlman's deli.

Many years ago, Lefty had cut ties with the shul. Nowadays he sold non-Kosher milk, but he still refused to carry ham.

"Lefty, give me one, will you."

"You got it. What's your lucky?"

"6,783: *I was with God, and I was with the Devil.*" Because if you took the most important line from this week's Torah portion and then computed the gematria value, you'd get 6,783.

"By the way," Lefty said. "I heard the beef."

"The what?"

"It's old news. Even the goyim know. When are you going to make the move? I know a matchmaker who can find someone for someone like you."

"Who told you?"

"Listen, if you want my advice: leave her to rot. You still got what you got."

Lefty tore off a pair of lottery tickets and passed them across the plastic enclosure.

"The second one's on me, because according to Latina numerology, *Morena Gonzalez is too hot to handle, too cold to hold.*" Lefty Pearlman winked at a plump woman selling coco frio outside the deli.

Mendel looked away. They'd followed the first rebbe's advice and gone out into the world. Sometimes, this was fine. Other times, it was like putting a cow in a room with a lion—you would get many things, but not milk.

. . .

Leah bought a pair of soft white gloves. She circled the corner of Fourth Avenue and Forty-sixth Street seven times before she went in.

What she'd imagined: that her partner would be named Ricardo, and though he was soft around the middle, that he was a good dancer, that he led her through the basic step, breaking on five, that he crisscrossed underneath her shoulder and turned her until she grew embarrassed with the way the conga tickled her collarbone. That at first she had her gloves on, which didn't seem to bother anyone, but after Ricardo dipped her for the first time, that they came off. That he picked them up and became the second man to touch her hands, her hips, the small of her back.

The class paused as she entered, and she quickly exited with a dog-eared flyer in hand. Afterward, she wrote in her diary:

*Things I thought I'd never do that I'll never do again.*

She opened the hole in the wall and peered through. In the milky dark, a bullock cart, or maybe the father of her sons, turned and snored.

. . .

Late at night, Mendel heard noises through the wall. It sounded like Leah was making an extravagant meal, shifting pots and pans, stirring stews, and arranging their good silver on the table. He didn't want much from her, a few leftovers would do. She could pass them through the hole and that would be enough. When he heard what sounded like the opening and closing of her front door, he held his blanket tighter to his body. It sounded like a line of strangers were coming in and going out again. Their voices were like woodpeckers in the trees.

He was tired enough the next morning that he considered

not going to work, but the roof under which they lived had to be paid for, and he was not a man good with excuses.

The job was in Brooklyn Heights, on a block close to the Promenade, with lots of maple trees and nannies who eyed him suspiciously. When he got to the house, he found that his client wasn't home, so he sat outside her stoop and laid out his tools. Many years ago, when he'd gotten Leah a chocolate box for her birthday, she'd said, *I wish you'd make me something from the heart.* So now he set about it. He began to carve and chisel a four-by-four block into a replica of Yankee Stadium. You'd look inside the wooden dome and see rows of tiny seats and imagine miniature figures in the crowd holding hands. When Ari was twelve, they'd gone to the stadium as a family, and who would've guessed that Leah would catch Reggie Jackson's bases-loaded home run?

When the outer ring of bleachers were finished, Mendel held his Yankee Stadium as if it were his grandfather's talis. From deep in his throat, he sang a nigun his rebbe had taught him when his hair had first been cut. With all the nannies watching, Mendel roared his wordless melodies into the air.

. . .

They did not belong here. If it weren't for his rebbe's rebbe, who had survived the war and the camps and the new country, where would they be? He'd always thought as you got older, as you did your duty and filled the world with decent children, that God would give you the right of way. A little Torah in the morning, some fishing in the afternoon, a hearty meal with family, and music in the shul.

Mendel paced outside his house and considered all the

things God might be trying to tell him. Then, he knocked on Leah's door.

She opened it partway. In the sunlight, she looked almost pretty. At least, he thought, they knew each other.

"I smelled your cooking," he said.

She shrugged and fixed her apron. It was covered in flour and stained with grease.

"Wife, how have you been?"

"Wife?" she said.

"Well, by the Torah, we are still husband and wife. If we wish to change that . . ."

"Listen, I need my red scarf. It's on your side of the room."

"What?"

"My scarf. Also bring me the typewriter. I need it."

"You, type? Do you even know the first thing of typing?"

"Mendel, you look skinny. Haven't you been eating?"

"Leah." Mendel tried to crane his head around her. "Is there a strange man in our house?"

"Listen, Mendel, is the shower broken? Because you smell like a wet dog."

"Me? I smell? You, you have chicken grease all over your face."

. . .

Shabbos evening, Leah went to the mikveh. It was something she'd done every month for twenty-nine years, even after her time of blood. Partly, she liked the quiet moments with her body: the filing of nails, the removing of wax from ears, the flossing even of back teeth, the washing of skin until every part was a pale gem. Also, she loved being submerged in the mikveh's waters, dipping herself seven times with slow, deliberate delight, but mostly, it was the feeling of coming home that had always made her go. When she returned to the house and touched her husband, after twelve days of being strangers, that was a feeling unlike any other.

Tonight, there was praying at the shul, and, afterward, dinner at the rebbe's. But there was also a party at Sunset Salsa, where the beginners would try their new moves: the basic step, the right-hand turn, the Mariposa, and the Figure Eight. Mendel had shut her like a book, shut the both of them out from their whole world. Yesterday his face had looked so pale, like a ghost from the old country.

Leah got dressed. She put on her wig and her special-occasions dress, a solid-blue gown that softly grazed her ankles. When God spoke the first word and there was light, it wasn't for the undoing. Mendel's wall was this kind of a word.

. . .

After a snack of herring and cold noodle soup, Mendel put on his Shabbos clothes. He'd gone to the dry cleaners to have his suit pressed, a task Leah used to do for him. It was a good thing, though, because now the dark suit sparkled. When Leah ironed, she was daydreaming this and that. She tended to leave wrinkles on the seam, his pants making him poorer than he was.

He took the longest time to wash his beard and to button his coat. In the bathroom mirror, an old man with too much forehead winked back at him. When he was ready, Mendel knocked on the wall. It was a studious knock, a knock that respected her privacy, but was, in its own way, quite firm.

"Wife," he said.

No answer.

"The rebbe expects us. Outside of the house, we are still man and wife."

He knocked with both his fists.

"Leah?"

He stopped knocking when he saw the sheet of paper caught between the wall and the floor. It was the frilly kind of stationery she used to make his grocery lists. He picked up the page. It said:

*Orange juice, salmon, sesame seeds.*

On the back, it said:

*It is not good that a man should be alone.*

*God said that it was mostly not good.*

*And there was nothing as subtle as the Serpent, which in the beginning was an off-putting comment, as was the way he discarded things such as Kleenex on the very floor where their child crawled.*

Mendel went for his sledgehammer. He aimed it at the wall. He struck three times. Each time the wall made a terrible groan, but it did not crumple. There wasn't a single dent where the sledgehammer had met the sheetrock. The surface still looked pristine, just as it had a week ago.

. . .

When Mendel reached the rebbe's house, he peered through the window. The Shabbos candles had already been lit. He couldn't make out the faces inside, though a couple of families were already seated around the table. The rebbe stood in the center of the room with a Torah in his hand.

He had come to this ordinary home on this holy night

countless times over the years, though on this night he came alone. After the silent prayer and the washing of hands, he'd have to give them a good story of how it all began. Mendel spoke the Shema under his breath and went inside. Until the end, it would be this way—his word against hers.

*Searching for Elijah*

Malini and her son were the last to arrive at the Passover dinner. Mrs. Cohen greeted them at the door, engulfing Malini in her silk décolleté caftan, and hurried them to the table.

"Now that we're all here," Mrs. Cohen said, "shall we wash?"

The family mumbled a collective *yes*. Around the table, there were four cousins, three neighbors, Stephen, his older sister, Elizabeth, and Mr. Cohen. Everyone smiled back at Malini, hiding what she assumed were varying degrees of suspicion and curiosity. Amar, who was waking from a cross-country sleep, buried his face in her lap.

"We wash before the meal," Stephen whispered.

"I know." Malini had researched the Passover seder via an audio guide that described the order and meaning of the ceremony. When riding the subway, she would wear headphones and mouth the Hebrew words as they were said. *Kiddish. Magid. Maror.* But now that she was here, it did not seem so simple, not with all the family watching and her son wondering what came next.

"We do it a little differently," Stephen said. "We wash each other's hands."

Her little boy tried to hide behind her legs, and she had to coax him to the kitchen, where Mr. Cohen, who Stephen had explained excelled at entertaining kids Amar's age and pined for a grandchild himself, lifted him onto the countertop and washed his hands first. Amar smarted at the feel of the cold water, but Stephen's dad was ready with a magic trick that ended with two red jelly beans. Amar laughed and splashed water.

"You, be calm." Before they'd left New York, Malini had Amar promise that he would be on his best behavior. "If you do," she'd said, "there'll be a new toy for you."

"Your turn," Mrs. Cohen said.

Malini presented her hands—a queen's hands, the color of molasses—fingers slender and long. Both hands were adorned: a sapphire ring crowned each one.

"They're beautiful," Mrs. Cohen said.

She'd bought the rings three years earlier, after her husband had passed away. The astrologer had told her the gems were for *love* and *persistence*.

Mrs. Cohen poured water on Malini's palms, three times on the left, three times on the right. She wrapped Malini's hands in a towel and dried them. It felt like an unearned intimacy, but Malini maintained her smile.

Mrs. Cohen leaned close to whisper, "I bless you for tomorrow's mikveh. That you may be purified, that you may be holy."

Malini recoiled from Mrs. Cohen's grasp. Tomorrow's mikveh, the purification ritual, had been on her mind ever since she and Stephen had become serious. She cut her eyes at Amar, who was splashing water again, but this time it was a welcome distraction from Mrs. Cohen's gaze.

"Thank you for the blessing," Malini said. Then she went to tend to her son.

. . .

Malini and Stephen had met at the farmer's market. In between nanny shifts, Malini worked a food stall called Brooklyn Masala Co., where she sold her simmering sauces and chutneys. She was there every weekend, and the other stall owners knew her so there was never a shortage of eyes on Amar. Her boy could wander through the market and be safe while she sold her cooking and chatted with her customers, though she could always feel when he ventured too far, when she'd call him back with her stern voice.

It was the tikka masala sauce, the simmer of coconut and cardamom-infused tomato, that Stephen came back for, again and again, but it was only on his sixth time, he later told her, that he'd had the courage to speak.

"Your sauce," he had said. "It's out of this world."

She had smiled as she did at all such compliments. It was not so difficult to see when men became smitten with her, and on that September Sunday, she knew Stephen was more than curious. What she sensed of him was that he was simple in his emotions, in his knowledge of love and loss, but that he was honest about his ignorance. He would be willing to alter his life to fit one more, maybe even two, and if she had told him then, *Go fetch me the moon*, he would've borrowed a ladder and tried his best.

They began to see each other. A dim café, the ferry to Governors Island, a stroll in the village, always Amar in tow, though that dampened the romance. Her boy was obedient, but even at three she feared he remembered Neel as a father and sensed this other relationship to be a transgression. At first when Stephen came around Amar wouldn't respond to any of his overtures.

Stephen was tender with her, and with her boy he persisted, learning how to play games they both grew to love. Often, he praised her beauty; he kissed her anklebone more than a hundred times once, stopping only when she told him it tickled. She enjoyed the smell of his shirts, with the collars crisp but not overly starched. His promenade apartment was spacious. She chose to ignore the way he cataloged his boxers into separate drawers, one for the whites, another for the blues, focusing instead on the hand-carved Buddha in the living room, who sat atop a mountain of water, whose Himalayan shape was sustained by a complex motor that produced a purring, nearly mammalian whir. The first time they made love in that room it felt to her as if they were floating in the middle of a pool, and she thought then not of her dead husband but of her childhood, when she'd skipped rocks into the endless Ganges, when all the boys had remarked on her looks. Though she was not so young now, nor as beautiful perhaps, she still believed that the Ganges in its morning light would see her that way—young and unmarred—until the man next to her began to snore and she was reminded of how far the river really was.

. . .

They reached the part of the Passover story where the Jews were trying to escape enslavement in Egypt. "It's a metaphor," Mr. Cohen said, "of any of us leaving the narrow place. Of any of us finding our way to freedom."

"It's not just a metaphor, honey. It's our history. Now eat some of the bitter," said Mrs. Cohen. She dictated and the family did. The next-door neighbor made a joke about the taste of the horseradish root, and Stephen's sister, Elizabeth, asked whether it was organic. The two cousins on the other side of the table resumed their conversation about the music industry. One of them, who had brought his guitar, began to strum a tune that sounded like "Amazing Grace." Amar dipped an asparagus into horseradish sauce and said, "Yuck." Malini smoothed his hair, but he said it again, louder, "Yuck."

"Don't worry, buddy. We're going to do a sandwich of sweet and bitter next," Stephen said.

"Yuck," Amar said. He maintained his look of offended pride.

Stephen's sister switched seats so she could be closer to Malini. It was the first time they were meeting.

"Anyway," Elizabeth said. "I love your sweater."

It was a black cashmere that hung loose off the tops of her shoulders, conservative, elegant, but with jeans still made her feel pretty. She'd agonized over her whole wardrobe looking for this exact outfit. "And I love your shirt," Malini said, though, in fact, she found Elizabeth's sequined stretch tee, inscribed with the word *Babe*, inappropriate for the occasion.

"Anyhow, little brother never said what you do."

When her husband Neel was around, she'd felt awkward

naming herself as a *housewife*, but that was what she'd become. Nowadays, explaining how she made ends meet, which was a combination of nanny work, farmer's markets, and loans from Stephen, was equally problematic. She was relieved when Stephen spoke for her: "She's a chef. A very good one."

Selling sauces at local markets had never, like the paintings she made, felt like a real job, but she didn't correct him. A couple of months earlier, after he'd spoken to his mother, he'd shared their big plans: she would quit her day job, she would write cookbooks that merged Jewish and Indian cooking, she would have her own webcast. Then again, Stephen's own job had never felt real to Malini. He blogged about the internet to only slightly more readers than she had customers. Still, it seemed to make him happy, and he was supported every month by a check from home.

"Well, you're a very pretty chef," Elizabeth said.

Malini could've sliced the horseradish with the condescension in Elizabeth's voice. She hoped the meal would start soon. Amar had begun to fidget. He was distracting Stephen with his *What's that?* game, where he would point to objects he already knew and say, "What's that candle?" or "What's that chandelier?"

"What's that maror?" he said, pointing at the bitter herbs.

The table laughed. Even the two cousins in the music business had stopped their shoptalk and were focusing their attention on Malini and her boy.

Elizabeth refilled her wineglass. For each blessing over wine, Elizabeth had allowed herself a good swig. "So you're older than little brother," she said. "Are you older than me?"

A hush settled over the table. "What kind of question—" Mr. Cohen started, but Malini could tell that even he was eager to know.

"Ma's thirty plus seven," Amar said. "She's really old."

"Look at me," Mr. Cohen said. He pulled the fleshy skin under his neck. "I'm the old guy."

Stephen was four years younger, and for an Indian family the age barrier might have been a serious issue, but for Mrs. Cohen Malini knew it wasn't.

"C'mon and make a sandwich, people," Mrs. Cohen said. She added the apple-sweet mash to the bitters and took a generous bite.

. . .

They'd been dating for six months when she met Stephen's mother. Amar was sleeping when her buzzer rang, her horribly loud buzzer that always threatened to interrupt his nap. That was another thing Neel had promised to fix but never did. She answered the door, out of breath, hoping Amar wouldn't wake for another hour.

From the downstairs intercom, a woman's whiskey voice answered, "You're dating my son. I'd like to talk."

In the time that it took Mrs. Cohen to climb three flights of stairs, Malini put on a clean sweater and tied her hair into a bun. She opened the door with as gracious a smile as she could muster. "Pleasure to meet you," she said.

"Did I disturb you," Mrs. Cohen said, but it wasn't a question. She was wearing a winter coat with a fur collar. Her boots were a knee-high black. She took off one suede glove, then the other. With her achingly blue eyes, she made her authority known.

Malini invited her in and made tea. She worried about what Mrs. Cohen thought of the space. It was a small one-bedroom with a hodgepodge of her art slung on the walls. The north wall had three different colors of paint because she'd never been able to decide on the right one. There were two fraying couches next to each other and an old black-and-white TV with bunny ears.

Mrs. Cohen took a sip of her tea. "I'm involved in my son's life," she said. "I know how deeply he's fallen for you. And he's a stubborn boy, so I also know that whatever I say won't change his mind."

When Stephen had talked about his mother, Malini had imagined a different woman, a haughtier version of the person who sat before her, but the real Mrs. Cohen, she could tell, was a pragmatist, a negotiator.

"What I want," Mrs. Cohen said. "What the *family* wants, is that you seriously consider conversion."

Malini's teacup missed her mouth. She spilled tea on her rug.

"It's not that we're especially religious," Mrs. Cohen said. "We're not. But it's the one thing that keeps us who we are. Without that, we're just Americans. Stephen didn't say—are you religious?"

The last time Malini had thought about God was when the hospital chaplain had helped her pray for her husband, that he should pass with ease into the afterlife. She hadn't minded then, though lingering on scripture wasn't her way. Still, she bristled when Mrs. Cohen asked about her faith, believing it was nobody else's business. "I'm a New Yorker," she'd said. "No time at all for God."

On that first meeting, they'd parted stiffly, but Mrs. Cohen had continued to call. Even after Malini had moved in with Stephen, she kept it up—*I hope you'll consider*—and finally exhausted and believing that it would not matter which religion she was known by, Malini said yes. She would meet the whole family at Passover, they agreed, and the day after she would dip in the holy waters and be named, almost a Cohen.

. . .

The Passover meal was catered by a Kosher restaurant. A small army of men and women in nondescript outfits brought the first and second courses, bowls of lavender-miso soup, rocket and fennel salad, the leg of a lamb, two kinds of North Atlantic fish filleted and glistening. For Amar, Mr. Cohen had arranged for a plate of chicken strips. The boy ate with his hands.

More and more, Amar was reminding Malini of her husband. He had her high cheekbones and her proud nose—in fact, in his body, he was completely hers—but it was in his expressions that he'd begun to echo his father. The way he chewed the first bite with his eyes closed. The way he winked at her when he wanted to share his enjoyment of the world.

Stephen made a show of taking away one of his chicken strips, and the two of them mock-wrestled until Amar squealed victoriously and raised his arms in the air. Watching them, Malini experienced a moment of jealousy. They communed not as adult and child but as companions, a relationship lived in early bliss.

Elizabeth forked a pair of roasted potatoes and pushed them into her mouth. "I thought Hindus didn't eat meat. You're not a vegetarian?"

Malini had a desire to end the conversation with a firm *No*, but she desisted. "Some of us do."

"You know Stephen was a vegetarian once. Back when he grew his hair out and had student loans," Elizabeth said.

"I was a vegetarian for one whole year," Stephen said. He had told her about that year—*the off year*, he called it—when between undergrad and grad school he had traveled India by commuter train, living as frugally as the sadhus who would brush by with sweet impenetrable blessings.

"Oh, I have pictures," Stephen's mother said.

In the glass almirah where the irreplaceable china shared space with little crystal dolls from Ukraine, there was a drawer for family albums. She pulled out one that said S-T-E-P-H-E-N in large hand-drawn letters, a woman's careful hand, and knew just where to look. She passed Malini a picture of Stephen standing between two long-braided sadhus. He was wearing a faded sky-blue Panjabi and his nose was bright red from sunburn.

"Oh, Stephen," his mother said.

"Yeah," his sister said. "It was great until they medevaced him out."

Stephen smirked, and Malini could see how as children together this would have translated into a pinch on the forearm or a kick on the shin.

As she continued eating, Amar swayed to a music only he could hear. The caterers came in and out of the dining room like ghosts. When Malini was thirsty, she found her cup refilled; when nothing was left of her meal but the skin of Alaskan salmon, her plate was cleared. The previous winter she and her boy had been subsisting on food stamps; a few times she'd made a game of taking him to the soup kitchen, where he refused to eat anything but the sweet potato mash. Sometimes, he was aggrieved by the monotony of his meals. Once he'd thrown his bowl of beans on her kitchen floor because he'd tired of the same dish, every night for that week, and after she'd scolded him and put him to bed, she'd made her dinner of what remained. Now they were feasting without a care—how remarkable was this life, the bittersweet turns of her fate. Amar had finished everything, even the ketchup licked clean from his plate. She stroked her son's head and then rubbed Stephen's back.

For a few moments, the only sounds were the contented sighs of the first meal. For those who wished for tea, there was tea, and for the others there was espresso or sparkling water. She could not imagine her family allowing a whole minute of silence, but the Cohens were savoring their after-dinner drinks with bites of marzipan. They were chewing their way into their own thoughts.

Finally, Mrs. Cohen broke the silence by clapping her hands: "Shall we let Elijah in?"

"Who's Elijah?" Amar said. He had been happy enough eating his cookie crumbs, but the possibility of a visitor got his attention.

Mr. Cohen opened the front door. "Every Passover, we wait for Elijah to come. He'll help us march to freedom!"

"Open it more," Amar said.

Mr. Cohen opened the door wide.

"What will he eat?" Amar asked. He kicked his legs under the table in worry.

Sometimes, Amar expressed a fear of hunger, but she didn't know why—he'd never suffered himself. She thought she'd shielded him. Even those nights she'd gone to bed hungry, he'd had something to eat.

"Oh, he's got his own plate," Mr. Cohen said, pointing out the empty place setting at the other end of the table with its decorative goblet, full to the brim with wine.

"Maybe he's lost," Amar cried.

And Mr. Cohen, whose deep love of children was the great artistry of his life, said, "Then we must find him."

. . .

The week before, Stephen's mother had texted Malini the address of a rabbi. He was based in Brooklyn, it turned out, and he was *deeply into Eastern stuff*. When she entered Rabbi Joseph's office in Greenpoint, she was struck by the scent of blooming hyacinth, which had been carefully arranged underneath a painting of Ramakrishna. He hugged her warmly. "Debbie told me all about you," he said.

He sat her down on a rustic divan to explain the situation. Jewish Law said that you had to visit the rabbi three times. Twice you would be turned away. Only on the third occasion, when your love for God and your knowledge of Jewish scripture was confirmed, would you be inducted. Since she had already been reading the books Mrs. Cohen had sent her, the knowledge part wouldn't be a problem, he said, but they would need to accelerate the three visits.

"Why don't you leave, get a coffee, and come back? That

will be time number two. Then I'll fly out to L.A. and you'll see me there. That will be time number three. Got it?"

She nodded. She walked around his block three times before she was ready to knock. Each time she passed his house she told herself that life was about cleaving yourself from the past, and this would be no different. Later that night, when Stephen asked her where she'd been all afternoon, she told him she'd been looking for a wedding dress. "I saw a beautiful handmade one," she'd said.

She hadn't told him then what she was up to. She would not tell him until after their wedding was what she'd agreed with Stephen's mother. This troubled her, but each time she'd broached the subject with Mrs. Cohen, her future mother-in-law had been firm. "It will be a sweet surprise," Mrs. Cohen had said. "Something to carry the fire into your new life."

Stephen had said he didn't mind if she converted or didn't, but Stephen did not hold the purse strings.

. . .

The Cohens lived a few blocks from the Marina, so if Elijah was to be found, it was agreed he would appear beachside. They split into groups. Stephen, Malini, and Amar twisted their long shadows under the light of the three-quarter moon. Her little boy stuffed enough shells into his pocket that his cotton breeches sagged. "Is he coming from the water?" Amar asked.

Malini had to end swimming lessons when Neel passed, and now she tensed up when Amar was near any body of water. "Elijah doesn't like the ocean," she said. "He'll be coming from up there." She pointed toward the sky, where it was that time of night when the dark crawled into the dark and a lidless moon hunkered between ash-blue clouds. Amar stared where she was pointing, turning his head to inspect each quadrant of night for Elijah's footprints. Stephen looked with him, as earnestly as her boy, because somewhere in his life, innocence had become habit.

"Have you found him?" Elizabeth had snuck up behind them. Her pants were rolled up, revealing a pair of pretty ankles.

"I'm still looking!" Amar said. He was squatting on the sand, following the walk of a crab.

"Bet I know where he is," Elizabeth said. She pointed toward the jetty, and the boy looked to his mother, who tried to hide the alarm in her face by looking at Stephen.

"It's all right," Stephen said. "We'll wait for you here."

Elizabeth took Amar's hand. They walked toward the jetty, which progressed like the tongue of the land, exposed to every whim of the ocean, eroded over time. She watched Amar's walk, duck-like; every few steps, he would gaze back until eventually, spotting a golden retriever, he forgot about her and ran ahead.

"He'll be fine," Stephen said. "Lizzie knows how to take care of kids."

"Of course," Malini said, but she did not believe for one moment that Elizabeth knew how to take care of *her* kid. Still, she didn't protest. The evening had been going well enough. There was no need to breach with Elizabeth. She watched the two run, holding her tongue, until she could no longer see them.

"I want to show you something," Stephen said.

He led her to a balustrade of man-sized stones, formations that had fortified themselves against the water a millennium ago. He smoothed his hand over the rock face. The cold water slipped underneath his feet, but he did not seem to mind. There was a name carved where the light touched the rock: *Stephen loves Malini.* And the sign for infinity.

She imagined him waking up early that morning to chisel the stone. Perhaps, Mrs. Cohen had asked where he was headed, and he had answered, *Nowhere.*

"If it's too corny," he said, "I can scratch it out."

She could hear Mrs. Cohen in the distance. It was difficult to see exactly where she was, but her laughter stuck to the air with the agility of an insect on a cobweb. "It's sweet," Malini said, which was not lying, exactly. She could love Stephen Cohen as one loves a troubled plant, nourishing him as needed. In time this caretaking might find a different bloom. Till then, she would be patient.

He seemed relieved. "So what do you want to do tomorrow? I've got buddies we could visit in the valley, or we could drive up the coast, or we could go sailing to Catalina. Whatever you want."

"Actually," she said, "your mother and I have a little date tomorrow."

"What for?" He seemed taken aback, before a confident grin rolled over his face. "Shopping, isn't it?"

She considered telling him everything—the sum of Mrs. Cohen's secret visits, how her husband's memory had begun to press on her waking life like an eagle circling its prey—but in that moment, his curly hair had become entangled in the wind and he looked like the twenty-year-old who ran with sadhus. She couldn't imagine telling that boy such a familial truth, because what if her honesty undid them? He kept three drawers in his apartment labeled *Malini*, had a section of his closet reserved for Amar's toys. No, it was better to leave him as he was. She loosened a few of the knots in his hair, kissed him on the cheek.

"Wedding stuff," she said. "Don't worry your head about it."

They sat down in the sand. She began to feel an ache in her belly, though there was the wind of the ocean to comfort her, though there was Stephen stroking the space between her shoulders, though the sky had turned perfectly cloudless.

. . .

*It's what I want*, he'd announced from his hospital room. *The rice ceremony must happen.* Amar was a year old. He had learned how to crawl over his father's body without hurting him—or so his father claimed. The doctors had said, *It's best to restrict movement.* The chaplain had said, *Anything to ease his suffering.* In the end, she heeded her husband's last wish: they wheeled him into the community room, which the staff had decorated with glossy posters of many-armed deities.

Someone had called a Hindu priest. He was a young man with a receding hairline and a flawless grasp of Sanskrit. "I am so glad," he'd told Malini, "that you are doing your duty in this difficult time."

She surveyed the evidence of her duty: a husband who had been propped into a wheelchair, his head balanced by the gentle hand of the afternoon nurse, a son who scrambled to take the priest's spectacles, and, of course, there was the rice.

It was arranged on a brass plate atop a foldout table, a little mountain of jasmine peaked with flakes of saffron.

The moment she took her eye off Amar, her little boy grabbed for the foldout table. In his wake, the rice toppled, the brass plate clattered against the linoleum, and the priest paused his prayer. When it was quiet again, her husband was the first to speak. She leaned close to hear, but his voice became lost in a rheumatic cough. The nurse checked his respiratory tubes and Malini tried to give her space, but her husband latched on to her forearm, his grip surprisingly strong.

He was unable to form a full sentence, so she was left to guess at what final advice remained. Over the years, she feared that her memory had transformed his look into something that it was not. Still, that was all she had of him: a few pictures, an hour's worth of memories, and what he was trying to say as he held her forearm, what she believed he would be saying to her now.

. . .

They sat by the ocean as the wind picked up and mussed her hair. She felt the whip of that memory, the dropped rice bowl, her husband's parched speech. Stephen didn't seem to feel her agitation. There was a cold spire in the breeze; she remembered her husband's touch.

She wished she could discuss the tremors she felt. But Stephen would not understand. He would blink a few times. Then he would wrap her in a hug. Though she'd acted for their mutual good, he would not understand why she'd been dishonest, nor would he understand why now of all the times in their relationship she felt threatened. It wasn't Stephen's duty to speak to her son in Bengali, as Neel had once done, or to teach him the notes of the musical scale, explaining the difference between morning and night songs. Soon it would come—she could already feel it—the tide of this family erasing whatever linked Amar to his father, his father's religion, and their old country. Was nothing to be done?

Stephen was fidgeting again, counting along his fingers. The night he'd brought up spending seder with his family, he'd also tallied the permutations of how such an evening could turn into disaster, he'd later confessed. She now crossed her arms over her chest and waited.

"There's just one thing I forgot to mention," Stephen said. "Since we're not official, Mom wants us to sleep in separate rooms."

She considered his age and hers, the sum of which equaled his mother's. Another test, that's all it was. She didn't bother to disguise her annoyance, which felt closer now to weariness than she would have admitted.

"There they are," Stephen said.

Mr. Cohen, Mrs. Cohen, Elizabeth, and her son were returning from the jetty. Mr. Cohen dragged his bad hip across the sand and everyone else slowed down to match his motion so that the whole group looked like a lopsided leviathan. When they got closer, she could tell that Amar was excited. A few feet away and she could see his pants had become soaked.

Stephen hugged his mother, as if it had been a long time since they'd seen each other, though it was only minutes, and in that embrace she saw the little boy come out in him, grateful for her affection.

"Ma, I stuck my feet in!" Amar squealed.

"The water is freezing, and you did more than stick your feet in," Malini said. She looked at no one in particular. "Why would you let him go in?"

"Mostly the tippy-tops of his toes," Mr. Cohen said. "We all got wet." With his hand on his wife's shoulder, he raised his foot with evidence of surf.

Malini took her son from Mr. Cohen's grasp. She felt his forehead. "He's quite warm," she said.

Stephen repeated her motion. "No," he said. "He feels fine to me."

"Loosen up, Mal," Elizabeth said.

"Maybe it's time we all went in for the night," Mrs. Cohen said.

Malini grabbed her son's hand, a little too firmly. The Cohens followed behind in nearly single file.

. . .

Malini went through her suitcase and made a little mountain of lingerie on the floor, as Amar looked on. It was past his bedtime, but Malini hadn't said a word since they'd gotten back to the house and Amar had known well enough to keep quiet, awaiting his bedtime ritual. This was the time for a lullaby, but Malini wasn't in the mood. Her mind was on Stephen, who had left her to sleep in his old bedroom on the second floor, parting with a quick kiss and instructions to wake him, if she needed anything.

She arranged the lace back into her bag. Each item she folded with care, as if bringing lingerie was for the purpose of quieting the mind, nothing more. When the suitcase was put back to order, she found Amar in deep sleep. His neck was at an odd angle, so she adjusted his body, listening to his breathing as he forded a dream. His little fists swooped mightily until the dream deepened and he settled into a pacific sleep.

There was plenty of room in the guest bed for her to lie down next to him, but she was too awake. Stephen's snore would often calm her, defenses yielding long enough for sleep to come, but without him here, she heard the tumult of the hour: the roll call of the ocean, the bells on a bicycle passing in the street, a few revelers yowling on the beach, a dog's persistent bark.

The first night she'd been alone with Amar, she had carried all the chairs in the house and piled them against the door. The door was already double-bolted, but the chairs eased her fears about what could come. She had the same impulse now: take the swivel chair, place the plush loveseat on top, make them more secure with the pile of *Esquire* magazines on the shelves. But there was a scratching sound at the door, a cat perhaps, who'd hidden from view so long as the crowd was thick, come to check on its room.

She put her ear to the door. Something that was not a cat was breathing on the other side. "Stephen?" she said.

"Ah, no, he's quite asleep."

Malini opened the door and found Mrs. Cohen standing in the hallway, pale in the luminescence of the night light. There was a flask of coffee in her hand and she seemed relieved that she'd not had to knock. "You know, I have a hard time sleeping myself," Mrs. Cohen said. "Always have."

At times like this, Malini felt uncertain about American etiquette—how was one to respond? There was her annoyance about the sleeping situation and then the upset about the ocean and her boy in it, but she was supposed to seem pleasant, make a comment about the floral sheets—wasn't that the way? After all these years, she wasn't sure. Finally, she said, "May I help you with something?"

"Well, you'd said the boy was feeling a bit hot and—"

"He's quite fine now, Mrs. Cohen."

"Does coffee keep you up? Me, I hardly feel it." Mrs. Cohen took a good swig.

"I could drink two or three cappuccinos with no concern," said Malini.

Mrs. Cohen seemed enlivened by this news. She took Malini by the elbow and led her to the back porch, where on a table of white linen another flask of coffee awaited. The second flask in hand, Mrs. Cohen looked piteous, an old sleepless lady. She asked Malini, "Won't you take a walk with me?"

Mrs. Cohen led by flashlight, and they found a dry spot on the jetty. No moon to be seen, just the ocean somewhere near, the calls of a lone gull finding its prize.

"I bet you think Stephen shrinks into a child when he comes here, but you have to understand his childhood." It was how he'd grown up, Mrs. Cohen explained. When he was young, she was working all the time, just like her husband, and the days when Stephen was under her care were a precious few. "It's like he's trying to make up for all that time."

"So it wasn't your idea," Malini said, "the separate rooms?"

"Well, we are old-fashioned about certain things."

"Why have you brought me here, Mrs. Cohen?"

"Darling," Mrs. Cohen said, sweeping a gesture that took in the ocean and the solitary bray of the seal who had followed them onto the jetty, "I'm not sorry I made you keep the conversion a secret from Stephen. Yes, it doesn't feel right, but it's the right thing to do. Stephen's a boy and you're a woman, so I can tell you this and I know you can hear me: Either you're in our tribe, or you're not. There's no in-between."

Removed of her makeup, a lone gray hair sprouting from her chin, Mrs. Cohen seemed old enough to warrant a handicapped seat, brittle enough to even deserve sympathy, but Malini couldn't grant her anything more than an adversarial smile. "Indeed," she said. "This is not something Stephen would understand."

"When it's time, Amar will have a bar mitzvah," Mrs. Cohen said. "You don't believe me, but it will be fun. It will be necessary."

When he came of age, there was a ceremony Neel would've wanted for Amar, but Malini didn't dare object to Mrs. Cohen's plan. For a while, they remained in their private languages. Then Mrs. Cohen produced a rumpled pack of cigarettes from inside the folds of her nightdress. The trail of ash, the faint scent of tar, seemed to wither her further. "What was he like," Mrs. Cohen said, after a lugubrious draw, "your old husband?"

Her first thought was that her husband was not old, that were he alive now he would be just a year older than she was, but of course that was not what Mrs. Cohen had meant. "He was," Malini struggled to offer something from her memories, "he was rather fond of nature. He liked to take walks in difficult terrain. His name was *Neel*, which means blue like the ocean. He wrote sentimental poems. He was not good with money."

"Harold was a poet," Mrs. Cohen said.

Malini imagined Mr. Cohen at his teakwood desk, carving sonnets into the frame.

"But he gave that up," Mrs. Cohen said. "To focus on things."

There it was again, the giving up—the essential cleaving. When tomorrow arrived, she would be expected to unbridle from her roots, as her husband in heaven had feared, but now in the final hours before conversion she felt the hook of an old life digging into her skin. She had loved what she had loved, and all the scars could not be hidden.

"We'll leave bright and early tomorrow," Mrs. Cohen said with a final swig from her coffee. "So get some rest."

After they'd returned to the house and Mrs. Cohen had retired for the night, Malini continued her nocturnal pacing alone. Careful not to wake her son, she went into the dining room, and, curious what spices hid in the cabinets, she shined Mrs. Cohen's flashlight and found evidence of fig jams, jars of saffron powder, anise seed, a can of truffle oil, three kinds of sesame paste. Deep in the fridge, there were even containers of her own Sunday Simmer Sauce.

There was evidence of morning in the night sky when she began to arrange a handful of spices on the counter. By the time they had been gathered and pestled into a paste, the earliest birds were awake. She worked faster. As the house slept, the cast iron pot glowed with the infusion of paprika; an eggplant was sliced into rounds; the shingles murmured as a northeasterly wind passed through. Soon, she had two platefuls of vegetables curried and steaming, her hands coated with the yellow of the turmeric. It was not the right food for this hour, or this house. She did not have permission to cook in Mrs. Cohen's kitchen, but if there was anything that could even the scales, it was this privilege—this morning where they would eat what she had eaten all her life.

When she heard the sounds from upstairs, the energetic tooth brushing, the low tone of rising banter, seven plates of food had been arranged on the table, each one decorated with a sprig of cilantro, flanked by squares of matzo. The Cohens were still upstairs when Amar walked into the dining room. He did not seem surprised by the pungent smells of the meal, or by the fact that she was sitting determinedly in her pajamas, her hair much too astray for good company. No, he did not mind her as she was. With eyes still poached with sleep, her little boy crawled into her lap and waited.

Moments later, she heard footsteps on the landing, a sated yawn, the creaking of the ancient stairwell. *Good morning*, someone said. And it was.

# A Mother's Work

Today's job involves the thirty-one-year-old Wall Streeter Shubho Chatterjee. Rani has reviewed the case notes enough times to know the young man's history and habits by heart. For example, Shubho calls his mother at nine thirty on alternate nights; when he was four he broke his wrist reaching for butter in the topmost cabinet; and he can recite several of Tagore's romantic poems from memory. Shubho has recently arrived from India, from one of those schools in the north that churn out soft-speaking financial engineers. But Rani has never actually met Shubho, only his elder sister Binodini, who at their first meeting slipped her wedding ring on and off and said, "This is what the family wants."

"Don't worry," Rani had assured. "I take care of everything."

Shubho's apartment is on a desirable block in Park Slope, overlooking gingko trees that are just beginning to bloom. Rani arrives at two thirty and uses a set of keys from Binodini to let herself in. The place is meticulously kept, and Shubho, it seems, has a taste for art deco, judging by the aquiline curvature of the armchair where Rani imagines she'll spend the next two hours. All the furniture is covered in plastic, which she finds odd, given that he's lived here for more than a year. His cupboards, however, are typical of her other bachelors. After scavenging, she finds only stacks of ramen noodles and, sitting out on the little table, a giant jar of peanut butter. No matter, she's brought her own ingredients. She takes a package of lentils and pours them, along with spices she's carried in her purse, into a saucepan. The room begins to smell of cumin and roasted fennel, the scent of home and motherlove.

She changes out of her jeans and caftan and into a starched white sari, applies makeup that accentuates the wrinkles around her eyes, then streaks her temples with wash-out gray and snaps on eyelash extensions. She takes another moment to fix her hair into a bun with two gilded bobby pins. The final touch is a red bindi placed in the absolute center of her forehead. She believes that her clients are often struck by the bindi's perfect symmetry, the high cheekbones it calls into focus. It's simple enough to transform into an elderly woman, so simple, in fact, that she has begun to wonder, at forty-two, whether she's actually taken on the accoutrements of old age decades before her time.

Rani expects Shubho's girlfriend to arrive between three and three thirty, as she does each Sunday, when Shubho returns from the gym. She sits in the armchair and waits. Early on, the waiting was unbearable, and she would bite her nails to bleeding and reconsider this new profession she'd discovered from a classified in the expat-Bengali newspaper. Nowadays, she can take this time to almost relax, as she rehearses her lines, and imagines the couple together, from their initial conversation to their first awkward sexual episode—the sort of preparation that's allowed her to make a name for herself in the local community of conservative Indian families.

At quarter past three, she hears someone approach the door and turn the key. She's got the deadbolt on, so the door doesn't give.

"Sammy, you there?" someone calls. "It's me."

Rani doesn't move. She lets the woman knock. She allows herself a deep breath, then another one. She studies her nails, which she has painted a proper navy blue. A third knock goes ignored. Then, in desperation, the bell rings. But if there's one skill she's carried from continent to continent, it's meditative stalling. She sits in her chair and remembers the crows who liked to perch on the ledge of her childhood house during the rains: they pined for each other in their dark, wet suits, stretching their necks across the grills of her open window while her grandmother told stories of gods and demons. Those days, it was enough to sing poems from Gitanjali until the evening lost its shape. An even louder knock. "Hey, you sleeping?"

Rani fixes her sari. Finally, she rises to open the door.

The woman on the other side of the threshold looks like the pictures Rani was shown—wide hips, windblown auburn hair—except in person and without makeup her edges become visible and her laugh lines age her. Melody Walker, Shubho's girlfriend of six months, is balancing a Pyrex dish in one arm, while, with the other, she's carrying a sleeping boy. Rani knows about the child. He goes to kindergarten in the city and qualifies for free meals. She also knows that he's the product of a music festival and the capriciousness of youth. She knows that he doesn't know his father and will likely never meet him.

Melody Walker is looking around the hallway, as if she's arrived at the wrong apartment.

"If you are another of the Jehovah's Witnesses," Rani says, "we don't want any."

"Don't want what? I'm here for Sammy."

Rani opens the door a few more inches so that the light from the stairwell falls across her cheekbones and illuminates her white sari.

"Oh my God," Melody says. "Are you—"

"I am Shubho Chatterjee's mother. And you are?"

"I'm Melody. This is Tyler." She looks down at the stove dish in her other hand. "I brought some food."

. . .

Rani has turned up the thermostat so high the hydrangea in the corner has started to droop. She offers an oversweet cup of masala tea. Melody sips, flashes what Rani considers an audition smile, the mouth upturned but the skin around the eyes tight. Tyler's still sleeping, now curled into Melody's lap, a line of drool making its way onto the carpet. If only she and her husband could manage the same, fall asleep anywhere and with a moment's notice, their lives might be a little happier.

"Have you been traveling—sorry, I don't know your first name?"

"You may call me Mrs. Chatterjee. Should I get something for the boy? A pillow perhaps?"

"No, he's fine, thank you."

Rani dunks a poppyseed cracker into her tea to lessen the sweetness, and, in the moment that she releases eye contact, catches the girl texting. She's likely messaging Shubho, asking him why in heaven his mother is suddenly in his apartment. It's a fair question, and Rani and the Chatterjee family have planned accordingly: Shubho has been taken to a coffee shop for what Binodini has described as an urgent family discussion; Rani's been promised two hours, during which time Binodini will do her part to sway her brother. "This requires combined effort," she always says to her clients. "You do yours, and I do mine." Which is all to say that Melody's text won't be seen by Shubho—Binodini will keep him occupied; she'll make her case that he shouldn't be with Melody, that his whole family would be mortified by his current choice, that more suitable women await.

"Weird weather," Melody now offers. "High in the sixties but with a chance of hail. Did you hear that too? Hail in the spring?"

"Is it the case, Miss Walker?"

"You can call me Melody. Don't mind me saying this, Mrs. Chatterjee, but you look really great. I can hardly recognize you from the pictures."

"The pictures?"

"Oh, Shubho showed me some photos from a family trip in the Himalayas."

Rani can't tell if Melody is harboring suspicions underneath her politeness, but she's faced this before. She keeps rope for almost every quandary. "Oh, Americans often think we all look alike. That's my older sister, who Shubho sees as a second mother. We are a very close family."

"Oh, I know. Sammy talks about his growing up. There was a lot of love there, I can tell. By the way, it's great to finally meet you, Mrs. Chatterjee. I've heard so much. All good things. Just can't believe Shubho didn't mention you were stopping by."

"Stopping by? I will remain for two weeks. Perhaps longer, if needed."

"Oh, that's great." Rani hears the slightest note of sarcasm in her voice. The girl is showing her weaknesses. In the last minute, she's crossed and uncrossed her legs, brushed away hair from her forehead five times, and adjusted the fake gold on her wrists seven. Natural signs of discomfort. At the kickoff meeting, Rani asked Binodini the difficult questions. Had Melody and Shubho consummated the relationship? Had they discussed possibilities of engagement, or of marriage? The sister, who'd discussed the matter with an aunt in Berkeley and another one in Kolkata, and, of course, the mother, stared at her tea leaves before answering. It was *probable*, Binodini said, that Shubho had had relations with the girl; it was *probable* that he'd said wildly optimistic things to her; it was *highly probable* that her brother felt the relationship was more serious than it really was. That was why they couldn't trust Shubho, Binodini had explained, on behalf of all the elder Chatterjees; he was blinded by an impossible love.

"So, tell me about your parents," Rani says to Melody. "Do they live here? I am so curious about people in New York City."

"My parents, what to tell? Well, they're good, decent people. I mean, they're recovering musicians. But with big hearts."

"And you—what do you do?"

"I act. I sing. I've done three shows, off-Broadway."

"That is what you do for a living? Acting? Singing?"

"Also I teach," Melody says.

Rani gives her a look, expecting more. Melody scratches at her earlobe—she's wearing long hooped earrings that steal attention—and continues, "Basic sign language. It's an okay gig, flexible, good pay. But no benefits. Plus I teach afterschool theater, two days a week."

Melody's audition smile is still unwavering, but her jaw has started to tense. Rani's getting closer, pressing the right buttons. "This child is one of your students? You are a babysitter?"

"He's my son," Melody snaps, then tries her best to reclaim her smile. "I'm surprised Shubho didn't tell you anything." She musses Tyler's golden-brown hair.

*Her souvenir of bad decisions*, the case notes anoint him. Rani dumps another cracker into her tea, waits till it's good and soppy, then spoons it into her mouth. The girl is visibly warm now, and the fact that she hasn't shed the sweater implies that what's underneath wouldn't be suitable for Mrs. Chatterjee's gaze, implies intimacy with Shubho, and indiscretion. Rani, on the other hand, remains comfortable. A childhood in Kolkata means she can now stroll through swamps without minding the heat.

"Do you understand why I'm here today, Miss Walker?"

Rani watches her expression shift from confusion, to doubt, to a barely shrouded hostility. They're aboard her vessel now; she's set the planks, but the girl isn't ready to walk. Instead, she's gone on the defensive: she's pinched Tyler awake.

"Ouch!" Tyler yells. The boy looks out through his stretched fingers in Rani's direction. He seems to be expecting something different. "Who are you?"

"My name is Missus Chatter-jee. What is your name?"

"Your fingers are yellow."

"Oh, that's from haldi. Americans call it *tur-me-rick*."

"Where's Daddy?"

When she met Binodini at the café, Rani asked how Shubho viewed the boy. The Chatterjee consensus was that the boy was a good boy, but that he had no serious attachment to Shubho and that Shubho had no serious attachment to him. Why didn't they tell her the boy calls him "Daddy"? It's an important fact, the kind of circumstance that, under duress, can jeopardize her ability to do her job. She tries not to pass judgment on her clients, but in this moment, it's difficult—she likes the Chatterjee family a little bit less.

The buzzer rings.

"Is Daddy home?"

"Oh!" Melody laughs. "He's at that age where he calls everyone that. The Butcher. The Baker. The Candlestick Maker."

The buzzer rings again. They hear the UPS man through the intercom that he has a package, but nobody moves.

Rani can feel her pulse quicken, her armpits starting to dampen. She must close the case, move on. "Miss Walker, I've come to interview suitable candidates."

"Candy? Candy dates?" Tyler leaves Melody's lap and wanders around the room. He zigzags to the kitchen and picks up the jar of peanut butter. He cranes his head and looks back to his mother, who winks *yes* at him, so he shows her he can twist off the lid, then goes at it, eating large globs of the stuff with his fingers.

"What's a candy date?"

"A candidate. Well, in our country, when the time is correct, all the family gets together. They choose the perfect man for the perfect woman. So now we are looking for the perfect woman for Shubho."

Melody gets up and wipes peanut butter from Tyler's mouth. "You want to do some coloring, Ty?"

"No. You want me to leave. So you can hold hands."

"Ty, animal crackers."

"I'm not going."

"Fine, an extra fifteen in the park."

Rani appreciates the child's understanding of bargains, imagines his mother regularly trades with him for moments of romance with Shubho. Tyler takes his coloring book and hops to the guest bedroom.

With the boy gone, Melody lets her audition smile fade. "Mrs. Chatterjee, you're in America now. In America, boys and girls do what boys and girls do without their mothers getting in the way. I don't mean to be offensive. What I mean is that you can't force us apart. We're soulmates. Someday, I'd like to know you better. Someday, I'd like you to know me."

Rani grimaces as she does whenever she hears *soul* and *mate* together. There's an emptiness to the combined word—no great sense in who falls for who—and the thought conjures a meanness in her. With some girls, it's enough for her to play the part of dutiful mother, cultural barriers good enough reason to cease and desist, but with Melody she sees that she must go further, scrape open an old wound. She can feel her skin crawl with all the small cruelties she's capable of.

"My dear, I lied a little," she says. "I already know

much about you. I know that your father is an automotive technician, that you supported yourself through two years of college, but never completed a degree. I even know that when you were a child your own mother spent two months in prison."

"How did you know about Mom? I didn't tell Shubho about Mom."

"Our family is thorough. We like to know what is committed by our daughters and sons."

Melody's lips quiver in what seem to be both confusion and rage. "Shubho is going to find out about this," she says, nearly shouting. "Then he's going to—renounce you."

This is the way the story unravels. A few uncomfortable moments in a sweltering apartment weighed against months of "passion." Who wins? To Rani, it hardly feels like a fair fight. She checks her watch. Forty-five minutes remain for her to clinch the deal. She is sure she will, but then what?

She's begun to feel that the long tooth of time has wormed its way into her veins. The days pass, all the hours. She and her husband were recent coillege grads when they met, a beach in Kerala that smelled of coconut rind, and now who can tell of their young love? "No," Rani says, gathering herself, "Shubho's not going to do anything. I have been married long enough to know a few things about love, and this I know to be true."

"Just because you've suffered doesn't mean we will," Melody says after a pause. "Anyway, I'm not typical."

"That is why I'm here, dear."

Rani watches as Melody struggles to keep her story alive. Her crow's feet seem more pronounced, there's a turn of red at the tip of her nose. She droops into her seat and takes a few

shallow breaths. She stands, says, "Excuse me," and walks to
the bathroom like an old, wounded bird.

Alone in the living room Rani is surprised to find that she's
sweating more than just under the arms. She dabs at her mask
of wrinkles, then curses herself, checking her face in a pocket
mirror to make sure she's still immaculate. Shubho's family
needs her to succeed, and in ways he doesn't understand so
does her husband. This is the marriage pact: what she works
for day and night.

In the morning she fries up rice cakes, which her husband
scoops with a bowl of warmed butter and chutney. Sometimes,
he wants American fare, and she's accepted this, turning out
oatmeal from the box, adding turmeric and ginger, a little
honey. After breakfast, he slides onto the sofa, where he
sleeps and listens to NPR on his headphones. One good hand
means that untangling the knots in the cord isn't easy, but
he labors through, each day a little more patiently, or so it
seems to her. That's when she brings him the Prozac and the
Xanax, which he swallows with a warm glass of milk. Lately
he's added another set of pills they purchase from a doctor in
Canada, or rather, *she* purchases, Rani being the sole earner,
and they are not cheap, not at all. But if the depression lifts, if
her old man once again fills her bed with hyacinths and sings
her Urdu poems, a few words here and there forgotten or
altered, then indeed it is worth it. Three months into the new
treatment, she still hopes, though the only change seems to be
a shared insomnia. Her husband up at the odd hours, and she
as well. They shut off all the lights and bump into each other
wordlessly.

Two years into her husband's depression, she still keeps

a journal of gratitude, capturing one or two moments from the waking hours. Yesterday, from the roof of their Queens apartment complex, she watched the moon rise at the same time as the sun fell, and that felt like a tiding. The sight was grand enough that she went to fetch her husband, but he was too weary. Someday, his depression will lift, and they'll observe the moon and sun together again. This is what she waits for, her patience a sword. In the meantime, she takes no pleasure in breaking couples apart, but when one out of two marriages ends on its own, isn't her work an expediency? Things fall apart, let them fail earlier, she tells herself; let the Indians be with their own.

Tyler comes in from the bedroom. "I made this for you," the boy says to Rani. He's holding a picture of a stick-figure woman and a dog.

"Beautiful, beautiful drawing," Rani says. She smells the talcum powder smell of him—he's still more baby than boy—and fights the urge to lift him into her arms. Five years ago, they lost a child in the third trimester of her pregnancy. Shortly afterward, her husband was injured on the job. That winter, they both fell into depression, but in the spring she came through and stayed afloat. She tried to bring him along and failed. Nowadays, she finds herself lingering at parks to watch toddlers experiment with slides and water sprinklers, finds herself trying to make sense of their garbled language, which seems to her as significant as mystical poetry.

"I like dogs," Tyler says. "What kind of dog do you have?"

"Tyler," his mother says, returning to claim the sofa, "Mrs. Chatterjee isn't here to make friends."

The boy stares at Rani, and she feels shame color her cheeks. There are parts of this job that leave her whittled, but till now she's never had to disappoint a child. "We might not become friends," Rani says, mostly to Tyler, "but we do not have to be enemies, either."

"What's an enemy?" Tyler asks.

Rani glances at Melody for direction—after all, a mother should dictate when her son learns the hard things—and sees only hostility. She says, "Why don't we finish our talk in private?"

"An enemy," Melody says to Tyler, "is someone who wants to take something from you that's not theirs to take." And to Rani, "Whatever you have to say, my boy can hear."

"As you like," Rani says. She can feel the sweat on her belly. Outside of these visits, she never wears a sari, and she wants nothing more now than to return to her jeans, have a cup of tea with her husband, who'll tell her all the sad things he learned that day listening to NPR. "Let us come to an understanding, Miss Walker. Shubho is of marrying age. It is no insult to you, or to your family. We are looking for the same caste, background, and education. When you are my age, you may do the same for your son."

"Is this because I have a son? Is this because of Tyler?"

"Miss Walker, this is not about your son. Candidates have exceptional beauty and education. Often, a candidate will have second or third degrees, from colleges like Harvard and Yale. For instance, I will be meeting tomorrow with a young woman who holds a doctorate in philosophy."

"Good for her. Does that make me ignorant?"

"Please, Miss Walker. To compensate for your troubles,

my family is prepared to pay you handsomely. What we ask in return is simple: That you leave our son alone. That you allow him his life. Our offer is generous and will pay your and your son's expenses for a year, or seed you to start your own business, or supply you the funds to begin anew. Somewhere else." Rani takes the check from her purse and lays it on the table. The amount feels obscene, though she knows that for the Chatterjees it's just the cost of doing business in a foreign country. Her portion is a small cut of that, which means the month's rent plus Rohan's medication.

Having delivered her offer, Rani pauses to study her adversary. She is expecting turbulence—a thrown object, a smattering of curses, perhaps a prayer to the Almighty, brief impious responses that quickly yield to pragmatism—but Melody hasn't glanced at the check, and the tension has left her face. "I dreamed you," Melody says. "I dreamed this would happen," she says. "Sammy and I took ayahuasca once in a sweat lodge. Sammy didn't see much, but I did. I saw how a woman would come to pull us apart."

"You're here to take Daddy away," Tyler says. He leaves Melody's lap and hisses at Rani.

"Please, calm down," Rani says to Tyler.

"Did he ever tell you how we met?" Melody asks Rani.

The case notes hadn't said, and this adds to Rani's nervousness. "It is best for you to take this money. It is best for you to end things with this boy, for it will not go well."

"It wasn't going to go well that night either," Melody says. "I was on a downtown train crossing through Harlem after the late show at Smalls. I'd come asking about a job as a hostess, but they had nothing for me. I was on that train, and this beautiful brown man in a suit sat next to me. He was so tired he started to fall asleep on my shoulder. At first, it bothered me, but then I didn't mind. I always want to help people, and this was such a small thing to do, give someone a shoulder to sleep against. My stop was coming up, and I had to wake him. He was so embarrassed he wanted to buy me breakfast. He was a whole borough away from his house. He wanted to get everything on the diner menu, but all I wanted was coffee."

Rani can imagine them, the shadow of Shubho's exhaustion following him until he falls into the lap of this woman who wants nothing more than to be kind to a stranger. He wants to thank her, and the only way he knows how is through money. A tender beginning that won't last, is what Rani thinks. For how can it across cultures, so little to hold them together when Tyler is older and Shubho wants his own child, when Melody tires of those quirks of his, hallmarks of his upbringing, which at first she found charming. "Romantic love is grand, but it doesn't last after year one," Rani says, thinking now of Rohan, of how they'd eloped to a smoky apartment in Jackson Heights, the both of them runaways from the same country.

"How would you know?" Melody asks.

As Rani is absorbing the shock of this question, Tyler takes the check from the table and tears it into pieces. His mother winks her love back at him.

"Oh, I wish you had not done that," Rani says.

"I was going to do the same," Melody says. "All my years in theater you think I wouldn't spot a makeup job? When you sweat like that, it starts to peel away."

Over the year and a half she's taken on this work, no one has doubted her identity. "I don't know what you mean,"

Rani says, feeling like a schoolgirl who's been caught with unfinished homework.

"Maybe you're my age, maybe you're dealing with my kind of problems. Whatever you are, you're not Shubho's mother," Melody says.

The other cases were simpler. The relationships were involved and maybe even a little complicated, but there was no child in the picture. "Yes, I'm not Shubho's mother, but everything I'm saying is still correct. Your love won't last. You're wild, and he's fastidious. Look at the plastic on the couch. His ways will grate on you, and soon . . ."

She wants to say, *Soon, he'll want a child of his own*, but she stops herself, seeing Tyler's expression, his mouth open as if what she'll speak is some great truth. But it's only her version of likelihoods, subject as much to the fates as any other story. Rani checks her phone, scanning the texts from Binodini:

*How goes? Time running out. Difficult to budge.*

"Shubho hasn't texted you back, has he?" Rani asks. "He's being persuaded by his sister as we speak. For him, family will always come first."

"I'm his family now," Melody says. "That's what you don't get."

"But soon he'll want to start eating more home food," Rani says, pointing at the pot of lentils that have made this apartment smell much like her own. She feels her weaknesses returning to haunt her. When she was in primary school, she kept to herself and didn't play schoolyard games, widening the circle of her aloneness; the other girls would whisper and taunt, pointing at her uneven pigtails, her frayed skirt. It wasn't till she was arm in arm with Rohan that the teasing stopped, but those early years made her feel afraid of the world, its ordinary interactions. With this job, she won't get her bonus, that's for sure, and word of her failure will spread. There are other women who are willing to do this work, and they will get the call.

"Your name's not Mrs. Chatterjee," Melody says. "What is it."

"Rani."

"Rani, I'm going to show you out now."

. . .

They've lived in the same apartment in Jackson Heights for their whole stay in America. She's proud that the fridge is always full of fresh fruits and vegetables, prouder even still of the satellite television she occasionally turns on to watch a Bengali soap, but returning home earlier in the day, the cracks in the linoleum offend, and all that dust makes her feel like she never cleans.

Her husband is napping in their bed, though when she enters he awakes, his eyes heavy with sleep. "I was worried about you," he says. His lame hand covers his face from the light. "I had a dream you were in some trouble. Were you?"

"No trouble," she says. "The office completed early, and I wanted to see you." Saying it aloud she realizes it's true. She falls into the bed beside him.

"I was looking for jobs today," he says.

"You'll find something soon," she says, though she doesn't believe it. Slowly, and with the burnishing of their long-standing affection, they begin to move toward each other like lions in old age. He stops to ask about the groceries, but she urges him on. She sees the boy in her head, the musical curve of his words as she left, *Bye, enemy*, such a sweet song from his chapped little lips, and her old man—for a moment, and he has few such moments these days, these years—is youthful beside her. His beard is soft. She clutches his good hand and thinks she'll put on her best perfume for dinner, a feast with candles that will burn till morning.

## When the Tantric Came to Town

Prem Chatterjee taught a class of thirty-three students. Of the thirty-three, one never showed, two dozed from 3:30 to 3:55, another couple held hands and texted amorous notes, one threw spitballs at the front of the room, one cursed Prem out, usually toward the end of class, one said his hair smelled like Lysol, one accidentally kicked him in the knee, one picked up a chair and threw it at another one, one put on her headphones and banged her head on the table four, five, seven times before he asked her to stop.

After a month of this, Prem called his mother in India. He said he loved her, and that he should have stuck with his programming job, like she'd said. He was sorry for what happened with Julia and for all the wrong he'd done over the years.

"When you talk like this, you sound American," she said. She told him not to worry: she'd spoken to their astrologer and help was on the way.

. . .

The help showed up one day before class, carrying a small knapsack. In the style of the Boronagor Tantrics, the woman had let her knotted gray hair grow down to her knees and smeared holy ash across her forehead. She was barefoot; the calluses on her feet had calcified into molds of new skin. She had a protruding boxer's jaw, lips covered with bits of dead skin. Prem tried to avoid her gaze, but he could tell, even obliquely, that she was disappointed in him.

"Where is the problem?" she said. There was a trident tied to her leopard-skin sarong; she released it from its holster and pointed in his direction. On its tip: rivulets of blue flame. The fire danced for a few moments until the Tantric doused it with her palm.

"I'm honored," he said, "to receive such a holy guest." Her body had all the scents of a cremation pyre—sweat and sulfur, creosote and cane pulp. He bowed deeply and offered her the uneaten orange he was holding.

"No," she said. "I am here for one purpose. Fixing the problem."

He described the discipline issues he was having with his algebra class. "Seventh period is the worst. I feel like they're in control and I'm just watching."

The Tantric squatted on the floor and listened to his lament. She nodded and squinted at his forehead from time to time, but mostly she stared at the equations he'd put up on the back wall. At the beginning of the year, he'd sketched Maxwell's equations in bright magic marker, only to have them covered over by graffiti the next day. When he finished explaining, the Tantric grunted and left the room. Long after she was gone, a smell different from her body odor—that of burning leaves—lingered by his desk.

. . .

It was no better and no worse the rest of the day. Before seventh period, a fight erupted outside his room. It didn't directly involve any of his students, but several of them looked like they'd been infected by it. Those same ones—Trevor, Miles, and Jere—deepened their swaggers and, heads cocked a few more degrees toward disquiet, slouched portentously in their seats.

"Today's lesson: Balancing Equations," Prem wrote on the board.

"C'mon, Mr. Chatty."

"That's stupid."

"Can't we go outside, man?"

"Mr. Chatty, Mr. Chatty, Mr. Chatty!" the students cried out.

Then there was something he'd never experienced in his brief teaching career: a full moment of silence. He turned back to the room to find the Tantric crouching on top of Trevor's desk. There was a lifeless squirrel in her hands, and she was pointing the squirrel head at Trevor's chest. A gargling, hissing sound escaped her lips. As she shook her head and chanted under her breath, bits of dried mud and pieces of acorn seed fell from her hair. She was good with balance, crouching on the desk like that. When she was done with her invocation, she dropped the squirrel in Trevor's lap, where it would lie the rest of the period, untouched.

After she left through the rear window, Prem taught the rest of the class without disruption. In fact, it became calm enough for him to leave the students to their worksheets so he could make his daily phone call. He tiptoed to the teachers' lounge and dialed his wife's number.

"Hello," she said. "Who's there?"

Julia's voice was always more serious on the phone than it was in person. She'd lived in Ukraine as a young girl and kept a hint of an accent he adored. Usually, when he called, she wouldn't pick up. He tried not to breathe. He tried to extend this moment with her as long as he could.

"Prem," she said. "Is that you again? I told you, you need to move on."

"Sorry," he said, then regretted having spoken. He hung up and waited a minute in case she decided to call back before heading back to class.

. . .

School ended; he drove the Tantric home. Since the separation, his housekeeping skills had waned. The small TV in the living room was balanced atop a stack of pizza boxes, and the foldout couch, which served as his bedroom plus office, was strewn with vintage porn and Kurosawa films.

The Tantric picked up *Amorous Gothics* and scrutinized the front and back covers.

"Are you hungry?"

She grunted back at him: perhaps yes, perhaps no. The problem was he didn't know the first thing about what a Tantric ate. In the burning fields outside Kolkata, he'd once seen a wizened Tantric skewer a bush rabbit and drink it down with tea. There were no such critters at the supermarket, though

he committed to buying lamb chops for the weekend. He set
about reheating macaroni and cheese and added a dollop of
ghee. Knowing she would eat with her hands, Prem did the
same. They sat on the floor, beside the kitchenette table.

"What you did today," he said. "It means a lot to me."

"Thank your mother. She came to Boronagor five times."
The Tantric licked her bowl clean.

After they ate, Prem squeezed the dishes into the
dishwasher, then called his mother from the kitchen phone.
"Ma, she's here. It worked."

"What is she doing now?" his mother asked.

Prem peered into the living room. "She's folding my jeans
into piles, and she's dusting the furniture with the end of her
sarong."

"Oh, that's a good sign," Ma said.

"When do I send her back?"

"Prem-shona, you need to keep her busy. She can help you
with your other problem."

"Ma, please."

"Listen to me, Prem. Take her to the house of Julia."

"I'm doing no such thing. Good night, Mother."

. . .

At quarter to midnight, Prem found himself hiding behind
an SUV parked outside Julia's lawn. She lived in a well-
proportioned pink house in the suburbs. It was the home
they'd bought to live in as a married couple, a house with an
almost-working fountain in the backyard and a mailbox with a
mechanical parrot inside. At three in the afternoon, the parrot

would come out from its case and spook the new mailmen: *Prem and Julia's house. Prem and Julia's!*

"It's not really trespassing," he told the Tantric. "Because this is my house."

He poked his head out from behind the car and through the window spotted Julia in pajamas, pacing with an open book in her hands. She worked as an editor at a publishing house and was likely sucking the life out of some new mystery novel, which meant he was free to stare at the shape of her body as it navigated itself between their antique turntable, the living room divan, and the granite countertop. Her exquisitely pale neck, her boyish shoulders. He only wished she weren't wearing flannel.

"This is your wife?"

"Yes," he said. "But we're *separated*." He winced as the word emerged from his lips. She had been the one to make the demand, but it wasn't so simple. Two months of courtship, one year of marriage, and now a month apart. He found himself on the lawn, where Julia's grass tickled his ankles. His knees wobbled, and he wished for rain—the kind he imagined the Tantric enjoyed back home, washing her hair in the fields thick with mist and tree song, in the luxury of the monsoon. What he wouldn't give to touch Julia again. Her painted feet, the tattoo of a shark swimming up her spine.

The Tantric followed him onto the lawn and stared at Julia. Each moment, it felt more painful to stand outside his former house for the sake of ogling his wife's flannel-clad body.

"Can we go home now?"

"I'm still inspecting her," the Tantric said. "These things take time."

While he waited for the inspection to be completed, Julia managed to head to the fridge, withdraw a milk carton, pour a cup, and heat it in the microwave, all without putting down her book, or taking her eyes from the page. The Tantric sucked air through her teeth in appreciation.

"Okay," he said. "Fine. What do I do to get her back? You can take your time thinking. We can come back tomorrow." He figured the Tantric would need a few hours to consult her divine ephemeris, but she only shrugged, as if the answer had been there all along.

"Simple," she said. "We must kidnap her."

. . .

The next morning, Prem called his mother from school.

"Beta," she said. "I've been trying to pin you all day."

"Listen, Ma, when does the Tantric leave? It's like taking care of you when you're here, only scarier."

"Beta, forget that. Did you go to the house of Julia? Did the Tantric help?"

"We did go."

"And?"

"We didn't talk. But the Tantric suggested we kidnap her."

He heard his mother light a cigarette on the other side of the world. She took a good long pull. "Kidnapping is a serious business," his mother said. "But this is your life. What could be more important than your life?"

"Ma, I don't get it. You could barely stand to be in the room with Julia when we were married."

"True," she said. "But now you're old goods. Which decent Brahmin girl will marry you now? A divorcée schoolteacher?

Not a one. Don't think I didn't advertise. I tried, beta. Damaged goods are better together. By the way, have you considered when I might next visit?"

"Goodbye, Mother." He hung up the phone and prepared for his first class.

The day at school went so well he didn't need a single Xanax. All his students, having either heard of or experienced the power of the Tantric, were docile angels. One even tried to touch Prem's feet, but he declined, while another one surrendered her love notes. The Tantric came to visit seventh period. All of the students greeted her by standing at attention.

"You may sit," he said.

She waved her trident at them. They sat, and he felt the pulse of his newfound power course through to the tips of his fingers. On the ride home, he said, "Listen, I've thought about it. We can try your plan."

The Tantric was sliding an acorn seed from one side of her mouth to the other. "Tonight we go," she said.

. . .

They stood on the crabgrass outside Julia's bedroom window. The air was turning cool. For a while they watched her move slightly in sleep. Early on in their courtship, there'd been so much sweetness. Once, she'd recited a couplet of Bengali poetry into his ear, having learned how to pronounce each of the sounds. He remembered this and chose to gloss over the fear that came later. Instead, he let the blissful evenings of their marriage wash over him, and he remained like this until the Tantric lifted the window screen, squeezed her body through, and beckoned Prem to follow.

When he stood beside Julia's bed, he couldn't help thinking that he was standing on *his* Persian carpet, next to *his* silk sheets. They watched Julia so quietly he could hear the animal breath rising from her body.

"American women are prettier in their sleep," the Tantric said. He looked at her face for guidance, but it was as unknowable as it had been all day. She rocked back and forth; at her waist, the trident swung like a pendulum.

"What do we do now?" he whispered.

The Tantric produced a long coil of thick white rope. With Julia still in her bedcovers, the Tantric tied her up until Julia looked like a mummy; thankfully, she was still a good sleeper; thankfully, the Tantric had extraordinary strength—she lifted Julia with one arm and carried her to the back seat of the car.

. . .

The apartment clock said 2 a.m. Julia was snoring peacefully on the couch. Prem was out of breath, even though he'd had little to do in transporting her. "Okay," he said. "What's our plan?"

The Tantric cracked her fingers. "I am hungry," she said.

"But we just stopped for tacos."

"Your food does not agree with me." She sharpened her toenails with his kitchen knife. "I require the meat of the woods." Then, in a fit of colored light—ambers and blues corralling her knees—she was gone.

He burned some sage to clear the smell of burning leaves

and sat down on a stool to watch Julia sleep. Except for her face and hands, her whole body was wrapped in white. He touched her hands and felt their lack of softness; her father had taken her hunting and fishing since she was a blond-haired toddler, and she'd never grown out of her calluses.

As he traced her fingers with his own, he noticed the lack of a wedding ring. Perhaps, in their month apart, it had simply slipped off somewhere. Maybe she'd searched every corner of the house, but it had eluded her. He couldn't be sure. All he knew was that when he'd bought her the diamond she'd puffed out her chest with pride. What followed were three days of Herculean lovemaking, afternoons of orgasms in the shed, with her body wedged against the typewriter she couldn't throw away and his family albums. In those interludes, she left marks on his belly, up and down his spine.

Julia fell more deeply into sleep. Her lips parted, momentarily, to produce a whistling sound, and he thought of the first time he rode a train with his mother, his knobby knees waggling ahead, his mother gripping his hand until they reached their seats and the final whistle announced departure. The memory of the train always left him feeling a little more loved, and also a little more sad. Julia snored on. He'd never wanted to be alone. He tugged on the rope that crisscrossed her body, at first gently, then with urgency.

"We don't want any," she said, without opening her eyes.

That was her line for telemarketers. He tickled her toes. "Julia," he said. "It's me."

Her eyes squinted open. He imagined them in the shed, pushing aside the clutter; he imagined burying his head in the musculature of her thighs, until she mouthed in her girls'-school Russian: *Dangle me.*

"What is happening?" she said. She'd noticed the bonds around her arms and was struggling.

He tried to produce soft cooing sounds from the back of his throat. "It's all right," he said. "The Tantric and I brought you back to my apartment."

"Why can't I move? You need to untie me right now."

"Because I'm afraid, if I untie you, you'll be mad at me."

"Prem, I'm not going to ask you again." Her whole face was red with exertion—the Tantric had done a terrific job with the knots.

He wasn't sure what to do. On one hand, Julia was squirming in a way that left him queasy. On the other hand, if he cut her ropes, she might punch him in the mouth, as she'd done their last Thanksgiving together, when he'd accidentally left the turkey in the garage. "Be right back," he said.

He sprinted into the kitchen and called his mother. She answered immediately. "What news, beta?"

"Big problem, Ma. Julia's in the apartment, but she wants me to untie her. What should I do?"

"Prem-shona, sometimes women say things they don't mean. Leave her as is, until she apologizes for kicking you out of the house. Remember: you are a prince among princes."

When he got back to the living room, Julia had stopped fighting the rope. She had managed to prop herself up on the couch. The color drained from his face—she was smiling a full-toothed smile and was, despite her bonds, the queen of the room. He grew afraid of her, again.

"Prem," she said. "I'm not upset. I just want to know why I'm tied up."

"The Tantric said it would be best."

"Who?"

"She's the one who leaves these." He pointed to the muddy footprints on the floor.

Julia bit her lovely lip. "So," she said. "Now we're here. Now we can talk."

He paced around the room. He couldn't deny that he'd imagined this moment so many times it was grooved into his forebrain, but now that she was here, what could he say? What came to mind was a simple moment: it was the start of spring; after they'd made love, when she'd torn through a pack of cigarettes, she'd announced, "That was the most boring sex I've ever had."

At the time, he'd covered his wounded pride with a grin. Now, he said, "Weren't we good together? I mean, in bed?"

She shrugged, as much as someone so bound could. "In the beginning, we were good. Afterward: no. You didn't want what I did."

In the beginning, there were keyholes, feathered masks, scarves made into whips, canine collars, bolts and clamps, tourniquets for every body part hidden in the walls. In the beginning, his heart would rumble so fast he would be afraid of losing his soul. When they'd met by chance in the doldrums of Hackensack, New Jersey, he'd had no idea of the worlds that awaited.

"Don't you agree," she said, "after a while, all you wanted was the missionary?"

He had to agree. He'd only outlived his astrology for

half a year. After that, whenever she'd come upstairs with the massage candle and the strips of whittled pine, he'd complained of an inscrutable pain in his side.

"I'm a boring guy," he said, in resignation.

"But this," she said, wiggling her knees suggestively, "this is new. This I might like."

"I don't think it's what you think," he said. "I just wanted to talk." Still, he felt inside himself the old pull, the galvanizing urge. He could let her out. They could—even if it meant him coming out bruised—recreate for a while.

"Let me guess," she said. "Your mother put you up to this."

"Not at all," he said. But he was a terrible liar. Dark-skinned as he was, he could tell she could tell that he was blushing.

Julia sighed. "You have something to eat? Chips? Crackers? Anything?"

"I'll check," he said. She was a fan of the midnight snack, but, as he rummaged around in the kitchen, his cupboards had only the slimmest of pickings. Behind the toaster, there was an expired package of peanut butter cookies.

He returned to the living room to find the Tantric standing behind the couch, eating the charred insides of a rabbit.

Julia opened her mouth, and he fed her a cookie. "This is the Tantric," he said. "She was hungry, too, but I don't recommend rabbit at this hour."

Julia shook her head to free the crumbs around her mouth. "She offered, but I refused."

The Tantric raised her palms in a manner that suggested she'd tried her polite best.

"But I like her vibe," Julia continued. "A sexy secret friend? We could play with that."

The Tantric continued her chomping of the rabbit; he hoped, dearly, that she hadn't taken offense. "Don't worry," he told her. "She doesn't mean anything."

"Excuse me?" Julia said. "Look, Prem, if you want me back, there are certain things you have to do."

"Tell me," he said. "I'll do anything."

"First, you must lick my toes," she said.

Julia had well-manicured feet and he'd never minded satisfying her in this way, but now he felt a little shy: the Tantric was watching; the expression on her face—a slight upturn of the lips—could've been called a smile.

"I'm waiting," Julia said.

He thought about the longing that can break a man, the kind that leaves him with what he will, in some afterlife, call shame, but which, in the moment, is simply the ordinary experience of a lover's feet, with its toenails judiciously painted blue. He got down on his knees; he licked her toes.

"Secondly," she said. "If you move back to the house, you must accept my hours."

There had been weeks where Julia would apply a coat of lipstick and leave after dinner. She would return in the early morning, dazed and enormously happy. Even though the Tantric was gleefully leering at him now, he still assented with a nod. "Fine," he said. "I'm not the jealous type." It was true: he had accepted the role of an ignorant husband for the sake of her pleasure. He had been a dutiful partner and would be again. He kissed the part of the rope where Julia's bottom hid.

"Lastly," she said. "You're moving back in, but she isn't."

"Who?" he said, knowing fully well the who and the why.

He looked to the Tantric for help, but she was engaged with chewing through the rabbit's paw. He was alone again.

"You know who," Julia said. "And I want to hear you say it to her."

Prem dragged the phone in from the kitchen. He dialed. His mother said hello. He said, "Mother, there's been some progress. Julia and I are getting back together."

"Beta, that's wonderful. That's the best news I've heard all day."

"So I won't be needing the help anymore." He snapped his fingers at the Tantric, who was picking the scabs off her knees. "You can go home," he said.

The Tantric looked at him, and, for the first time, he allowed himself to stare into her eyes, and in so doing, Prem experienced the peripatetic passing of his own life, its orderly combustions and rhythms—the heart's last mile—which, while it struck him as being extraordinary, was nothing more than walking with Julia on the boardwalk, chasing, with his cane, the seagulls into the air. The Tantric saw that he saw. Then, without another word, she stuffed the rabbit carcass into her knapsack and left through the kitchen window.

His mother said, "Are you still there, beta?"

"Yes, Ma." He felt the breath constrict in his throat, so he swallowed a few times before he spoke. "But there's one more thing. You can't stay with us anymore."

There was a pause on the other end of the line, but it was mercifully brief. He held the phone against Julia's ear, so she heard, as he did. "Of course, beta," his mother said, sounding resigned. "I completely understand."

Afterward, he sat next to Julia. Their fingers grazed, and for a while they were silent. "I'd like to untie you now," he finally said.

"You did good," Julia said. "You did just fine."

He started loosening the rope. After the final knot was undone, Julia cast off the sheet herself—revealing a terrifically sheer slip—and stood up to her full height. He was six feet and so was she, but, somehow, she always seemed taller. She leaned close—he smelled her mouthwash and cigarette smoke—and kissed him, at first, softly, then with more pressure, involving both the tongue and the teeth. When it was over, he was out of breath and his lower lip was bleeding, but he didn't complain, or even say *Ouch*.

Instead, as she held him tight, he thought of the afternoon when she'd tried to teach him to fish. He wasn't fast enough for the river that nearly dragged him under. He wasn't agile with the line in his hands while she piled one catch on another, making a little mountain of carcasses next to their picnic basket. She gave him the eye—it was their sixth date, and he knew what it meant, how the affection would dry up and the calls stop, how he hadn't earned himself a place in her mythology—so he took off his shirt, sucked in his gut, and dove into the water.

## In the Bug Room

At the airport the maid flagged down a taxi and then sat next to him in the back seat. Chinmoy smelled her bodily mix of talcum powder and mustard paste and realized something was off: she, being the maid, should've been riding in the front with the driver and not lounging in the back with him. He cleared his throat, but she didn't get the hint.

When they reached Maniktala Junction, the maid turned to face him. Her skin was pocked with the evidence of a childhood disease. "Chinmoy-babu," she said. "Too many years have passed since you last came to visit Mother."

"Mother?" he said, counting the years—*eleven*—since he'd visited.

"Your mother is like a mother to me."

"I don't remember you."

"Of course you don't," she said. "All those years you were outside playing, I was working in the kitchen. I am Shefali, only daughter of Gopalji."

In the heyday of the house, a dozen servants had lived on the ground level, but he'd rarely paid them much attention. Still, if he subtracted her muscular forearms and her betel-stained teeth, there was something familiar—a young girl who had this woman's cheekbones, who'd hid behind the long dhoti of Gopalji, his father's bearer.

In any case, Ma had let standards slip. Maids did not have the right to speak to their employers in such a tone. He was considering the proper way to scold Shefali when their taxi pulled up in front of Chatterjee Lane.

"Your house," she announced. The house before him was a version of the house of his childhood: it was four stories, and the windows and doorways were of the same colonial footprint, but all along the facade the paint had peeled and the plaster had cracked. The upper verandas leaned dangerously. Absent now were the street sweepers who removed the first signs of dirt; the fruit sellers who saved the family the choicest fruit; the wandering musicians who sang ghazals in his father's name.

"What happened," he said. "Did Ma not use the money I sent?"

She shrugged. "Who will coordinate the repairs? Me? Ma? We are ladies only."

He couldn't tell if she was mocking him or just complaining. He reached to pull his suitcase from the trunk, but then remembered the hundreds of times he'd carried bags for his thankless American customers. "You may carry my bag," he told the maid.

Shefali turned to the taxi driver, who was still waiting for his tip. "Driver, carry the babu's bag," she said.

The three of them took the stairs to the first floor of the house, where all the rooms were locked. He peered over the railing and spotted someone on the ground level. "Who's there?" he asked.

"My father," Shefali said.

He made a mental note to oust the freeloader as soon as possible.

The second floor was equally depressing. Here the doors were double padlocked. He stood in front of his old bedroom and said, "Let's have a look."

Shefali said, "This room is to remain closed. Ma has set a bed upstairs."

He didn't like being told what was to remain closed or open. He studied the ring of keys on her sari hem, the same ring his mother had once worn, and imagined what it would take to wrestle them free. "Where is Mother, anyway?"

"She is finishing her bath. You may take rest, then come to the kitchen for lunch." She tapped her feet, and the keys chimed like Christmas bells.

But he had no wish for rest. He had returned to the house that had made him feel wanted. *A boy of incontrovertible brilliance*, his father had once proclaimed. He wished to roam his old haunt without anyone to impede him. To see, to touch, to smell again the grandeur of his childhood. It was entirely here. All of it—if only beneath a layer of dust.

. . .

Over the years of his living abroad, there was one room that had become enshrined in his memory. He'd sit with his thesis and remember how peaceful it had felt inside the bug room, as it was called. The bug room had been built by his father, an orthodox Vaishnav, who wouldn't kill an ant. When insects wandered onto the premises, he gave them food and lodging. Walling off half the prayer room with a wire mesh, he created a sanctuary for the tiniest creatures. They could leave from the open window, but if they remained within the Chatterjee walls, his father treated them as his guests.

Walking up to the topmost floor now, Chinmoy found that the bug room had suffered less than other parts of the house. The mesh that kept the bugs inside the room looked like it had been recently replaced, though the walls within were cracked and chipped. The window slats at the back of the room, through which the bugs could return to the wildness of the city, were painted and polished. Overhead, a ceiling fan had been installed; a cool breeze encircled the room.

What's more, the bugs were still in residence. He did not know how they had survived. Surely, Shefali wouldn't have taken over his childhood duty of carrying all manner of insects, along with small piles of stale sweets, into this very room. But somehow a population had maintained itself.

Chinmoy lifted the mesh and sat cross-legged in the center of the room to admire a child-sized clay statue of Krishna, which had long ago been brought by an ancestor from Kashmir to serve as a protector. Oh, it was all coming back now. At first glance, he could see that there were roaches, beetles, moths, and ants all around. They seemed healthy, but something was off. In his memory, the roaches had lurked in one corner while the ants had built colonies in another; between them the beetles would haul their dung enormous distances and the moths would patrol the ceiling, observing the landlocked with nonchalance. Now, several of the roaches had learned

to fly, and they were upsetting the dung rolls of the beetles.
The beetles were sending missions into the colonies of the
ants, and the ants were marauding across the surface of the
room, forming lines as striated as the ones on his palm. In his
memory, the bugs had lived in partnership. Now it seemed
that they kept their crumbs to themselves, as if sustenance
were scarce.

. . .

His mother was waiting for him in the kitchen. The slats of
sunlight coming through the stained glass highlighted the lines
of her face. So much worry there, all that passage of time. He
stared at her face, the gullet underneath her chin, hair the
texture and color of fresh snow.

"Oh, beta," she said, remaining in her chair. "Come closer."

The thought that he ought to impress her went through him
like an arthritic pain, followed by a deep guilt at having her
genes and amounting to nothing. He remained at a distance
with his hands in his pockets until Shefali shoved him; he
touched his mother's feet in respect. Ma stroked his forehead
in blessing and studied his face without rising.

"It makes me so happy to see you here. If I could cry, I
would be crying right now."

"Ma," he said, gathering his strength. "We need to do
serious talking. The house needs a great deal of repair. And I
need to tell you about my own plans."

"Oh, beta, don't be in a rush. Shefali ran to the bazaar twice
so you could have proper lunch."

"Oh, I can hardly eat a thing," he said. In truth, he'd been
looking forward to this moment for weeks, but it was a custom

in their family to pretend otherwise. "The food on the plane was so heavy. They serve you a meal every two hours."

Shefali ignored him and brought out the meal. What food, he thought, what glorious fat food. A whole hilsa: head, tail, and body bubbling in a rich mustard sauce. A kilo of jasmine shaped into a perfect cone. Squash and bitter gourd and chickpeas arranged in small bowls. Each dish with its own secret sauce. Plus two plates of milk sweets, pistachio and that other kind, bulbous with rosewater.

He ate everything, mixing the sweets with the meat, the honey cream dripping down his chin as Ma watched. He remembered her words from long ago, "The most important thing is family. Right after that is food."

When he was finished, he said, "You were right, Ma. Nothing like home food."

"But beta," she said. "You are mostly thin now." She touched his sternum and poked his ribs. "Why? And what are these on your face?"

"Just sunspots, Ma."

"Is it the teaching? Are you working too much on your research?"

"No, Ma." After eleven years of slaving on his doctoral thesis—*Qualia in a Materialistic World*—he'd finally quit. In any case, his adviser had threatened to cut funding the next year, measly as it was. Over the years, he'd had to complement his allowance by running night shifts as a livery cabdriver, where he'd grown to enjoy the stories of his passengers and the camaraderie of his fellow mostly Bangladeshi drivers more than the writing of his thesis. But this was not what he'd explained to his parents on the phone, six months before Baba passed away.

"I am defending my thesis in two months. Any day after that they will hire me as a lecturer," he'd said.

"Is it tenure track?" his father had wanted to know, and he said *Of course*, forcing the lie into its current mold. When Ma had called to announce his father's passing and impending cremation, he'd remained in the States, explaining that he was at the critical juncture of his studies. "Your Baba would have wanted you to remain in America and to succeed," Ma had said. "Think not once of coming home."

He considered unseating this lie now, but so much had happened since. His mother's health had turned, and there was Shefali by the door. Any disgrace that would befall him he could not allow her the pleasure of witnessing.

"What we need to talk about now is your health, Ma," he said. "I heard you fell in the bathroom. Is it true?"

Shefali clucked her teeth in admonishment. "Ma, don't strain. Take some rest now." And to him she added, "Ma will take rest, and so will you."

. . .

After his mother retired for her afternoon nap, Chinmoy went to the main road to have a smoke. He relaxed into a colored Bengali with a hawker who divulged the street gossip. The hawker kept rows of a milky, unfiltered liquor on display, and Chinmoy purchased two bottles at the price locals paid.

When he returned to the house, he had an urge to open the almirahs and hunt for the paisley shirts he'd left behind. He had a longing to find his lesson books, where in the margins he had upbraided his headmaster in limericks. Where were his hand-me-down mystery novels, and the watercolors he'd painted of girls bathing in the Ganga?

He didn't go down to the ground floor to get the keys, because it would have been beneath him to ask Shefali in her own domain, so he remained on the first-floor landing—and clapped. This was his father's preferred mode of communication. The sound of his father's clapping had been loud enough to wake the dogs sleeping on the street, but his own version was quickly drowned out by crows fighting over a mango peel. He waited until the crows were finished. Then he resumed clapping. After a minute, the elderly lady next door opened her window to tell him to keep it down.

The stairwell to the servants' entrance needed work. All the light bulbs had burned out and cobwebs encircled the cracks in the wall. Everything in the house was on entropy's short list, but the condition of the entranceway made him feel guiltiest that he'd stopped sending money over the years. In the beginning, whatever he could scrounge from his night shifts driving the livery cab, he would send back home, and every month he would receive an aerogram with the news of what had transpired with the extended family along with the refrain: *No more, we have enough.* But this wasn't true. What with the increasing cost of upkeep, his father's pension was just barely covering groceries—and that after they'd let go of most of their staff.

He put his ear to the door of the servants' quarter and listened. On the other side someone was snoring and someone else was bathing in the cistern. When he was fourteen, he'd secretly watched a servant from this very keyhole, as she'd poured soapy water from buckets over her body. He didn't dare take that risk now: the sight of Shefali's nude, lopsided form would have diluted memories of that sweetness—that early, laudatory ejaculation.

When the sound of the bathing stopped, he cleared his throat and knocked on the door.

"Maid," he said. "I need the keys. Quickly now."

Shefali opened the door a crack, so he could only see her face and the tops of her shoulders, which were suntanned and a shade of brown not unpleasing to the eye.

"Speak quietly," she said. "Baba is taking a nap."

"Sorry." As soon as he said it, he regretted having apologized. He stepped into her personal space to balance matters.

"What do you want?"

"The keys to my old room, and the key to Uncle's room, and the keys to the storage closet. Turn them over."

A look of suspicion crossed her face, and the mole on her right cheek began to twitch. "Have you been watching me bathe?"

"No, are you serious? Me, watch you? Seriously?"

"You come-again Americans," she said. She gave him a shove and closed the door on his face.

. . .

As evening arrived prayer bells rang from every direction. This hour had always been special for Chinmoy: books in hand, he would retreat to the bug room, leaving sweets in piles for his special guests, then lotus pose to study. For a few breaths, he'd peruse the school subjects, then move onto *The Invisible Ant*, his beloved comic. Now, he sat and waited as anxiously as he had as a child.

They came back to him. First, a pair of beetles poked his toes—the beetles had always been the friendliest ones. Next, a wasp alighted on his chin, and something with wings stirred around his ears. But the roaches refused to come closer, and in time, even the beetles wandered from his lap. After a few more breaths, he was alone again. Alone with the spirit of his dead father, who, being just as much a Vaishnav as his own father before him, had kept this house sacrosanct. Whenever Chinmoy had tried to escape vegetarianism, his father's spirit had bored a hole into his skull: *In a past life, stupid, even that bug was your mother.*

That voice, its wise swagger. With his father no longer around, it was as if the clay statue of Krishna before him had assumed his father's bearing. The conquering smile, the beautiful, delicate hands. Good that he'd brought along a few bottles of the hawker's brew. The liquor tasted as if it were coated in honey. He thought of bees, how they labored from veronica to hyacinth, all for the sake of the queen, but for what end, for what higher duty, did they keep on, he wondered, as his sips became gulps, and the sunset hewed the room into the color of a sweet burn.

His body felt lighter, weightless even, as he began to sway, careful to avoid harming the other guests in the room. During the evening, as he finished one bottle and worked on the next, he found himself dancing with Krishna as if he were a newborn, and, in fact, the statue was the size of a small infant.

A decent container, also, for his grief. Grief for the father he had not properly mourned; for the career that had defeated him; for the spent promises of this grand house.

. . .

The next morning Chinmoy found himself prodded by calloused feet, but he kept his eyes closed, hoping the interruption would pass.

"Why are you lying in filth?"

Shefali's voice brought him to his senses, available as they were this morning through the headache that was beginning to announce itself. He rose as gracefully as he could. Somehow, his zipper had come undone and there was a mosquito bite on his upper lip. "I was meditating," he said. "I must have fallen asleep."

"What a big mess," Shefali said.

He looked around, unsure of what she was referring to. While sleeping, he saw that he'd crushed a beetle. This would require a proper cremation. Perhaps he'd knocked over the statue of Krishna, but no, the blue-skinned God was smiling just as he had been.

"Why have you not changed out of your clothes? And what are these liquor bottles doing in the prayer room? Did you sleep here the whole night?"

There were the two bottles he'd purchased from the hawker on the street. He remembered their honeyed taste, how they slipped down his throat like spring water. Both bottles were empty and sat lewdly without their caps. He forced himself to look Shefali in the eye, though the effort worsened his headache. "Remind me why you are challenging me in my own house?" It came out a question, though he hadn't meant it to.

"Because I am Ma's keeper," Shefali said.

"You are not Ma's anything," Chinmoy said. "I doubt you even lived here when you were a child. Probably, you lied about that. Given your bearing, I wouldn't be surprised."

"You are one to talk, American-babu, waking with tadka liquor and all these bugs."

"The bugs are part of this place, but you are not. When I run this house again, things will change." As he spoke, an ant bit his chin. He crushed it without thinking—then, ashamed, glared at Shefali, lips quivering in rage. "You've made me kill a living being. I'm done with you in this house, done also with your freeloading father. We'll find another maid for Ma in no time at all. Now, pack your things and get out of my sight!"

"I could smell your bad heart from the first," Shefali said after a long silence. "But soon you will see what is what."

· · ·

He stopped at Ma's room before Shefali could accost her, but Ma was sleeping on her back with her arms on either side of her body, heels touching. Next to her on the bed lay a portrait of Baba. He'd heard that Ma had started sleeping with Baba's portrait right after the cremation, but it was still strange to see her hands graze the frame, as if the wood were the flesh. The artist had given Baba a shiny black head of hair and the expression of a general swaggering into war, but it was unquestionably the man Chinmoy had loved and feared—that frown that knew the world.

As he leaned in to kiss her brow, Ma curled her body toward Baba's picture. He could see her breath fog the frame. Someday she would die, as Baba had, but for now Chinmoy enjoyed this vision of her breath on Baba's features. He resolved to buy fresh garlands to tie over the portrait. Ma would like that a great deal, Shefali wouldn't object, and the room wouldn't smell so much of medicine and naphthalene.

He left her as she was and washed up. He ran a razor over his face. He even combed his hair into order—it was thinning at the top these days, but no matter, with just a shower and shave, he appeared more vital—before he jogged down to the kitchen, where he found Ma already at the breakfast table, and Shefali beside her.

No kingly spread awaited him, not even a cup of tea to soothe his headache.

"Beta," Ma said. "There's been a serious accusation of your behavior last night."

"Oh, I can hardly sit here," Shefali said. "I fear for my life."

"In this house, no harm will come to you," Ma said, putting a hand over Shefali's.

The gesture surprised him, so much so that he struggled to understand the meaning of her words.

"Beta, did you accost Shefali last night? Did you ask her to leave the house? Did you push her out of the room? Did you say you would throw her from the window of the bug room if she did not leave? When she did not listen, did you grab her by the arms and shove her into the hall?"

"Not in the least. No, not at all. What is this nonsense?" Chinmoy slammed his fist on the table, but this seemed to only confirm his newfound tendency for violence. "Ma, obviously she is lying. I told her to leave this house, but I didn't lay a pinkie on her."

"Any further atrocities were avoided because the assailant fell asleep, or so Shefali has reported to me." Shefali confirmed this by snorting.

"Jesus, Allah, Krishna. Could we please speak alone, Ma?"

Shefali shuffled her way out of the room while keeping her eyes on the ground, as if she were a demure bride. When it was just the two of them again, Chinmoy noticed the unkemptness of his mother's sari. She'd always dressed in crisp attire, but this sari hung from her shoulders like a bunched rag. Surely, the morning's news had upset her. Likely, Shefali had woken her from her light sleep, and in her haste she'd dressed, all the while considering what to do. Ma was a woman of rules and order; he would need to appeal to her reason. Then she'd see how ludicrous such an accusation was.

"Firstly, Ma, have you ever known me, your only son, to commit any violence on the help? Secondly, have I ever told you a serious lie?"

"Beta, where were you last night?"

"Where was I? Where could I possibly be? Ma, you don't seriously believe."

"Beta, I am on your side. Last night, were you in the bug room?"

"Out of habit, yes."

"There, did you have drink?"

"Ma, it was a long flight. Absurd, Ma, absurd."

"Beta, please, don't shout. I will try, as long as possible, to

keep this from the neighbors, but these days we can no longer
ill-treat our help."

He felt the blood freeze in his skull. The tips of his fingers
went a little numb. Never had he been so afraid. Not only the
accusations against him—looking Ma in the eye, for once he
didn't know if he was still her precious little boy.

"Beta, listen to me very carefully," she said.

But he had not done the maid any harm. "Ma, she is making
this up."

"Apologize," Ma said. "This has nothing to do with her
makeup. She may come from lowly class, but so what?"

Ma's wit was as sharp as ever, but her hearing seemed to
have hit a cliff, which helped to calm him. Perhaps, this was
simply a misunderstanding, a few words uttered in the wrong
order. "Hold on, Ma," Chinmoy said, raising his voice. "I will
make this right."

. . .

He knocked on the door to the servants' quarters.

"If you open up willingly," Chinmoy said, "I might forgive
you."

A fossil of a man opened the door. It was someone who had
long ago carried baby Chinmoy on his shoulders. "Gopalji, my
old friend," he said.

"You remember me," Gopalji said. "But still touch my
daughter?"

"Please, Gopalji, it's me. Remember that time a scorpion bit
you? We went to the hospital together. Remember?"

"Babu, tell me the how please?"

"Gopalji, what is this babbling? I did not do a thing."

"Convince Ma, babu. There's a hurricane in the bowl."

"Where is Shefali?"

"Would I tell the one who touches my unmarried daughter?"

"Gopalji, think of all the good times we had."

"Exactly," Gopalji said. "That is what I am saying."

His father would have known what to do. He would have been able to produce the right question and to inflect his eyebrows at just the appropriate angle to unseat such an accusation. It upset Chinmoy that he didn't remember the whole of the night. There were moths fluttering by his eyelids, and then it was the habit of darkness. How he got from dusk to dawn was a mystery as deep as the hymns his uncle had sung to empty floors.

"Gopalji, let's come to some understanding."

Gopalji scratched under his chin. In his old age, he'd turned into a raisin of a man. The children used to compare him to Bhimsen, the strongman of the epics, but some time ago he'd exchanged his muscles for a set of false teeth. The way he showed his dentures made Chinmoy think he was smiling even when he wasn't.

"What I am saying, Gopalji, is that misunderstandings can be compensated for." It was the family way. Once, his father had paid a fortune to see a diver jump a hundred feet into the imperial ponds of Fatehpur Sikri; he remembered the sound of scissoring water, the after-smell of algae on the diver's dark skin as he'd stood for pictures beside the family, the sweet musk of the man's moustache as he'd leaned in to kiss the children. When both sides were willing, it was all right to bargain. It did not matter that he had not touched her. She had played her hand well enough to earn his respect. "My checkbook is upstairs," he announced.

"Oh, wait one minute," Gopalji said. "Just wait one minute."

Gopalji returned with a broom in his hand. He gave Chinmoy a woeful glance—one that carried the shared love of the buffalo milk sweets they'd eaten together when the power was out for the night and the servants were called to sit on the kitchen floor and gossip but mostly to praise God and family until both hearts and bellies were full—such were the ways they had loved one another. Gopalji lingered on that look before he raised his broom and brought it down on Chinmoy's head.

. . .

Ma was good and kind and full of reason. She held the icepack to his head and sang something under her breath. Her singing comforted him; when he touched the stone of this house, there were songs he remembered from his childhood, lullabies she'd sung into his ear to carry him to sleep. When had that feeling left him—of wholeness, comfort, of a complete lack of loneliness?

"It didn't go well, Ma," he said. "Not just Gopalji. I mean, my whole life."

"Beta," she said. "He hit you, and now we're even. We have a case. One eyewitness versus another."

"I don't care about that, Ma."

"Beta, please, no despairing."

"My studies, Ma, my dissertation. I never completed it."

She looked at him with what he thought was understanding

and forgiveness but what may have only been the light against her worsening cataracts. "Studies are never complete," Ma said. "To be a scholar is a lifelong journey."

She hadn't understood him, but perhaps that was for the best.

"Whatever came of Linda?" she asked. "When will we have the joy of dancing at your wedding?"

In his early twenties, he'd briefly dated a girl by the name of Linda, and ever since, though he'd casually seen other women, he'd always maintained the Linda facade, a woman who was getting her legal degree, who, like his father, would one day move into private practice. His current girlfriend was thirty-six and a clerk at an insurance firm. He'd been performing oral sex on her with the regularity of the obituaries. On the weekends, she would pull down his sweats and reciprocate, and overall they had a nice time, talking about Graham Greene and how their bodies were becoming more like their fathers' or mothers', but neither of them ever entertained the possibility of something serious.

"Linda is having a tough time in law school," Chinmoy finally said. "Anyway, it's no time to speak of marriage. What do I do now? What's the next step?"

"Keep a low shoulder, beta. Your flight is only a few days away. If nothing else happens, Shefali has said she will not go to the police."

He didn't have the heart to tell her that he'd planned on missing his return flight, that back in America he was immersed in a quagmire of his own making, and that this stunt that the maid had pulled was ruining everything.

. . .

The next morning Chinmoy loitered on the first-floor veranda until he heard Gopalji leave. Then he went down to the ground floor.

"Shefali, open up. There is no more time for nonsense. Speedily, now."

After this offering, he heard the approach of her feet. As she lingered on the other side of the door, he smelled her perfume. It was the kind of scent he'd smelled on a career waitress in a pit stop in Ohio. He knocked where he imagined her face was, and she opened the door partway.

"You have nerve," she said. "Coming down here. Know that I have not yet involved the police, out of respect for Mother."

"I see you are still lying through your bones. What is it that you want?"

"This is our home now, Chinmoy-babu. Many years ago it was yours, but now we are ready for you to leave."

"You cannot be serious. You realize I have a legal right over this house."

"The man you purchased the tadka liquor from, he is my friend. He would be happy to inform others of how many bottles you took back to the house."

"You could not possibly think people will believe you over me?"

"That is not the point. Ma will never allow the family name to be soiled."

She was right. Ma would rather have him back in America than embroiled in a lengthy public hearing. He considered

Shefali anew, her bronzed skin, the key ring that jingled as she tapped her foot, the single loose lock of her dark, oiled hair. "I think we started on the wrong foot, you and I."

"You have three seconds. Then I scream till the crows shit."

"I won't evict you or Gopalji. You will be safe under my watch. You have nothing to fear."

"Watch your nose." She tried to slam the door shut, but he held it open with his foot.

"There is something else," he said. "There is a way in which you could, in some time, not immediately, of course, have legal claim on this house."

She stopped trying to push the door closed. "What is it that you mean?"

"I mean, there are laws I could explain to you, simple laws even you could learn." He hadn't planned on offering her legal claim over the house, yet it had come out nonetheless. Good thing his forebears hadn't heard these words. Once said, though, he wouldn't take it back. If that's what it would take to make peace, so be it.

She looked at him for a long moment. "Have a nice flight," she finally said, kicking his foot from the doorstop. He fell back into the hallway, marveling at her strength.

. . .

No better place than the bug room to consider his situation. The stone floor was cool to the touch. The room pungent with sweetness, all those years of sugar. A wasp flirted with his knee but did not sting. He nudged it aside and thought of all the critters he'd saved during his childhood. Hundreds, perhaps thousands. Each one had been brought to these walls and cared for. Karmically, that had to count for something.

When he closed his eyes and imagined the sum of Shefali's karma, he saw a kaleidoscope, a shape-shifting bruise he failed to understand. He thought of what he'd left behind, which was not more or less than loneliness, the trail of insignificant things he'd done to whittle away his time. What did it mean that he had not loved?

Even in his peace, Shefali's words haunted him: *Then you will see what is what.* She had lied to protect herself; he had done the same, over and over again in America, imagining the life his parents would have wanted. Perhaps she'd known from their first meeting that he would try to bring new order to the house, leaving her and Gopalji displaced.

He tried to meditate, bringing the statue of Krishna close and working his legs into lotus pose, as a roach hopped from one of his ankles to the other. When he closed his eyes and imagined again the sum of Shefali's karma, he saw the silt of the Hooghly and the minnows swimming upstream and the old men who fished with old bait. This was Shefali's karma: mud and fish and bait. But she had taken care of his beloved room. She had saved thousands of bugs over the years. She'd kept Ma alive.

As he brushed away the ants that were circling his knee, he knocked over the statue of Krishna. Before him the blue God lay broken in several asymmetric pieces, and as he tried to put them back together he felt his heart skip a beat. Generations ago a forefather had brought this cheap little thing, which over the decades had received a thousand prostrations, garlands, and offerings of cow's milk, and now it was he who had done away with all that. He carried the pieces to the windowsill for the crows to claim.

. . .

In the house's heyday, his father had kept cows on the ground floor so fresh milk could be had by everyone, and there was a path only the calves were allowed to take. Long ago, Chinmoy had taught the calves how to climb the back stairwell to reach the roof, and he took that path now, down past Gopalji's room to where Shefali was combing her hair. In the shadow of the doorway, he took a moment to study her anew. She wore red and white bangles that made music as she combed. The red sari she was wearing was one of Ma's hand-me-downs. The room smelled of coconut oil. On the floor was a stack of *Tintin* comics.

"I didn't know you could read," he said before he could stop himself.

"You again," Shefali said, pausing with her comb in her hand.

"Thank you for keeping the bug room intact. I know Ma wouldn't have cared either way, but you kept it as it was."

She stared at him, unsure perhaps of how to treat such a compliment.

"Father would have liked it. It was a special place for him."

"Bah," she said. "He liked only the idea of it. When it was time to feed the bugs, it was you or me." She put down her comb and, without using a mirror, set a bindi on her forehead, perfectly centered. He marveled at her sense of geometry, her ease in her own skin.

"I am not leaving for America," he said. "There's nothing there for me to return to. I've been lying to Ma. I am no professor. I drive a taxi to make money."

"American-babu, you drive taxi?"

"Only the night shifts. Listen, I won't kick you out. You and Gopalji can stay."

"I don't believe you," she said. Stone-faced Shefali, tough enough to crack a conch shell with her glare. Except, she was tapping her foot out of time. Her key ring that could unlock any door of their house jingled and betrayed her nerves. He wished to calm her, perhaps even to show his gratitude. For years, she'd cared for all the insects who'd wandered into the bug room, and she'd watched over Ma, while he had turned away.

"I'm going to tell Ma I'm staying," he said. "For a few weeks, then we'll see what happens. Will you come upstairs with me to share the news?"

She remained where she was. Though they'd spent their childhood under the same roof, how little he knew her. He moved toward the stairwell. The window there was caving into itself and would need to be repaired. Perhaps, he would attend to it himself. Shefali would do what she would do, but he would go on; he would transform himself as he had in America, only this time into someone he could love.

## The Overnight Bus

To do good things in this world you sometimes had to leave your old life behind, Tara came to believe, even if that old life included a wife and child. So on the first day of the new year, Tara boarded the overnight bus from Kolkata to the seaside, even though it was the slowest and, at times, the least reliable of options. His younger brother Mintu came along, carrying bathing towels, two woolen blankets, a reed flute, and several packs of playing cards. Tara loved to play gin, but recently Mintu had been on the kind of winning streak that threatened their pastime.

When the bus came, Tara pushed through the line of passengers and found seats across from an old merchant from Kabul. The Kabuliwallah, who had just enough teeth in his mouth to gossip, was passing a hookah around, and soon the whole bus smelled of Kush tobacco and the many odors of sleep. But Tara resolved to stay awake. He dealt another hand.

"Please, Mintu," Tara said. "Stop looking at me and play."

"Brother, I feel you will be mad at me, but I need to ask," Mintu said, taking the hand.

Tara could smell the antiseptic cream on Mintu's neck. He'd have to teach Mintu again, show him how to hold razor to chin.

"There will we still be able to play cards, or will they tell us always no?" Mintu asked.

"I have not asked Govinda specifically, but I can assume," Tara said.

"What can you assume? What about the ocean? Will we be able to go to the ocean at times?"

"Of course, at specific times, yes."

"Bhai, I have never seen the ocean. I would like to go for my seventeenth birthday."

"Mintu, play your card now."

"I have never seen the ocean," Mintu said. "But when I imagine, I think of Sonia."

Tara pinched Mintu on the fleshy side of his forearm. He disliked his brother bringing up his two-year-old daughter. "Bhai. Please."

The Kabuliwallah, who'd clearly been eavesdropping, offered them his hookah. Tara accepted it as a courtesy to old age.

"What is the way of this new generation," the old man said. "Why do you name your children after the Raj?"

"The idea of my wife. I agree it is too British, but now it is late to change," Tara said. It was true he'd argued with Nita for a more Bengali name, but there was something fetching about the sound of *Sonia*. She would be two when winter lifted, and whenever he said her name aloud, he felt a pain in his chest.

Mintu took out a picture of Sonia and passed it across the aisle. Tara tried to look anywhere else, but there she was in her pink dress, crowned with three pigtails. He imagined her tiny hands on the floor ruffling his papers, then chewing an invoice or two. She had an appetite for pulao with raisins and for his receipts.

"What a pretty," said the Kabuliwallah. "You two are going for business?"

Before Tara could say yes, Mintu blurted it out.

"We are leaving our house. We are going to be monks."

"And the girl? And the wife?"

"We will not see them again," Mintu said. "But Tara has told me they will have a nice life."

"You Hindus. You strange people."

"In our dharma such things are allowed," Tara said. "My great-grandfather also became a sadhu."

"Well," said the Kabuliwallah. "God metes everything in time."

. . .

Tara and Mintu had grown up in a house where the only people who seemed to work were their servants. But that all changed overnight. One moment they were the sons and daughters of zamindars, and the next they were scurrying across a border carrying satchels of family gold. In the dark, men with scimitars were howling at the night, men who had been fishermen and good cooks, who knew their names and wouldn't strike them down—Tara thought—if the moment came. Still, they fled.

Tara had met Nita again on the march from Dhaka, when she still wore her knee-length hair down, which he liked, but for his eyes only. He told himself he was afraid the wrong kind of man would take her, so he stepped in and tried to carry her things.

"You have no extra hands," she'd say. "I don't want your help."

Their attachment grew out of refusal. He was constantly offering her what little he'd managed to bring, the better half of a jackfruit, a cool jug of water, a story of how their fathers knew each other and once did business before the revolution, and she was always saying, "No, it's not needed," until they crossed the bridge into Bengal and he became her last, best chance. Also, he thought she loved Mintu. He came to believe that his little brother reminded her of a sibling lost.

. . .

On board the overnight bus, Mintu was the one who did not sleep. As Tara snored, Mintu unwrapped one of Nita Baudi's narus and put it under his tongue to savor the sugarcane juice. Early that morning, before Tara was out of bed, Nita had given him the box of treats.

"Don't let him see," she said. "If he sees, he'll know you know more than he thinks."

He was a boy who had been underestimated all his life, but only recently did he appreciate the fruits of this station. People told him things. They expected him not to understand, or to forget as soon as he'd heard. He was not stupid in the ways of the world, but he was slow with words. He'd have a word on the tip of his tongue, like *electricity*, and it wouldn't come for minutes.

That morning, Nita had told him she knew all about their plan.

"He's a complete idiot," she said. "And it was all because of soap on the floor."

"Soap, accha."

"He said clean it up. He said the house was always dirty. He said I did not feed Sonia at the proper times. Can you imagine a man saying this to his wife?"

"The house is not dirty, sister."

"But of course it's dirty, Mintu. It's dirty because Sonia is two and she smears banana. The house is dirty because we don't have money, and I am not a maid."

"This is true, sister."

"And what does Tara do?"

"What?"

"He runs. He runs like his father, who was also no good at business. What will happen to the tea shop?"

"Will you run it, Nita?"

"Mintu, listen to me closely. If you don't bring Tara home, I will take Sonia, and I will go to Puri. I will find your shaved heads, and you will see what I will do to you then."

"Like that old man?"

"Yes," she said. "But only longer. With more suffering."

He'd seen an old man die on the road from Dhaka. The man's chest was bloodied from a swarm of fleas; no one wanted to touch him. Mintu stood by his mud-caked feet until the smell crawled into his lungs and became the ants in his throat. It was why they were going to become monks—to understand more about death and life, Tara had said. He'd explained it piece by piece. When they arrived in Puri, they would take their potlas directly to the ashram. A man by the name of Govinda would be waiting. Tara said Govinda was round around the middle, but kind to strangers. Govinda would lead them to the ocean, where they'd dip as many times as needed. Afterward, Tara would shave Mintu's head, and Mintu would do the same for him. It was as far as Mintu needed to see without actually arriving.

. . .

The bus stopped many times. Each time, its eyes would illuminate something: the front teeth of a village, the gleaming cowbell around a cow's neck, but more often than not, Mintu couldn't see anything beyond the darkness. Mostly a single stake in the road separated a bus stop from overgrown country. Impossible that anyone could live in such jungle, but then someone would step out from the darkness, board the bus, and quickly fall asleep. When they first came from the cold, Mintu could see their breath and smell the ash of jackfruit smeared on their clothes. Once, there was a whole family: a pregnant woman with twin sons and a man who looked like he hadn't eaten for days carrying a suitcase on his head. More often than not, they'd stop and no one would board. The bus driver would honk and drive on. Such was the way of the night.

At one of these stops, the Kabuliwallah turned to him.

"I think we're in trouble," he said.

Mintu smiled as he did whenever he was nervous.

"There are dacoits on the road. See here."

The Kabuliwallah passed a newspaper. *Will Nehru Ever Hand Power?* And: *Thousands Die in Mudslide.*

"No, no, other side."

In the back corner ran a small heading: *31 Killed by Dacoits on Road.*

"Rubbish. Just rubbish," Mintu said. He'd heard his brother

use the phrase with Nita. It seemed to calm the Kabuliwallah a little, and it helped him as well.

"Where are you from?"

"North Calcutta. We come from an old family." Mintu enjoyed the aftertaste of his lie.

"Good, good," said the Kabuliwallah.

"But recently we have lost some wealth."

"Troubles? Is it to do with the silk industry?"

"Oh, no, we are not in silk. We sell . . . fish. We sell the best fish. Packaging also."

"There is money to be made in that."

"But the fish have been spoiling. Our fishermen receive the fish as they normally do, but the catch dies too quickly. Our customers, who are smarter than us, do not want dead fish. They want the ones still kicking in their buckets. We want that also, but it is in the wind, I think. Sometimes I smell too much salt. Too much salt can kill a grown hilsa. A hilsa needs to feel the difference between salt and blood. This is what makes them the lucky fish."

"Do you smell it now? Do you smell trouble?"

"I do. My brother will be mad if he overhears."

"Take some bhang, my friend." The Kabuliwallah passed the hookah. Mintu swallowed the smoke into his body and closed his eyes, but he did not sleep. In the dark, he lay still and heard his brother's heart. He tried to imagine its other rhythms, but there were only the two he knew: Tara the brother, beloved, and Tara the fighter, the one who woke up with sore ribs and cursed the lights on.

At Dhaka University, Tara had been a fearless boxer. He'd fought all the weight classes and taken everyone's medals, but now Tara didn't dare lift a hand, even when the men drank the special tea and rowdied up their shop. There was something askew in his head, the doctor said, after eating all those wallops. Nita knew it too. Mintu had watched her stare Tara into a corner and threaten to beat him to an inch of his life. She was spectacular like that, with the broom raised above her head like a premonition.

He pressed his ear to his brother's chest and listened; there was no asking for more.

. . .

Sometime after Malda, the bus came to a shuddering halt. Tara looked at his watch—2 a.m. He thought they'd hit a giant pothole, and that the conductor would need to bring the tires back to form. But it was not that.

"Get off," the conductor yelled. He came around and gave the sleepers a decent shove.

"Are we arrived?" Mintu asked.

He was not answered.

"I've seen this before," the Kabuliwallah whispered.

The bus driver cut the ignition and the lights, and they were led outside. Tara shined his light into the rows of dark fields and pinned rows of rotting jackfruit hanging in the trees, but he didn't have the gall to speak and in this he was not alone.

After what might have been half an hour, a constable car pulled in front of the bus. It was one of those vehicles reclaimed from ambulance service to aid the new Bengal police. Several around him recoiled from the brightness of the constabulary lights, and therefore missed what Tara saw. As soon as the pair of constables stepped out from the car, one of the passengers ran deep into the field. Nothing remarkable about him. At least, Tara hadn't noticed him before, though now he admired the grace of his flight: in full sprint—the legs outstretched and the elbows close to the body—not a motion wasted.

Two shots rang in the air, and the man fell into the tall grass. The constables didn't bother to check the body. They returned to their car and drove toward the city.

When the passengers were back on the bus and the bus was moving again, Tara offered Mintu a date from a stash he kept in his coat.

"Sometimes when a country is becoming itself, it's hard to tell the wrong from the right," Tara said in what felt like an apology. Surely that man had been a criminal, a trespasser on their route.

For a while Mintu said nothing at all, joining everyone else in a funereal silence. Then he said, "I don't understand this country, bhai. But can we talk about Nita? Is it time?"

"What do you want to know?"

"I want to know, bhai, are we in the wrong or the right?"

"Do you think I was wrong?" Tara said. "Leaving her?"

"If we catch tomorrow's bus, I think Nita won't be so mad. We'll say we were drinking the special tea and there was a fight at the shop. Such was our delay."

"I don't care what she thinks, Mintu. I'm asking: Do you think I am in the wrong to leave her?"

"Bhai, now you're yelling."

"Mintu, I was married too young. That is the problem. But not the only problem. Another problem: I was married without

Ma and Baba. If Ma was still alive, she would have found me someone obedient."

Nita was the one who sent the punches flying. Even with her tiny frame, she could defeat Tara in minutes, sometimes lifting a hand, sometimes with only her mouth. The final straw—she'd used the same voice on him she used with Mintu, a baby voice, a beat-me-if-you-can voice, a goading, out-of-bloom voice no decent man would accept.

"I do not like a woman who is always going about with her teeth," Tara said. "Do you know she cannot recite even a single poem?"

"Bhai, does Sonia know poems?"

"Sonia is two. She cannot know poems. Unless, of course, when she is speaking with God."

"I would like to return and teach Sonia a poem."

"Perhaps we could loaf back when she is a little older. Like when she is sixteen. Then she will be able to understand why some men become sadhus." He had meant what he'd said in jest, but now he saw that Mintu had believed his every word.

"Fourteen years is a long time, bhai," Mintu whispered.

Tara wanted to say that it might be longer than that—perhaps they'd never return at all—and even if they did, they wouldn't receive a warm welcome. He didn't, for knowing this might break Mintu's heart. He thought he'd lied for good reason. Had he left Mintu with Nita, she would have stripped him of his joy and his youth. A boy in a house with a witch couldn't last. Now Mintu ached for Sonia, maybe even a little for Nita, but he'd soon forget them. "When we're monks, each year will go quickly. You'll see."

"Every year I become a sadhu," the Kabuliwallah interrupted. He'd rejoined them in his seat without Tara noticing. "In the winter, I leave Kabul, and in the summer, I go back."

"That is not renouncing your life," Tara said.

"But it is. I take only a single potla, a hookah, and one wool blanket. Fine, I sell a few things, but along the way and back, I do not see any one of my four daughters."

"We are doing this for spiritual reasons," Mintu added.

"Insha'Allah," the Kabuliwallah said. He relit the hookah and passed it to the two men. They each took a generous draw and allowed the smoke to drain into their lungs.

. . .

When Mintu awoke, it was already morning, the bus had come to a full stop, and most of the passengers were already gone. He smelled the salt in the air and knew they'd arrived in Puri. The sea wouldn't be far, and if they were good and lucky, there would be time for playing in the ocean. Tara had promised.

Except Tara was in a fuss gathering the things.

"Get up, quickly."

Mintu stood, swaying, as Tara scrounged under their seat.

"The son of a pig!"

"What?"

"I just knew I couldn't trust him. The old bastard took our money."

Tara stormed up and down the aisle, and when he was done with that, he punched the seat where the Kabuliwallah had been.

"How do you know it was him?"

"Hand of a whore, lice butt, pig fucker. Mintu, I shouldn't have fallen asleep."

They dragged their belongings into the terminus, where a handful of rickshaw pullers were milling with tea brewers. A few of the passengers stood with empty teacups while others were ordering porters around. The bus driver, who had been quiet the whole trip, was telling a dirty joke. There was no sign of the Kabuliwallah.

"We don't even have money for a rickshaw," Tara said.

"But bhai, we don't need money. We're monks."

"Mintu, don't talk about what you don't understand. Now we have to walk three kilometers."

"Bhai, I have a few annas." Mintu took out a five-rupee note from his pocket.

"Where did you get that?"

"On the floor." Mintu did not want to explain that Nita had given him some money in case they ran into trouble.

Tara took it and called over a rickshaw to load their potlas. The rickshaw took them off the main thoroughfare into narrower side streets and then finally onto a dirt road, where Mintu felt each pothole. He was sore in his thighs and bottom when they stopped in front of a tire shop, a place as far from the ocean as he could imagine. At least there was the smell of hyacinth from flower beds in the lawn. The grass around the beds was browned and nearly dead, but the hyacinths had survived.

A man lumbered out from the shop. He kept his hands on his hips to support his large belly, and when he said hello, he spit out the red juice of a betel leaf.

"Mintu, you remember Govinda from Dhaka?"

Mintu had a memory of a Govinda loitering outside his school. That Govinda would take your lunch money and turn it into more money, and though he wore a cologne like naphthalene, he'd give candies and sweetmeat to all the boys. That Govinda and this one didn't seem so different: a little heavier, a little more of the smell of money coming from him, though this one wore a prayer mark on his forehead.

"Look at you," Govinda said. "Last time, you were a medium shrimp. Now you are mostly a man."

"Give us a minute, Mintu."

While Tara and Govinda spoke inside the shop, Mintu waited and stared at the sun until his eyes burned and his hands stopped feeling cold. He closed his eyes and soaked in the warmth until Tara returned for him. His brother steered him into the shop and then into a hallway in the back that led to a series of rooms. Mintu followed Tara into one and watched as his brother cleared cobwebs with a painted hand fan someone had left behind.

"Bhai, I need to tell you something serious," Tara said. "I need to tell you that sometimes people don't always say what they mean. This is a way of protecting. In our case, bhai, we ended up married to a strange woman. I once saw Nita talking to a cat. Can you imagine that? A wife talking to a cat? To escape such places, a man must make decisions. In our case, bhai—"

"What about the ocean?" Mintu interrupted. He was feeling hot and disoriented. He didn't understand why Tara was unpacking their things inside a tire shop. "Can we go there soon?"

"Yes, bhai. Except I must start working here. It will keep me, and it will keep you."

"What about the monks?"

"Get some rest now. I have a little work."

"What about—"

"Bhai."

Mintu knew better than to continue his questioning. He joined Tara by the car hoist, where Govinda barked instructions to his men. They'd been tinkering around a vat of boiling rubber, which smelled like the rotting dead at Mymensingh but also a little like fresh, sweet curd.

It turned out that there was a lot to do. First, Govinda told Tara to stack a set of tires, and then he had him undo the stacks into smaller columns by the main hoist. The final instructions were delivered by one of the men into Tara's ears.

Tara looked like he was going to either throw up or hit someone, but then he got on his hands and knees and doled out pushups. Govinda counted the rise and fall of Tara's body out to twenty; the other men counted from twenty to forty. It was over when Tara collapsed at seventy-two.

"My little boxer," Govinda said.

The men laughed to stamp the name.

It wasn't the first time Mintu had seen Tara's show of strength. Nita had permitted such displays on the road from Mymensingh, when he would heave a trunk on his shoulders and balance a full water jug at the same time. How Nita had stared at his brother bathing in the Hooghly. That look had been the difference between the days of the road and the days of marriage that came after.

. . .

The first few days they got up before dawn to eat two chapattis
with a cup of goat milk. Tara would work till noon and then
lie in the sun with the other men, while Mintu played the flute
and counted the last of Nita's narus. For dinner, they had
dal and rice in clay bowls. They didn't speak during the day
because there were signposts on Tara's face of all the things
they couldn't talk about, and after dinner, Tara would crawl
into the bottom bunk and quickly fall asleep. Mintu thought
he'd failed in some way; his job had been to bring Tara home
to Nita—to dip in the ocean but ultimately to serve as a
peacekeeper.

It wasn't easy for Mintu to hear his thoughts during those
first few hours, which turned into the first week. On the eighth
day, his seventeenth birthday, he began to work in the shop
for two hours every morning, carrying hot tea from person
to person. Mostly they ignored him, but sometimes they
squeezed his shoulder or pinched his bottom.

"Sing me a song, baccha," they would say, and he'd comply,
singing the lullaby he'd written for Sonia. Often, he'd weave an
extra verse and include the names of the tire men. Other times
there would be a stanza about the dogs that lurked around the
shop. He could smell the sea on these mutts; they gathered
and bayed into the twilight hour.

It was only on the ninth day that Mintu accosted Tara.

"Bhai, I turned seventeen yesterday."

"You did? We did not celebrate."

"I imagined we would be swimming in the ocean for this."

"Listen, bhai, I am protecting you. There is no Sonia and Nita here, and there is no monastery."

"Why did you lie?"

"Because, Mintu, in one year I'll be free. No more debt, and Govinda is going to give me extra to start my own business."

"And then we go back?"

"No, Mintu."

"Why? Are you afraid, bhai? Your own life, does it make you feel unsteady?" Sometimes Mintu felt this way himself, but he went further. "Are you afraid of Nita Baudi?"

Tara rocked on his heels like a dumbfounded schoolboy, opened and shut his mouth a few times with a possible answer, smiled with teeth to show he wasn't mad at the accusation. Then he struck.

Years later, Mintu would come to think of that punch as a little mercy. For as the blow landed under his right eye and he was knocked backward, he found the anger that felt like a shiver in his belly. It was the first time he could have responded in turn with a raised fist to his brother, though he didn't. Tara could punch through a brick wall. With Mintu he'd drawn only a thimble's worth of blood—such was a brother's love—though Mintu's anger remained, then dulled into the normal work of his heart.

The next morning the men in the tire shop jeered at him. "Your wife beat you?"

Govinda was there to witness the taunts. "Shut up," he yelled to no one in particular. "And you," he yelled to Tara, "get back to work."

Govinda extended a long meaty finger and called Mintu

into his office. It was the first time Mintu had been, and the room's furnishings filled him with a nervous delight. There in one corner was a brackish aquarium with two giant turtles knocking into each other's shells, while in another a gramophone with gilded handles reflected the sunlight.

"Tell me what happened to your face."

"A dog attacked," Mintu said.

Govinda studied the evidence, then offered sugar cubes from a bowl. "Why don't you sing me a song?"

Mintu couldn't think of a melody. He was transfixed by the drops of sweat on Govinda's forehead and by the circles of sweat that were staining the armpits of his rose-colored shirt. While his belly was large, his forearms were those of a boy's, hairless and small enough to fit a child's bracelet.

Govinda balanced the bowl of sugar cubes on his lap and, staring into some middle distance, hummed a tune Mintu found familiar but couldn't name. While Govinda hummed, Mintu focused on the prayer mark above his forehead: a red smear stamped a little unevenly between the eyes.

"Did you just sing? I wasn't attending."

"No, I didn't," Mintu said.

"Come here." Govinda unbuttoned his shirt halfway, took Mintu's hand and placed it on his chest. "What do you hear?"

"I hear a dog with three legs. Nothing steady." Was this what it felt like to be inside the ocean? Mintu's hand touched the wetness of skin and measured the timeliness of Govinda's breath. He would have preferred reaching into a sack of dead fleas, but there was something in Govinda's voice that made him keep his place.

"Don't worry, child. Only the beginning is difficult."

Govinda rose to lever the gramophone, and static joined them, drowning out the drawls of the shop workers. He closed the window slats, leaving the gramophone in shade. The static was not so far from the whirr of a conch shell, and it began to feel like they were in the middle of a body of water. It was quiet, but the turtles in the aquarium were upset again, climbing atop each other for the morsels that hadn't dissolved.

The thing Govinda produced from his trousers was not extraordinary. A piece of flesh so uncertain of itself it had turned a grown man into a shy schoolboy. Perhaps it was the despair in Govinda's face that let Mintu stay—that prodded him forward for a closer look.

. . .

Late that night Mintu awoke with a start. He had been chased by a dream that led to an alleyway with no light, and in that darkness an old wolf cornered him. An old, fat wolf with no teeth. Next to him Tara snored, and no wonder, every day Tara worked himself to the bone. Mintu drew a sheet around his brother's body. He poured three cups of water, then put on his sturdy leather shoes. The contractions in his belly would pass, and perhaps one day he'd forgive his brother the good lie. Even then, he wouldn't tell him what happened with Govinda. No, it would be his wound to keep.

With his things stuffed into a knapsack, Mintu left the tire shop. Though he'd never been far from the grounds, he figured he knew the streets from the men describing the way to the market and the station. Still, there was no telling—a man had to find his own feet.

As he walked, a thick mist rose to his knees. Twice, he had

to stop and ask shopkeepers for the way. It took him several hours. When he reached the ocean, he waded into the water and felt the life swimming around his legs. He thought he would write a song about that moment, but the tune was like the water that wouldn't stay in his cupped hands.

. . .

When Mintu made it to the bus station, his clothes were soaked, and he had to huddle himself against a family of sleeping cows to stay warm. Shame helped him onto the bus, and the cold settled him against the men in the back who hauled fertilizer and drank sour brew from bowls. Halfway to Kolkata, there was another breakdown. This time, the passengers waited by the side of the road as the conductor inserted a coil between the pistons and the water tank, which coerced the engine back to life. Only then did Mintu take out Nita's last naru. A zigzag pattern of mold had grown over the sweet's surface, but he thought of putting it in his mouth, having had nothing in his belly all day. He scraped the mold off the surface but decided to save the core to show Nita he could keep things.

By evening, he was in Kolkata. By nightfall, he'd reached their house. He stood in the alleyway outside their bedroom window. He waited with his ears to the closed window and was rewarded by the beat of a hand fan and then by Sonia's voice. She was resisting going to bed, so Nita sang her a lullaby. Nita didn't have a melodious voice. She floated in and out of pitch, but her singing still called to him.

The morning she'd put the pack of narus in his hand, Nita had pulled him close.

"You are the reliable one," she'd said. "Don't let anyone tell you otherwise."

When she'd said that he remembered the evening he'd had to fill a kolshi in the riverbanks near where an alligator was known to make its bed. He'd been the one who'd stepped up to do the deed.

They were in the part of the house that never allowed sunlight. A cool breeze had lifted Nita's sari from her shoulder, and one of the stray cats from the neighborhood had found its way onto her lap. All he had to do now was knock.

. . .

Tara awoke before daybreak. His calves ached, as did his arms, and every crease smelled of kerosene. He wondered if he should have struck his brother and concluded that he'd been in the right. The men on the grounds would give Mintu no quarter, and it was time his brother learned the worth of a punch. In less than a year, he would lead his brother to the ocean to thank him for his unquestioning love.

"Bhai," he called to that empty room. "There is work to be done."

## The Fortunes of Others

The Kabuliwallah, angling for a spot near the front of the train, noticed little around him. He was passing through one of the busiest stations in the world, but these days the journey felt as familiar as the cup of ginger chai he would permit himself in the evenings. A little boy was tugging on his pants, but little boys had tugged on his pants hundreds of times over the years, each with their own mantra of need. It was only when this boy said *ice cream* or, maybe, it was only *cream*, that the Kabuliwallah stopped, for it was said with such fierce candor.

"Ice cream," the boy said, shoving against his kneecaps. The Kabuliwallah realized that he was being ordered by this dirty creature, who he doubted had a penny in his pocket.

"Cream," the boy said again, pointing his finger at the freezer with cones and cups and several flavors of ice cream.

The Kabuliwallah rarely attended to beggars; for one, he himself subsisted on the slimmest of margins, and, moreover, the children who begged on behalf of their families disturbed him in ways he didn't care to admit. Still, he considered the price: a cup cost two rupees and a cone three. He bought the little boy a cup of chocolate and vanilla.

The boy's name was Sundar, which meant *beautiful*. He was

too dirty to be considered beautiful, though if a guardian were to thoroughly scrub and wash, one could imagine if not beauty then at least a note of sweetness in that face with a mane of curly hair. He watched the boy savor his ice cream. Perhaps he was used to favors from tourists, but not one from a man as poor as he. "I'll have another," Sundar said, as if he owned the train tracks and the trains that ran on them. It was enough to make the Kabuliwallah laugh; he would have bought the boy another if he could've spared the change.

"Where is your family?" the Kabuliwallah asked.

The boy pointed at a solitary goat chewing on the grass between the tracks. "Sister," he said. Then he pointed at a stray puppy who was bounding toward them. "Brother."

"But where do you come from?" the Kabuliwallah asked. The boy's eyes were as green as his own.

Sundar shrugged and gave his cup a final lick before relinquishing the container to his puppy. "I go where he goes," the boy said, scratching the little mutt between his ears.

That night the train was delayed by fourteen hours, for a low fog had settled over the north and everything south of Varanasi was running with a limp. The Kabuliwallah unrolled his bedding and shared space with the little boy, who curled up beside him with such ease that for a moment the Kabuliwallah believed they were related. He wanted to ask how old the boy was but knew the answer wouldn't matter. Five, he guessed, maybe six. Sundar's hair smelled of gunpowder, and when the boy began to snore, the little pup settled his body over the boy's legs like a blanket.

. . .

As a young man, the Kabuliwallah had traveled the Hindu Kush with his burlap bags of cardamom and perfume, work that had served him well enough to eventually finance a wife and, afterward, a child, a boy who hardly cried, or so he remembered, the decades having turned his firstborn increasingly cherubic. When the Taliban came, the Kabuliwallah took up arms. Kabul fell. Music became a memory. Every woman wore a purdah, and there was little work to be found. One winter evening, his family perished, struck by mortar shell.

He crossed the border a final time with his bag of cardamom and perfume, a skeleton of a man by the time he reached Kolkata, though each morning he applied attar and smelled as fresh as the housewives who'd sample his wares.

. . .

When the train finally arrived, the boy put his hand in the Kabuliwallah's. "We travel together," he said, indicating the pup, who was mewling at his feet.

"I cannot support you," the Kabuliwallah said. "Myself, I barely eat most nights."

"His name is Arun," the boy said, taking the pup into his arms. "He has a good nose. We will find what we need."

The Kabuliwallah bribed the ticket checker when he came, paying a slightly higher fee for Arun, who howled like a wolf whenever the train sped through the fog.

. . .

Though it had been his habit to travel the spice circuit, with a boy and dog in tow the Kabuliwallah decided to stay in

Varanasi when they arrived, at least for a while. He called in a favor with an old merchant friend and, in exchange for half the profits, was set up in a shop painting the busts of Hindu deities. It was simple, mindless work that paid just enough for a sparse meal for the three of them. If they wanted more, Sundar would lead his dog to the riverbanks, where he often found something half-eaten and delectably so—a box of almond pastries just a day stale, sweet lentil balls that someone had wrapped in newspaper and dropped by the water, only a little wet. In this way, approaching his fiftieth birthday, the Kabuliwallah felt that he had come close to restoration—that something worthwhile from his youth had once again been revealed.

They found lodging in the attic of a garment warehouse, where sometimes the owner would let the boy in downstairs to peruse the thousand colors of garments. He learned that his name meant *beautiful*, and since Sundar didn't know his birthday they agreed the day of their first meeting would serve as that. Sundar turned seven and began to work for the Kabuliwallah and to attend school one day a week.

. . .

The shop stood next to a monastery that was popular with foreigners, and the Kabuliwallah had sold more of his painted Parvatis and lacquered Ganeshas to the clientele of the monastery than anyone else. Now that he had a child and pet to support, he was wary of wasting time with the wrong customers. When the fair-skinned walked into his shop, he would abandon whatever conversation he was having with the locals who came, most often, just to peruse. He'd devote his attention to the English or the Americans or the Germans and praise the spiritual quality of his pieces. He did not believe in God, certainly not in a many-armed one, but he believed that the fervor he held in his heart for his family would prompt his customers to open their wallets.

Sometimes he used Sundar to help move the merchandise. Sundar's English-language skills had quickly surpassed the Kabuliwallah's, so the Kabuliwallah would assume a mystic's pose while Sundar worked his charms. His boy would say, *This one is most spiritual* or *This one have good energy*, and with the exchange of a wink and a smile he'd have the foreigners in his palms.

They'd been having a slow month when Hannah first came. Arun the mutt was napping in the midsummer heat, and the boy had skipped school to help add detail to his statues of Lakshmi, the goddess of wealth. Hannah strolled around the shop, lifting trinkets, then setting them down. She seemed to have little interest in what they offered but smiled whenever Sundar smiled at her. The Kabuliwallah guessed that she was a familiar of the monastery from the wilted look she'd donned when she'd first passed by their store. He knew that look, having seen many a foreigner in the haze of the unmoored.

"Explain, explain!" the Kabuliwallah whispered.

Sundar did as told. He walked her from aisle to aisle, holding her hand while narrating the spiritual benefits of the statues and prayer paintings. Though he went to school less and less, spending most of his time in the shop and walking the mutt in the evenings who knew where, the boy's English had continued to improve. Not even eight and he could slang-talk a smile out of anyone who passed through. Perhaps his father—the original one—had been a charmer, a teller of tales, though it was impossible to know, the boy having largely forgotten that first life. There was only the life of the shop with its ever-growing collection of statues, and their family, or so the Kabuliwallah believed. Sometimes, they shared an ice cream and relived their first meeting. The boy had never asked for anything more. Hannah lingered until the boy grew impatient, then left the shop, having bought one of the smaller statues they had—the bust of a frog with no religious meaning whatsoever, though he guessed that Sundar had fluffed even this, added the frog into some modern pantheon.

She returned to the store several times a week. As the monsoons approached, some days she was their only customer. The Kabuliwallah would see her tall frame crouching through the entrance and immediately stand to greet her. He'd silently praise the seeming infinitude of her pocketbook, for by buying what Sundar showed off she paid for their evening meals. Each afternoon, she stayed longer at the store, until her visits became ritual, the Kabuliwallah arranging a chair with a cushion, where she would sit to chat with Sundar while sipping tea from their sole porcelain cup.

. . .

The gatekeeper at the monastery was a fellow refugee from Afghanistan, who shaved and pretended to be a Hindu, and the Kabuliwallah began to ask about the American. He was grateful for her purchases but began to grow curious and even a little wary of her intentions. In an early awkward exchange, she'd offered her name. There was little else beyond that, for Sundar grew coy when asked about the substance of their conversations, which happened now not only at the store but sometimes out, elsewhere in the neighborhood, when hand in hand his boy would cart Hannah around like a prize. She was long of limb and muscular in the arms. Perhaps she had played some sort of sport? Sometimes she would come to the shop with a prayer marking on her forehead, a white shawl wrapped around her shoulders, despite the heat. Other times, she would come in her faded jeans and a shirt that showed her arms to full effect.

The gatekeeper relayed what he'd learned. Their best customer was a divorcée and rich to boot—though weren't they all, the ones that bought? She hailed from a part of America where snow covered the streets more than half the year, which made the Kabuliwallah think of his time passing through the Himalayas, of the lonely yaks he'd chained himself to in order to navigate the storms, the fires he'd lit in the bellies of trees to thaw. Once, Hannah had thought of becoming a monk, the gatekeeper said, but now she mostly came to the monastery for chai and a chat.

"How long is she to stay?" the Kabuliwallah asked, for they had seen her every day for the better part of a month.

"No one knows," said his fellow refugee. "She pays for her room week to week."

That night when the Kabuliwallah came home by the side door of the garment shop, Sundar wasn't there. Arun the mutt, who had grown plump on scraps, was restless, so he led the dog to the riverbank, where after scavenging for his meal his old friend lifted a leg and released a long stream into the river. The Kabuliwallah circled from the riverbank to his shop in search of Sundar. His boy knew the streets but almost never stayed out past dusk. He had made a few friends at school but always had dinner with the Kabuliwallah, before taking Arun for a stroll. The Kabuliwallah searched for an hour, lightheaded with exhaustion and worry. When he returned to the garment shop, he found Sundar asleep on his cot, something curled close to his body. Aiming his flashlight, he saw the evidence of an intruder: his little boy was holding a stuffed tiger in his arms; the dog sniffed and licked the soft fur of the thing as the little boy turned away to snore.

In the first year of their acquaintance, the Kabuliwallah made it clear that he needed his own bed. The little boy kicked, and, in the beginning, released pockets of gas from turn to turn. But that was not the reason. The Kabuliwallah had grown used to the solitude of his sleep and wished for Sundar to appreciate the same. But on this night the Kabuliwallah placed his body—nowadays his neck nearly always stiff, his knees hardly suitable for long walks, his chest hair all turned gray—next to his little boy, and when the rains came to cool the air, still felt warm from bone to bone.

. . .

The Kabuliwallah did not approve of Hannah's gift. His own son had died before his fifth birthday without ever having such a toy. Sundar would walk with the tiger as if they were conjoined twins, at all hours the fur grazing his hip. *Tiger Friend*, he named it, striking long, elaborate conversations in multiple languages. After a week of this, the Kabuliwallah made his displeasure known.

"This is not manly," he said. "You are losing your heart."

Sundar scoffed, though by the way the boy avoided his gaze he could tell his words had an effect. What he had wanted to say was that attachment to such things was dangerous. Again and again he had seen the world take and not give back; it was better to swim without stones. He took Tiger Friend and placed it on a high shelf.

That evening, as they were closing up, Hannah came by the shop. "Why did you tell him the wrong thing?" she asked. She seemed upset, but he had only understood half of her words, her English sometimes delivered too quickly to parse. He looked to Sundar for a translation. "She doesn't like that you took Tiger Friend," the boy said. "She thinks it's bad fathering."

He was too shocked to speak. What would a customer have to say about the way he raised his son?

"Go now," he said. He was a tall man and dwarfed nearly everyone in town, but this woman stood eye to eye with him. In his country such a statement would have been unforgivable. They were no longer in Afghanistan, though this fact did little to soften his gaze. He worried about all the days of abbreviated meals ahead. "No need you," he finally told her. "No need money."

"I'm sorry," she said, perhaps realizing her mistake. She made a motion of apology that he'd seen as a child—she touched her hands to her forehead, then to her heart, leaving with a muted goodbye.

Sundar walked to the back of the store and made a show of dusting off the statues, and the Kabuliwallah tried to ignore his boy as long as he could. He fed Arun the mutt, tallied the day's paltry earnings. The air between them grew so thick that the dog whelped his anxiety.

"Quiet!" the Kabuliwallah cried.

"Baba, how will we eat?" Sundar asked.

It was the first time the boy had called him *Baba*. He thought of his firstborn, those pale little hands, serpentine eyes. What a wound it was to have known that love. Now, there was another, who cared for him as much or more, and he, in turn, had given the whole of his affection, without regret. To protect this boy—this life—he would've walked into the bullets of the Taliban.

"We have always managed," the Kabuliwallah said. "We will not go hungry."

That evening the Kabuliwallah took a few rupees from his special stash. He went to the bazaar for goat meat, stayed to watch the halal slaughter, the blood flowing. When he came home, he found that Sundar had lit a kerosene lamp to study. They had one table with three legs, so half his energy went into keeping his notebook from sliding off.

"I should study more," his boy said. "For what will I become?"

The Kabuliwallah would have laughed had Sundar not spoken so earnestly. Of course, the boy would take over his business, the crow's nest he'd built himself twig by twig. He'd take over the trade, and with his bright eyes he'd do better than his old man. Arun the mutt would gracefully age under the boy's care. When the time came, the boy would find a bride. Sometimes, the Kabuliwallah dreamed of the wedding, the garish pandel, the sweets made with ghee, and him in the center of the room; he saw himself dancing—oh, he'd moved like that only once before in his life—with a younger man's heart. He told his boy none of this, fearing that the words spoken aloud would rob them of a certain happiness.

"Do not worry," the Kabuliwallah said, finally. "You will be poor like me, only less so."

"But Auntie has said I can do more," the boy insisted.

"Oh, what can you do?" the Kabuliwallah asked, as he felt his anger beginning to boil.

"Be a teacher, even a doctor."

"This is not possible. You will run the store when I die."

"I can do better than you, Baba. You can't read a single letter on this page."

His boy had never spoken to him in such a tone, and the shock made him momentarily recoil. He felt his collar grow hot with rage. The book before him was filled with the uselessness of the city rich, and he took it from his son's hands. He tore it cover to cover. "Now you can't read it either," the Kabuliwallah said, tossing the mess into the coals of his stove.

The boy stared at the remains, then began to cry. Immediately, the Kabuliwallah felt sorry for what he'd done. He could not afford to replace the book, which the boy had so treasured.

"I cannot pay to replace," the Kabuliwallah said quietly, which made the boy cry harder. He left to prepare the goat meat, though his heart wasn't in it. If love didn't make a meal, his mother had said, nothing else mattered; no amount of expensive spices could compensate. So it was that the Kabuliwallah oversalted the goat, and when they finally ate together by lamplight, the pleasure he'd hoped for was not there. The boy's eyes had swollen, even the mutt avoided the Kabuliwallah's gaze. It was not the way of a father to apologize. Not knowing what to say, the Kabuliwallah kept quiet till the meal was finished. "Next time I put less salt," he said, taking the boy's dish.

. . .

The next day Sundar went to school instead of tending shop. The Kabuliwallah didn't complain, and in any case the morning was slow. There were a few customers who grazed without committing to a sale. He sanded the back of a goddess listlessly. Around noon, a merchant asked if he'd take a day's wages to paint a sign, and he agreed, though without Sundar it meant he'd have to close the shop, which he did, though he regretted the lost business.

It felt like more work than a day's wages, but after a few hours he managed to paint faces for what would become a ladies' hair salon. It was welcome, for he thought of nothing but rendering a well-shaped eyebrow, or an aquiline nose. His father had performed a similar job, drawing signs in the theater district for performances wealthy men went to see.

Returning to his shop, he saw Hannah and Sundar sitting together in the monastery garden. They hadn't noticed his approach, so he retreated behind a tree and watched the two of them talking. They were like old friends. From the way Sundar was using his hands he knew the subject was a matter of significance. Hannah listened, not saying much at all. Whenever he'd seen her at the shop, he'd remarked at her gray hair. Sundar had assured him that she was no older than forty, though all her hair had turned gray. He watched her twisting the ends of her long hair, listening to his boy rant about who knew what.

He returned to his shop and looked through his accountings for the month. Aside from the regular sales to Hannah, which he'd marked with an *H*, it was fair to say that their enterprise had come to a head. It was the country changing, though the Kabuliwallah didn't know why. Perhaps, the foreigners no longer queued for religion, which meant his statues had lost value, or maybe there were other cities more desirable in the tourist's lore than Varanasi. It had felt like a stroke of genius when he'd planted his flag three years before with his boy. He remembered the first thing he'd bought in the city: a meter-wide tin tub where he'd bathed Sundar, then the mutt, then finally himself of all the ills of their long travel. That night, as they fell asleep still wet in their cots, he thought they'd reached their place of non-migration. Except now their livelihood was challenged. Before the boy and the dog, he'd made do from city to city. But how would he go on now—how would they eat?

The Kabuliwallah was not easily given to despair, but as he rued the second fall of his happiness—the first almost a lifetime ago in a city of veils and myrrh—he began to feel sorry for what the world had given him. It was then that he saw Sundar lope toward the store, and his heart burst with gladness. He'd found this boy with half of his baby teeth and raised him through episodes of confusion and longing. Where before he'd been all bones, the Kabuliwallah now saw blooming muscle, the sweet curve of his back. With air to grow, his boy's hair had erupted into fierce curls, and it was well coiffed, the barber a few doors down giving him trims for half price. He had not done well in business, but he had done all right with his boy, who'd learned to read with only a day of school a week.

"Come, let us tend shop together," he told Sundar, who'd walked through the door. "I have ideas on how we can do better."

"Baba, we are invited for dinner tonight," his boy said.

"By who?" They had few friends in the city. Aside from the barber and the neighboring shop owners and Sundar, the Kabuliwallah hardly exchanged a word with anyone else.

"Hannah Auntie," Sundar said. "At the restaurant."

Though he'd frequented roadside stalls, the Kabuliwallah had never sat for a meal at a restaurant, and the thought filled him with anxiety. Were utensils required? How would he know what to order? Sometimes, when he walked by the restaurant next to the monastery, which was the one he assumed his boy was referring to, he would see the would-be monks waste copious amounts of food, the dried pieces of chicken stuck to their plates like spirits from the past. He would sigh and cluck his tongue at the fortunes of others.

For all his reservations, he knew it would be foolish to reject a free meal. "Even if I wished to say no," the Kabuliwallah said. "I must say *yes*."

His boy smiled, his light illuminating the statues in their dusty coffins. It was a father's right to receive such love. He stroked Arun's head until the mutt wagged his tail with enough exuberance for them all.

. . .

The restaurant in question was not the one frequented by visitors to the monastery. Instead, it was next to a five-star hotel on the riverbank, close to where the minions gathered for the evening aarti. For the occasion, the Kabuliwallah had washed and ironed Sundar's one good shirt. He'd done the same for his own outfit. Though he lacked Western clothing, he'd carried a sea-blue kurta his father had worn from country to country. He trimmed his beard, oiled his hair, and fastened the buttons of his kurta. Now he was older than his father had been when the Taliban had come to take the capital. Now, he had a boy of his own, who tried to insist on bringing his stuffed toy, though the Kabuliwallah said it would not be proper. "Arun will watch Tiger Friend," the Kabuliwallah said. The mutt bared his teeth to confirm this duty.

They walked hand in hand to the restaurant by the river. Without Arun at their side and with their clothes specially chosen for the occasion, the Kabuliwallah believed they were as respectable as any other father-and-son pair.

"What did you learn at school today?" the Kabuliwallah asked, feeling a little giddy.

"The ring of fire," the boy said. "The place of many volcanoes and earthquakes."

What strange, delightful subjects his boy was learning! In the future, he would try to send Sundar to school at least two days a week, and each night he would ask about the discoveries of the day. The Kabuliwallah could not read, but in other ways he could still help his boy with school.

Hannah was waiting for them outside of the restaurant. She seemed pleased to see them so finely dressed, though she herself had come in a white tee shirt and blue jeans, which he found odd and a little upsetting, given how much care the waiters of the restaurant would give to the serving of the food, how rare an experience it was for Sundar and himself.

"You must be hungry. Come with me." She took Sundar by the hand and left the Kabuliwallah to follow.

The restaurant was cavernous, two stories full with the conversations of foreigners and well-dressed Indians, a stylized English in the air, which along with the perfume of many bodies left the Kabuliwallah feeling lightheaded. They were seated by the window, where they had a view of the water. All that current evident through the haze of the settling dusk, the priests wading in to stir their prayers into the water, the tourists gathering by the shore to witness.

First there was bread, with the crusts hard but the innards soft. The Kabuliwallah tried to eat slowly. Across the table, Hannah watched them. From time to time she spoke, and he tried his best to understand. Sometimes, he would look to his boy for help, and Sundar would whisper into his ear. *She was asking about business* or *She wants to know how you came here.*

*Good*, he said. *So long ago*, he said, relieved that he could find the phrases in English.

Mostly, it was his boy and Hannah talking, exchanging phrases in English rapidly as if they were playing some sport. With all of the other conversations in the room and the sight of those priests in the water readying for the evening prayer, the Kabuliwallah found their talk difficult to follow. He did not complain, for food appeared without his having to worry. For his boy, there was pasta with tomato sauce, and for him Hannah had ordered a dish of curried lamb, the sauce thick with cream and coriander.

He thought he would need to show his boy how to use a fork, but Sundar already knew, the pasta a familiar friend, which he scarfed down with no reservations. Watching his adopted son, the Kabuliwallah felt that Hannah and Sundar had done this before. He'd always assumed that they only walked around the neighborhood during their afternoon sojourns, but perhaps they'd feasted at this very restaurant without the Kabuliwallah knowing, the boy's belly full with delicacies as he returned home and was offered a bowl of puffed rice, a cup of tea. He had always thought the boy told him everything of import, but as he watched Sundar roll pasta with a fork, he conceded his ignorance.

He looked at the table next to them, where a group of men with gelled hair and blue suits drank from long-stemmed glasses. They'd hardly taken a bite of their kebabs. One of them laughed with the delicateness of a caged bird. They were all doing their best to ignore him, his blemished face, his robber's beard. With his outstretched arm, he could've knocked a glass off the table, stopped their mirth in its tracks. The lamb on his plate began to taste sour.

"Something wrong?" Hannah asked.

"Beta, I am feeling a little sick," the Kabuliwallah told the boy.

"He is already full," the boy said in English.

"But we haven't even had dessert," Hannah said.

"No need," the Kabuliwallah said, though he wondered what sweet treats lay hidden in the kitchen. He watched as his boy slurped the last of the sauce from his plate.

"They have the best ice cream," Hannah said.

"Baba, please," his boy said.

At least tonight he hadn't needed to worry their meal to life; maybe he would take the scraps of lamb back to the mutt. His boy was bursting with gladness, but for him sitting through the meal had felt like a kind of reckoning. The men at the next table, the waiters, everyone they'd passed had given him the same look; he wasn't meant to be here, to be among the rich, and never was he to return. But the boy hadn't noticed—he remained eager to have his treat. "What kind do they have?" the Kabuliwallah finally asked, consenting, for Sundar's sake, on dessert.

"Twelve flavors. My favorite is pistachio." Hannah signaled to the waiter, and soon they each had a bowl of pistachio ice cream.

The Kabuliwallah had carried pistachios early in his trade, tiny burlap bags full of the exquisite drupes, some shelled and salted, others roasted and honeyed, but he'd never tasted ice cream with pistachios. He took a good whiff to confirm the invention before him. What was it the boy had that first day together? Chocolate and vanilla, that was right, hands dark and sticky with the sweetness. Some had gotten into Sundar's hair, leading to a cowlick that remained for days.

The waiter brought the bill, and Hannah slipped him a card without checking the amount. "There's a question I have to ask you," she said.

The Kabuliwallah waited, uncertain if she was expecting to be thanked for the meal, if he'd missed some note of etiquette.

"I'm returning to America," Hannah said. "Sundar's told me his story. I want to take him home with me. Will you let me?"

The Kabuliwallah wasn't sure if he'd understood, so he looked to Sundar for help. Word by word, the boy rendered the message in their own language. He was squinting at the Kabuliwallah, as he said, *Will you let me?*

What a question to consider over a meal, what a strange question to even ask at all. He had suspected that Hannah's affections for the boy were strong but couldn't have imagined this precipice. *Will you let me?* The boy's words played through his head and left his throat unbearably dry. It took him several moments to understand the import. During his silence, he could feel the men at the next table pause their conversation to eavesdrop. He wanted to roar, give them all the benefit of his voice, but his throat was parched.

"No," he finally muttered, repeating it to be sure he was heard. He watched Hannah's face grow old hearing his answer. Then he stared at her bowl of ice cream.

As the ice cream melted, his heart softened. What wonders his son could learn in her homeland—from the lives of frogs to the lives and fortunes of others. He looked to his son, as serious as when he studied for his exams.

"Baba," his little boy whispered. "You can come too. So can Arun."

"Maybe," said the Kabuliwallah. "I think more. Now, we go home."

The color returned to Hannah's face. "I'm here another week. There are things to be sorted out, but I'll come back for him. Promise you'll think it over?"

He nodded. He had meant to ask her to replace the boy's schoolbook, but now that request felt out of place.

When they left the restaurant, they found Arun the mutt waiting outside with Sundar's stuffed tiger in his mouth. He had a good nose, which meant he could've found them a city away. When Sundar took his toy, Arun sighed and barked a wistful hello. Hannah shook the Kabuliwallah's hand. "You'll let me know?" she asked.

He nodded. When she retreated toward the monastery, she walked with hunched back into the unfamiliar dusk, a smaller version of the person who now loomed so large in their life.

That evening, he and the boy and the dog watched the aarti by the riverbank. It was an ancient ceremony, older even than the journey of merchants from Kabul to the cities of Hindustan. A dozen priests had rolled up their dhotis and were wading in the water, waving candles, and humming scripture. He had no room for God in his heart, but there was beauty with all the lights in the water. When he squeezed Sundar's hand, his boy squeezed back.

Even if he was invited, he was too old for another country, but this boy beside him, this fast-talker, this learner of words, this bearer of many fires, would experience worlds he couldn't imagine.

"Baba," Sundar said. "Why don't we come here more often?"

"Don't know," the Kabuliwallah said. All this time that they'd lived in Varanasi, they'd mostly missed this daily ceremony by the river, the songs sending the paper lanterns into the sea. It had been many years since he'd seen Kabul, the beauty of its blue veils, every so often a street opening to a glimpse of the mountains. But this was a country of water. In making this second life, he'd once again come to believe that love could not be taken. Until this hour, as the paper boats with their blessings burned into the tide, it had seemed like a good myth to live by.

## Acknowledgments

My first published story appeared in the Kolkata daily *The Statesman* when I was fourteen. Faced with my youthful existential angst, then features editor Michael Flannery gave me a piece of advice that I've always remembered: *Just use your imagination and have fun.* The stories in this collection have been in pursuit of a deepening of my own imagination and in the pursuit of joy, and through this I've been blessed to work with some amazing guides and editors: Beth Blachman, Hannah Tinti, Patrick Ryan, Jonathan Lee, Polly Rosenwaike, Brad Morrow, Tayyba Kanwal, and of course Tom Pold at Knopf, whose kindness, wit, and deep questions improved each of these pieces. Thank you to the entire team at Knopf, especially Emily Reardon and Emily Murphy.

Julie Stevenson: I am so grateful for your belief and support of my work. I'm indebted to my writing mentors and communities, Joshua Henkin and the Brooklyn College MFA program, A Public Space and Elizabeth Gaffney and Mary-Beth Hughes, the Craftwerkers Katie Belas, Maria Villafranca, Harris Solomon, Chris Griffith, Carol Ko and the Quarantine Writers Group, Claire Cox, Steph Skaff, Clare Needham, and Jane Breakall.

I am the beneficiary of my parents' stories and of their love, which you may find in each of these pieces. And I am lucky to be the life and artistic partner of poet Elana Bell, my first and most trusted reader. I dedicate this book to our son, Surya, in eager expectation and witnessing of his own story in the world.

The math problems in "Lilavati's Fire" are from Bhaskara's twelfth-century text *Lilavati*, adapted from the H. T. Colebrooke translation.

A NOTE ABOUT THE AUTHOR

Jai Chakrabarti's novel *A Play for the End of the World* was
long-listed for the PEN/Faulkner award and received the
National Jewish Book Award for debut fiction. His short
fiction has appeared in numerous journals and has been
anthologized in *The O. Henry Prize Stories* and *The Best
American Short Stories*, and awarded a Pushcart Prize.
Chakrabarti was an Emerging Writer Fellow with A Public
Space and received his MFA from Brooklyn College. He was
born in Kolkata, India, and now splits his time between the
Hudson Valley and Brooklyn, New York.


He can be found at jaichakrabarti.com.

A NOTE ON THE TYPE

The text of this book was set in Freight Text Pro Book,
designed by Joshua Darden (b. 1979) and published by
GarageFonts in 2005. It was inspired by the "Dutch-taste"
school of typeface design and is considered a transitional-
style typeface. Legible, stylish, and sturdy, Freight Text
was designed to be highly versatile, belonging to a wide-
ranging "superfamily" of fonts, including many versions
and weights.

*Typeset by Scribe*
*Philadelphia, Pennsylvania*

*Printed and bound by Berryville Graphics*
*Berryville, Virginia*

*Book design by Pei Loi Koay*